The Town

and

the Troublesome Strangers,

1880-1980

The Town

and

the Troublesome Strangers, 1880-1980

By

M. H. Neuendorffer

*To, Joe Halpin,
for all your help,
Thank you!
Mary Helen Moore Neuendorffer
08-16-2017*

Copyright © 2015 by M. H. Neuendorffer.

Library of Congress Control Number: 2015918384
ISBN: Hardcover 978-1-5144-1324-1
Softcover 978-1-5144-1323-4
eBook 978-1-5144-1321-0

All rights reserved. No part of this book may be reproduced or transmitted in any form or by any means, electronic or mechanical, including photocopying, recording, or by any information storage and retrieval system, without permission in writing from the copyright owner.

This is a work of fiction. Names, characters, places and incidents either are the product of the author's imagination or are used fictitiously, and any resemblance to any actual persons, living or dead, events, or locales is entirely coincidental.

Any people depicted in stock imagery provided by Thinkstock are models, and such images are being used for illustrative purposes only.
Certain stock imagery © Thinkstock.

Print information available on the last page.

Rev. date: 11/23/2015

To order additional copies of this book, contact:
Xlibris
1-888-795-4274
www.Xlibris.com
Orders@Xlibris.com
720505

Preface

BEFORE I STARTED this book in 2002, I had had a persistent urge for years to write a story about a small New England town, Northfield, Massachusetts—that I knew well. Six generations of my family have gone there. The first ancestor of mine arrived in 1890; and for more than a hundred years, family members returned in the spring, summer, and fall seasons. As a child, I remember overhearing my parents speaking of the rich historical past of Northfield and also discussing the daily activities of the hardworking, firmly established New Englanders who lived there.

The main theme of this book is the recurring interaction between the permanent townspeople, some of whose family names date back to 1672, and the different and often troublesome groups of people that made their way to Northfield and settled down, less for farming than for other reasons throughout the years 1880 to 1980. Many stayed for a long time, but eventually, the groups broke up and moved away. All except for a few.

The story also includes the travels of young people from Northfield to US cities such as New York City; Corona, Long Island, New York; Washington, DC; and the world—such as France, Germany (1939), and the South Pacific during World War II. But most of these returned to Northfield and to familiar sights. The tall trees still line the wide main street in front of the colonial-style houses, and the Connecticut River still flows south. And Northfield Mountain still rises high above the town.

I hope this book proves interesting and highlights the puzzle of human nature compared to the pleasantness of natural scenery.

This book is a work of historical fiction. Any reference to historical events, real people is used fictitiously. Other names, characters, places, and incidents are products of the author's imagination, and any resemblance to actual events or persons, living or dead, is also used fictitiously.

For my daughters Carol, Esty, and Jeannie.

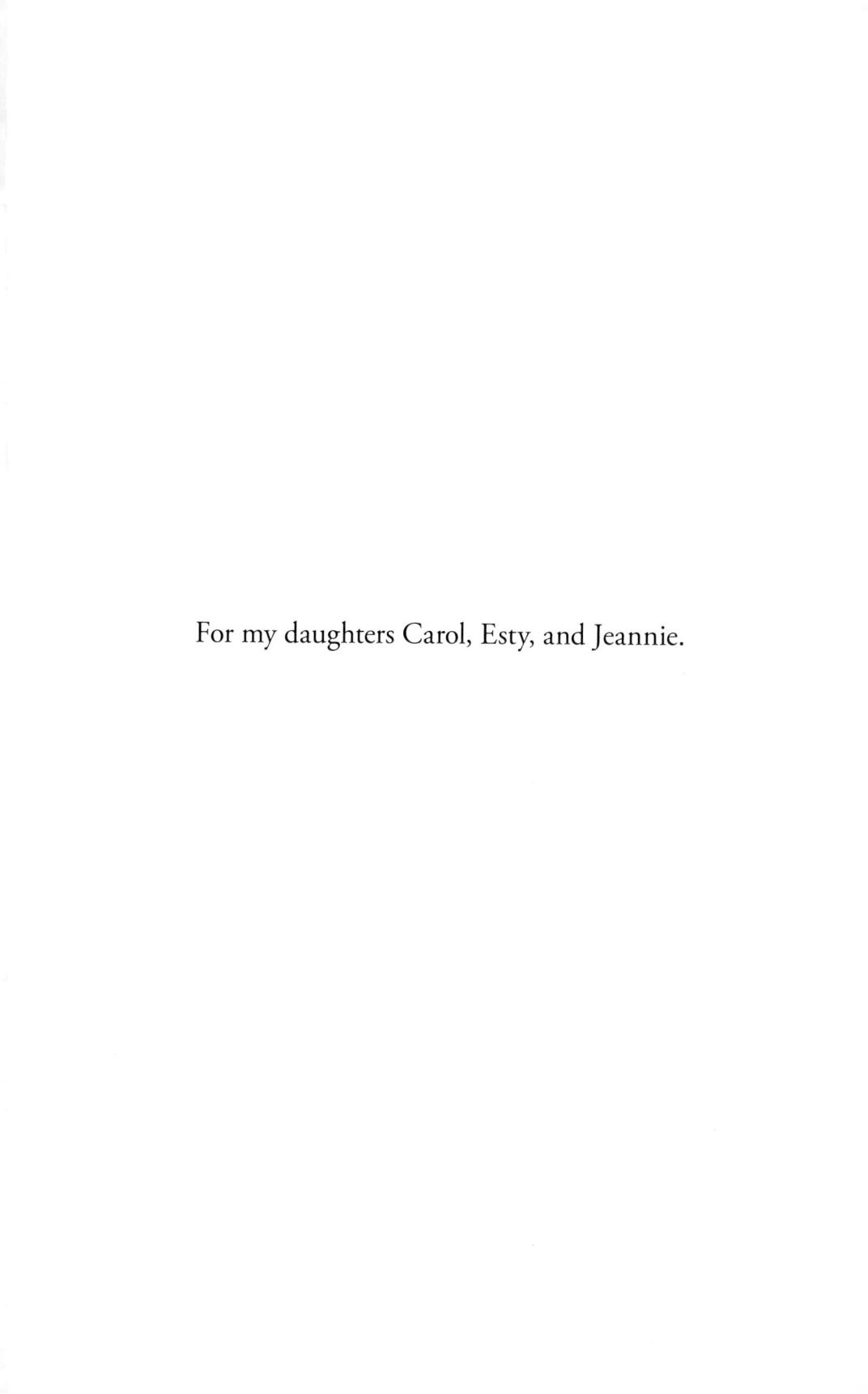

Chapter 1

EVERY WINTER, THE frost appeared first on the mountain rocks above the town of Northfield, Massachusetts. Later, the snow would fall and cover the roads and fields. Strong winds would blow it against the farmhouses and barns. Deep drifts would form on the sides of the houses on Main Street, and snow would pile up high on the rooftops.

There was a small farm three miles up the mountain from the town. It belonged to James Crawford. He had been born there in 1847. As he grew up, he worked hard on the farm with his father and two brothers.

His grandfathers had worked the land there before him. Now they lay in their graves in the family cemetery, not far from the house. There was a low iron fence around the burial ground, and inside, some of the old tombstones had begun to lean sideways.

After his father died, James's two older brothers went to Boston and found jobs, but James stayed on. Ernest Nelson, his cousin who had a farm down the mountain from his, was the only person he cared to see.

James was in his late thirties when an elderly woman from town had come up to him. She said that she would die soon and asked if he would marry her thirty-year-old daughter, Maria. She explained that Maria was a little slow. The woman told him that all her possessions would go to him when she died. James agreed, and the two were wed. Maria was plain looking, but she had a willing disposition and was a hard worker. She accepted her new life with James with no complaints. Soon she was expecting a child.

On a March morning in 1888, a snowstorm started, and it soon turned into a blizzard. It wasn't the first snowstorm of the winter, but the ferocious winds that accompanied this one were stronger and more menacing than any others. James and Maria watched from the kitchen window of the farmhouse as the snow drifts grew higher and higher. All the branches of the trees became encased in ice from the lashing sleet.

The second day of the storm, Maria told James that she was in pain and thought the baby was coming.

"I can't go out in this storm and get help," James said.

"I'll be all right," Maria assured him, and she went into a small room off the kitchen and lay down on a narrow bed.

James sat down outside the room and waited as the wind whistled through the trees. Then he heard another sound. It was a shrill animal cry. He went over to the side door and cracked it open and then slammed it closed.

"What was that?" Maria called out weakly from the small room.

"It's the barn cat. He wants to come in. What do I care if he freezes? We can't have him in here now."

"Don't let him freeze!" Maria said, using what little strength she had to call out.

James opened the door, and the cat was in the kitchen before James could look down.

Twelve hours later, Maria was dead—as was her stillborn infant son.

Several days later, James's cousin Ernest and two men from town came up to help him bury Maria and the baby. James was grateful to them, but he was silent, which didn't matter. No one expected him to go around thanking anyone because he was well-known in town for not saying much.

Chapter 2

AS THE YEARS passed, James kept mostly to himself. His life had become a lonely one. Each day was the same as the day before, but he continued to work hard.

One June afternoon, James was standing outside the barn when he saw Sarah Nelson, his cousin, Ernest Nelson's wife, and her sister, Ruth, climbing up the hill toward the house.

As they walked, the wide rims of their bonnets shaded their eyes from the bright summer sun; and the hems of their long gray dresses swept the ground, dislodging the small stones on the steep dirt road.

Ruth turned to Sarah and said, "It's possible that James might tell us to go away."

"Oh, he's not that bad!" Sarah said. "Anyway, he has to listen to what I have come to tell him."

"He's been known to chase people off the land with a pitchfork."

"Well, I have to give him this message. I promised Ernest that I would."

Suddenly, the dogs that were tied to a tree near the house started barking. James ignored the noise and took a few steps toward the women. Seeing him coming, Ruth whispered to her sister, "Look at him. His beard and hair are so long, and his overalls are dirty."

"Be quiet, he'll hear you," Sarah said and turned and walked up to him. "I have something important to tell you. Ernest wants you to know that there are several hundred people coming by train to the Northfield station from New York City tomorrow. They will be attending the religious conference here. Carriage drivers are needed to take the people from the station to the meeting grounds at the school. The drivers are supposed to get the horses and carriages from the school barns tomorrow at 3:00 PM. The train gets in at 4:00 PM. Each driver will get paid several dollars. Ernest says they need more men. Will you do it?"

The dogs continued to bark. James picked up a stone and threw it at them and yelled "Quiet!" They stopped barking.

"You may remember William Ford from Corona, Long Island, New York. He came here last year?"

James shook his head and then looked at Sarah for a few minutes, and he said, "Maybe, I'll do it. Is that all?"

"Yes."

Then he turned and walked back toward the barn.

The two sisters called out their good-byes and started down the hill. When they came to a spot on the road with no trees on either side, they stopped to admire the view. The mountain ranges in the distance were purple and gray under the cloudless sky as they stood and looked out.

"It's beautiful here," Sarah said. "What a view."

"I suppose so, and it's easier walking down the hill than walking up," Ruth mentioned.

"You are right about that."

Then Ruth asked, "Why do these city strangers keep coming here every summer and camping out at the girls' school?"

"The people that come are mostly ministers, and they have meetings. They bring their families too. The good part is that townspeople get jobs because of this, and that puts money in their pockets. Tents have to be set up, dormitory rooms cleaned, kitchen help is needed, grass-cutting, barn chores . . . all this has to be done. It's like we just told James Crawford. Drivers are needed to take these strangers from the railroad to the conference grounds," Sarah explained.

"James is an odd one. Do you think he will show up tomorrow?" Ruth asked.

"You don't know him. He'll come," Sarah replied.

They continued walking down the hill with Ruth whispering, "Not to know him is to know him well."

Chapter 3

THE NEXT DAY, at the Northfield railroad station, the drivers waited with the horse-drawn carriages for the train from New York City to arrive.

Some of the drivers got out of their rigs and stood together on the station platform.

One of them, looking down the tracks, called out, "No sign of it yet!"

"That train is always late!" another said.

James Crawford remained seated in the open carriage, slightly away from the others.

Back on the platform, one man said to another, "Do you know that tall young German man standing over there?"

"Yes, that's Otto Kirschheimer. He's the foreman for a construction job that's being started off Highland Avenue."

"I heard he is meeting some foreign workers he needs, who will be on the train."

"That's right. They will be working on the big mansion that some rich man is building. The man is a friend of Dwight Moody. Moody is very famous now because of his preaching, his founding of the schools, the religious conferences he has started, and his trips to England."

Then, behind them, someone shouted, "I think I heard a train whistle!"

"I didn't hear anything," another replied.

Meanwhile, on the train that was approaching the Northfield station was a bachelor minister named William Ford. His Congregational Church was located in Corona, Long Island, New York. This would be the second year he had attended the summer religious conference in Northfield.

William walked through the passenger cars of the train, which was his habit—so that he could renew old friendships with the ministers and others he had previously met. As he did this, he came across a fellow minister from Long Island named Otis White. They greeted each other enthusiastically. Otis's pretty nineteen-year-old niece was sitting next to him. Otis introduced them, "This is my niece Grace White from Boonton, New Jersey. Grace, this is William Ford. He has a church near mine."

"I'm glad to meet you," Grace said softly.

"This is a pleasure," William said, never taking his eyes off Grace's face. Then he asked Otis, "Do you mind if I ride the rest of the way with you?"

Otis immediately agreed. "That would be fine," he said, smiling as William sat down on the seat facing them.

The train finally arrived at the Northfield station. Steam belched from the engine, and the breaks screeched as it stopped. The conductors hurriedly lowered the steps of each car, and the passengers got off the train. Soon a large crowd filled the platform and the surrounding area. The women held tightly to their bags. Some carried pillowcases stuffed with clothes and bedding. The men began leading the way to the waiting carriages. The children, who had been there before, shouted, "We're here! We're here! We're in Northfield."

From the back of the train, about thirty foreign workers jumped down from the boxcar they had been riding in. Kirschheimer began getting them in line to go to the camp where they would be staying.

Suddenly, three of the workmen left the others and raced down the tracks.

"Come back!" Otto Kirschheimer shouted.

But they kept going. Soon they veered off into the woods.

Otto gave up. "There's no stopping them now."

William and some others came up to him and asked, "Why did they run away like that? Are those men dangerous?"

"Oh no, they are not dangerous. But one of them is a maverick. He kept talking about his relatives in Boston, and he must have talked the others into leaving with him. Don't worry about them, I'm not going to. They have no money, so they will probably come back."

So the people returned to finding seats in the carriages that would take them to the conference center at the Northfield Seminary for Girls.

James noticed the commotion and saw the three men running away but didn't think much about it.

Chapter 4

JAMES WATCHED THE crowd from his seat in the carriage. The city men were dressed in black frocked coats and black derby hats, and the women wore long dresses with shawls around their shoulders. Suddenly, a boy ran over and patted James's horse on the nose. James grabbed the whip from the seat beside him and flicked it in the direction of the boy, shouting "get away from there!" The boy pulled back quickly.

Then William Ford appeared with Otis and Grace and asked James if the three of them could ride with him.

James gave no answer but lifted up the reins.

"I guess that means we can get in," William said.

But before they could climb in, William heard his name being called out.

"Pastor Ford!"

He looked around and saw Clara Lovett, his landlady from Corona, and her daughter, Liza, running toward him. Clara's large hat was set askew on her head, and she was dressed all in black. She was a large woman and was breathing heavily and struggling with her bundles as she came up to him. "Pastor Ford, is there room enough for us in this carriage?"

William introduced Otis and Grace to Clara and Liza, and then said politely, "As you can see, this is one of the smaller open carriages. And it is at the end of the line. I can see there is more space in the ones up front. You will be at the conference ground way before us if you take one of those."

"If you think so," Clara said dejectedly, and she and her daughter turned around and left.

"That woman and her daughter are members of my church," William explained.

"They seemed nice," Grace mentioned.

"I have been boarding in Mrs. Lovett's house for five years, so we are well acquainted. Actually, Miss White, you will probably be staying in the same building with them. The single women's dormitory is in East Hall. The families sleep in tents on the campus of the school. Your uncle and I will be at the men's camp in the woods, also in tents."

James steadied the horse as the three climbed up to the seat behind him, with William helping Grace. Then James flattened the reins on the horse's back and guided it to the end of the line behind the other carriages. Slowly the procession moved away from the station and out onto the River Road.

After a short while, Otis called to James, "One of the back wheels seems to be wobbling."

James slowed the horse and looked back.

Soon the other carriages in front of them pulled out of sight.

William realized the driver's concern and said, "I think it will hold!"

Meanwhile, Grace glanced at William and thought to herself, "He is a very handsome man." She liked his thick wavy brown hair and deep-set blue eyes and broad shoulders. Then she noticed a scar on his cheek.

William saw her looking at it and explained with a smile, "I acquired that scar in a saloon in Corona. The owner didn't like me coming into his place and giving a temperance sermon by the bar. So, one night, he threw a glass at me. It broke and cut my face. But I still go in there occasionally and preach about overdrinking."

Otis commented, "Will is known all over Long Island for his adventurous ways."

"You are brave to do that!" Grace said quietly. Then she straightened her hat and smoothed the front of her black skirt and looked straight ahead.

James made a clucking sound to start the horse moving again.

Chapter 5

AS THEY WENT along, Otis noticed that the high marsh grass on the right side of the road was swaying. "There is something in those reeds," he said to the others.

Suddenly, three men burst out from the tall grass and said in broken English that they wanted to steal the horse and carriage.

"They are the runaway workmen from the station," Otis said to William.

William stood up and shouted, "Stay away! Keep back!"

Ignoring the warning, one of the men grabbed the horse's harness while the other two jumped up to the driver's seat. They tried to push James off. He struggled with them until one of them drove his fist into his face. James fell backward off the carriage and rolled over and over down the steep incline to the edge of the river.

William attempted to grab one of the men by the shoulder from behind, but at that moment, the carriage began to tilt and rock, and then it pitched over. They were all thrown out onto the ground.

As William and Otis got to their feet, the assailants tried to wrestle them down, but they fought back. Grace crawled to safety under some low bushes. Then the attackers began punching William and Otis with quick blows, and they fell down. They could hear the men shouting back and forth to each other in Italian as they righted the carriage and harnessed the horse. With scornful looks back, they jumped into the carriage and started to drive it up a path that led across a field to Main Street.

"Is Grace all right?" William asked, getting to his feet.

"I think so," Otis said as Grace came out from the bushes and stood up.

Then they turned and saw James trying to climb up the riverbank. He was obviously in pain. William hurried down the slope to assist him. He held out his hand to him and inquired if he was hurt badly. Crawford shook his head but refused to take William's hand. When William looked into James's eyes, he could see only animosity, not gratitude. James made it to the top of the bank on his own, and ignoring the others, he started walking back along the river road in the direction of the Northfield railroad station. They could hear him muttering as he went. He was grumbling about strangers and outsiders.

"I'm afraid there are some in Northfield who dislike the people that barge in on them summer after summer," William said, and then changed the subject. "It's not far to the conference ground. It is not a long walk, if Ms. White feels up to it."

He turned and looked at her. She was shaking, and there were tears on her face. Then William realized that she had been badly frightened. "I'm very sorry this has happened to you," he said kindly, and there was deep concern in his voice.

"I'm all right, they are gone now," Grace said. Then she picked up her hat from the ground and put it on and then tried to roll her tangled hair back under it, but it kept falling down. So she took off her hat and let her hair hang straight.

The three started off toward the campus, with the men carrying the bags. As they walked along, they noticed how strong the current of the Connecticut River was as it flowed southward. Soon the tower of Stone Hall (of the Northfield School) could be seen ahead of them, and they knew they were getting close to the conference grounds.

Chapter 6

ON THE CAMPUS outside Stone Hall, Clara and her daughter, Liza, stood in line, waiting to register for the conference. Suddenly, they saw William, Otis, and Grace coming up the hill from the river.

"I wonder why they are walking. Where is their carriage? Let's go down and meet them," Clara said.

"We'll lose our place in line."

"That doesn't matter. Come on," she said, grabbing her daughter's arm, and they hurried down the hill.

When William saw the two women running toward him, he held up his hand and said, "Be calm. We are all right." Then he told them that the horse and carriage had been stolen. "It was the men that ran away from the station that took them. They rushed us and were too strong for us."

Clara noticed Grace's disheveled hair and the dirt on her dress and said, "How terrible for you, young lady!"

"I'm fine now," Grace said. And she added, "But I must look a sight!"

Then Otis spoke up, "I hear the single ladies stay in East Hall. Perhaps that is where you will be staying."

"Yes, and we'll see that she is with us. I will arrange to have her room close to ours. We'll take good care of her," Clara said to Otis and turned to William. "Aren't you going to tell the conference leader about what happened to you at the hands of those ruffians?"

"I believe the driver of the carriage in front of us saw something. He will probably report it. I'll mention it to them myself when I have time. Let's get registered now."

"The conference cost seven dollars a week per person, and the food is included," Clara informed them. "You register over there where the crowd is, just follow me."

After they had registered and paid, a leader announced that the conference would officially open the next morning.

Then the people went off to find their rooms and tents.

William, Otis, and the three ladies started walking up a hill toward East Hall. Halfway up the hill, William asked them to turn around and look at the view.

"From here, you can see the green field sloping down to the Connecticut River," William said. "Now, if you look to the east, you can see the southern mountains of New Hampshire. And over to the west, you can see the green mountains of Vermont. Now look back and you see a high wooded ridge. That's known to be a good place for afternoon walks," William said and smiled at Grace.

When they reached East Hall, Clara stomped up the stairs to the porch with the two young women behind her. "Let's hurry so we can get a good room," she said. Then Grace and Liza turned and gave the men a hurried wave good-bye.

William and Otis started off in the direction of the men's camp. As they went along, Otis asked William, "What kind of membership do you have at your church in Corona?"

"It is somewhat diverse. There are many farmers that come, and we have day laborers, shopkeepers, and some people that go to work in the city every day. But there are more and more immigrants from Europe coming into Corona each year. A great many of them come from Italy. They get off the boat in New York City, and when they hear the word *Corona*—which means 'crown' in Italian—they settle there. Some of the immigrants start up small businesses like restaurants or corner bars, but the majority of them are hired on to the building trade. They are hard workers."

Then Otis said, "I remember at the last ministers' meeting, we were asked to send in a report on the crime perpetrated in our parishes."

"I remember that too, but I didn't send in a report. I believe it is the duty of the police to fight crime, not the clergy. But I have watched the new immigrants gain control of the liquor business. And I have seen how ruthless they can be if anyone opposes them."

The two old friends continued on slowly without talking. Other men passed them.

Then William asked Otis if he would help him guide the men and boys on a mountain hike the next day. "Every year, the conference people climb the mountain behind the school. It's a tradition. We would be the leaders. Now that I think of it, the trail goes past James Crawford's farm. Maybe we will see our carriage driver again."

"I'd be glad to help, if you are sure you know the way."

"I do."

After a while, they arrived at the men's camp in the woods.

Chapter 7

THE MEN'S CAMP was filling up fast. William and Otis selected a tent at the far end. There, the tall pine trees stood together so thickly that the rays of the sun could hardly be seen through the branches. The tent they chose was on the edge of a deep ravine. There was a rushing stream at the bottom. The sound of it could be heard above.

Inside the tent were two canvas cots and a small table with a kerosene lamp on it. The men threw down their bags on one cot, and Otis immediately stretched out on the other and was soon asleep. William went outside and began introducing himself to the men he did not know. William's friendly ways soon made him popular with all the others, and they selected him, informally, as their leader.

That night, when the last kerosene lanterns were extinguished in the camp and all was quiet, few heard the pat of the paws of the woodland animals. The raccoons, skunks, and fisher cats made sure that their nocturnal routes had not been disturbed. Some bravely circled the large trash bin at the center of the camp. Low-flying bats swooped down over the tents, gobbling insects; but none of this bothered the sleeping men

The next morning, the camp began to empty out as the men left for breakfast at the conference center and for the first meeting. They walked together across a wide field toward Stone Hall. Suddenly, William and Otis noticed a man leading a pair of yoked oxen and a cart in the distance.

"Is that James Crawford?" Otis asked, as he strained his eyes to see the man who was a ways off.

"I am not sure," William said doubtfully. Then he turned to a man near him and asked, "Who is that?"

"That's Ernest Nelson," the man said. He explained that he himself lived in a small town south of Northfield and knew most of the men in the area. "The Nelson farm is not far from here. Ernest does odd jobs for the school. You mentioned James Crawford. He is Ernest's cousin and has a farm up the mountain from him. Crawford has lived up there by himself for years."

"I would like to talk to Ernest Nelson and ask him if James Crawford was injured yesterday when he was thrown off a carriage," William said. He then he began walking quickly toward Ernest and the oxcart.

"Leave him alone," Otis called after him, "the man is working." But that didn't stop William.

Ernest saw him coming and yanked the yoked oxen in the opposite direction.

William shouted for him to wait, but Ernest didn't raise his head or look around. He did hit the oxen with a stick he was carrying to get them to go faster, but he acted as though he hadn't heard William call to him.

Finally, William gave up and came back. "Strange, he wouldn't stop," he said to Otis.

"He didn't want to talk to you."

"I thought he might know about our driver from yesterday—and also if someone had caught the men who had stolen the horse and carriage."

"If he knew, he probably wouldn't have told you. Remember, these New England farmers like to keep to themselves. I wonder where he is taking all that wood in the back of the oxcart."

One of the men standing there explained, "Those logs on the cart are for the bonfire Saturday night. That man will deliver the load to an open field by the pond down from Stone Hall. A large pyramid of logs, branches, and boxes will be erected. Some other men will be helping them. Saturday night, they will set the whole thing on fire. The conference people will gather around the fire in a large circle and watch it burn. Everybody likes bonfire night."

Otis looked at William and said, facetiously, "Don't worry. Grace will be there."

William smiled and then shouted out so all could hear as they walked along, "There will be a mountain climb tomorrow afternoon. We'll start from the auditorium."

Chapter 8

THE NEXT MORNING, the sun was shining brightly as the Stone Hall tower clock struck eight. Grace and Liza sat on the front steps of East Hall. They were waiting for Clara, who was to join them so they could go to breakfast together at the main dining room in Gould Hall.

"This will take some time," Liza said. "Mother is a slow dresser."

"I don't mind," Grace said, looking across the campus. "It is so beautiful here."

Suddenly, Liza got up and ran to the side of the porch and pointed out, "Look, the men are arriving from the camp."

"Can you see my Uncle Otis?" Grace asked as she hurried over to her.

"No, but he will find you. Women have to sit at different tables than the men at meals, but your uncle and Pastor Ford will be looking for you," said Liza. She added, "I think Pastor Ford took quite a shine to you."

"Oh, don't be silly. He was kind to me when the bad men attacked us on the way from the station, but he is a very important minister. You said that he is thirty-five years old. He wouldn't be interested in someone like me."

"You are very pretty, Grace," Liza said, looking at her. "He noticed you, I could tell. Did you know he was stabbed in the face in a saloon in Corona, Long Island, New York? He had gone in to give a temperance talk. He was attacked and thrown out. Ever since then, the Italian children in Corona throw stones at him. But he is never vengeful. The church people respect him and admire him, and he is well liked by all the other townspeople."

"Yes, he told me about what happened at the saloon, but I don't understand why he has never married. He is so handsome and likeable."

"I probably shouldn't say anything, but I feel like I know you well enough now. It happened that he almost had to get married a few years ago," Liza said.

"What do you mean 'he had to get married'?"

"Oh no, it wasn't that," Liza answered. "But there was a young unmarried woman, named Charlotte Wagoner, who lived with her parents in the house right next to ours in Corona. She began to get ideas about him. You know that Pastor Ford boarded with us. Well, the Wagoners are very important church members. However, when their daughter Charlotte started waylaying Pastor Ford whenever he walked past their house, trouble started. Of course, he was polite to her when she stopped him, and would listen to what she had to say. But she began waiting for him more frequently and sometimes after dark. There is a lamplight right near there, so I could see her from my upstairs window. She would beckon to him when he tried to pass. Then she would come up and walk with him a few steps and whisper in his ear."

Grace frowned at Liza. "Wasn't he just being courteous to her?"

"You would think so," Liza said. "But one afternoon, a lawyer came to our house and asked for the pastor. Mother called him down from his room upstairs, and he and the lawyer went into the front parlor and closed the door. Mother was worried that something was really wrong, and listened at the door. She heard that Mr. and Mrs. Wagoner were planning to sue Pastor Ford for alienation of affection in regard to their daughter Charlotte."

"Oh no!"

"Oh yes! Well, the story got out, and the church people were all in a storm about it. Most people sided with the pastor and thought the Wagoners were just trying to marry off their aging daughter. However, some of Mrs. Wagoner's women friends took her side, and there was gossip, and some criticized him."

"What happened then?"

"Well, it looked like he might be taken to court. But fortunately, the richest man in our church—Mr. Levering, who is a bank president in New York City—went to the judge and did something to settle it because no one heard anything more about it after that."

Heavy footsteps signaled the arrival of Clara. "How do I look? Am I presentable enough?" she said in a loud voice.

"You look just fine."

"Well, let's hurry. They are gathering over there. There is a line forming already. If we want to get the best of the breakfast, we had better hurry."

Chapter 9

IN THE EARLY afternoon of the next day, the men and boys of the conference met at the auditorium for a hike to the top of the mountain. They started off with William leading the way. Otis walked at the rear to make sure the stragglers didn't get too far behind.

Halfway up the mountain, they passed the Crawford farm. When the hikers approached the farm, some of the group wanted to go into the old family cemetery, in order to read the writing on the tombstones. But William waved them away.

"It's better not to go in there," he said, and then pointed out toward a large field beyond the barn. "Do you see that man out there raking hay? I believe that is James Crawford, who owns this place."

A few looked in that direction, but most just continued up the mountain.

The trail narrowed and was partially overgrown with vines and bushes near the top. The higher they went, the steeper the climb. Some had to grab saplings and roots to pull themselves up.

"How much farther?" a man called out.

"Not much," William answered. "It's all rock from here on up."

Finally, they reached the summit, and all turned around to look at the view. There were mountain ranges to be seen in all directions. Down in the valley, the cornfields, the cow pastures, and miles of woodland spread out before them.

"There's the Connecticut River!" someone said.

"It looks so small from here, just a thin silver line."

Then Otis suggested they all sit down and rest.

William went over to a group of boys and pointed to the cracks in the rocks. "Do you see those small red stones in the cracks?"

"Yes, what are they?"

"They are garnets. Garnets are jewels of a kind. They are not valuable like diamonds, but they shine up well."

Immediately, the boys knelt down and began collecting the garnets.

After a while, the group started back. The walk down was easy compared to the climb up. Otis joined William at the front of the line. They passed the Crawford farm without making any comment.

Four of the young conference boys held back from the others. When they saw the barn door was opened at the farm, they decided to explore the inside. They ran in, and two of them climbed up a ladder and began to throw hay down on the others; they were yelling back and forth. The noise scared a horse that was tied in a stall. The horse reared up and broke loose. Then the horse galloped out of the barn to the field behind as the surprised boys watched.

James, who was working in the field, was startled when he saw the horse running free. Then he saw the four boys dashing out of the barn and running quickly down the hill. He raised his fist and screamed at them, but the boys were already out of sight.

Sweat poured down James's face. He began to breathe heavily. The heat of the sun bore down on him.

"I have to catch that horse!" he muttered to himself as he started chasing it.

Chapter 10

SATURDAY NIGHT, THE glow of the bonfire lit up the sky. The conference people had hurried down to the field to watch it burn.

William had asked Grace to go with him, and he came for her at East Hall. Otis, Clara, and Liza had left earlier to find a good place near the fire. When William and Grace arrived, Clara waved to them.

"Come over here," she called out to them. "I've saved some room for you, Grace, between me and Liza. The men can stand behind."

Grace did what she was told as William and Otis joined the men in the back.

There was laughter and animated talk as the crowd watched the wooden logs and boxes being consumed before them. Children raced around the fire, and anxious mothers jumped to their feet to grab them when they got too close to the flames. At times, the spectacular sight of the raging bonfire and the heat coming from it left some of them speechless.

"Look at those huge sparks flying upwards," William said to Otis.

"It's something to see, all right."

Then William's attention was drawn to two men standing by the edge of the woods, apart from the crowd. He pointed them out to Otis. "I suppose they are Northfield men that are here to make sure that the fire is out at the end," William said.

"They look like two of the drivers that were at the station."

"Are they James Crawford and Ernest Nelson?" William asked.

"No, they are some other Northfield men."

"I wonder what they think of us."

"Not much, if you ask me. These New Englanders are a tight-lipped bunch. It's hard to know what they think. But don't worry about them. They are being paid by the conference people for setting up the bonfire."

William glanced over to where Grace was sitting. The glow of the fire threw light on her pretty face and soft brown hair. Suddenly, he felt like he wanted to go over to where she was, but he thought better of it and stayed with the men.

A conference boy, sitting close to Liza, turned to her and said, "I saw a crazy man yesterday!"

"What?" she exclaimed.

"Yes, he was out in a field. And when he saw me and my friends coming out of the barn, he started yelling at us. A horse had broken loose and ran away, and the farmer raised his big sickle over his head and shouted that he would kill us."

The boy's father, sitting nearby, quickly said to Liza, "Don't listen to him. Those boys shouldn't have gone into that man's barn. Most of the hikers had gone past the farm, but the boys had lagged behind and had gotten into trouble. I wouldn't blame the farmer for being annoyed with strange boys trespassing on his property. He told them to leave."

"That's not right!" the boy insisted. "He didn't tell us to leave. He said he was going to kill us. That man was crazy!"

"That's enough!" the father said in a tone that quickly silenced the boy.

Chapter 11

LATER, AS THE flames from the bonfire began to die down, the people started to leave. Some carried lighted oil lamps.

Otis escorted Clara and Liza back to East Hall, while William and Grace followed behind them. Then Grace said, "Look how all those lighted lanterns, carried by the people, flicker and sway in the dark. They remind me of fireflies."

"They need those lamps to get back to their rooms and tents," William commented and surprised Grace by taking her hand. She stopped and looked at him thoughtfully, but she left her hand in his.

When they came to the front steps of East Hall, Otis reminded William that they still had a long walk to the men's camp. So they said goodnight, and the men left.

Liza asked Grace why she seemed sad.

"They could have stayed longer."

"You'll see him tomorrow," Liza said smiling at Grace.

As the two entered the men's camp, Otis asked William if he heard dogs barking.

"Yes, I was wondering about that," William answered. "The barking seems to be coming from the direction of the mountain road. Do you suppose they are James Crawford's farm dogs?"

"I don't know, but we will have a hard time sleeping if that racket keeps up."

"I remember hearing dogs barking like that when I was a boy on my father's farm in Connecticut. It always meant that something was wrong. I think we should go up there," William suggested.

"Do you really think that it is necessary?"

"Those dogs aren't barking for nothing."

"Well, if you want me to, I'll go with you. But it's pitch black up there, you know!" Otis said.

William got a lamp from their tent and lit it. Then they started off.

They followed a dirt path out of the camp and soon turned onto the mountain road. They started climbing, with the lantern bobbing up and down.

"Watch out for tree roots and animal holes," William warned.

Otis nodded.

When they were halfway up the mountain, they could see the outline of the Crawford barn. Coming closer, they saw the post to which the dogs were tied. The barking continued as the dogs pulled on the ropes that held them.

Then, suddenly, William and Otis noticed that the barn door was open and that there was a light inside. They entered the barn and could dimly see two men standing at the other end, looking down at something on the floor in front of them.

"Who are they?" asked Otis.

"That's Ernest Nelson. But I don't know the older man with him," William whispered.

"What's that on the floor? It looks like a body."

William stepped forward and called out to the men, "Is that James Crawford on the floor?"

"It is," was the gruff reply, "but you keep away."

"Is he hurt? Can I help?" William asked.

"He's dead! We figure he dropped dead in his field yesterday. It was probably a heart attack or heat exhaustion, because he was chasing his horse. The horse showed up at my farm, so my neighbor and I came up here and found James in the field. We brought him into the barn," Ernest said.

"But make no mistake we don't need any help from you out-of-towners. Keep back!" the old man said vehemently, and he shook his fist at them. "Someone let that horse loose. It might have been one of you people. You city-folk don't belong here. You should go back to where you came from!"

"It's better if you go now," Ernest said.

William and Otis left the barn but stood nearby. Soon they saw the two men carrying the body out and taking it into the farmhouse.

Otis whispered, "Should we tell the conference men about this?"

"I don't think so—at least not now," William said. And he added, "There's nothing they can do here now."

So they turned and walked down the mountain road. William paused and looked back. Silhouetted against the starlit sky was the Crawford farmhouse and barn. Nearby, the tombstones in the cemetery seemed to shine brighter in the night than in the day. Soon, James Crawford would be laid there with his ancestors.

Chapter 12

THE NEXT TWO weeks passed quickly. During that time, William and Grace met every afternoon. They would walk around the frog pond that was located down the hill from the conference grounds.

One afternoon, when they were sitting by the edge of the water, William said to Grace, "See those town boys on the other side of the pond?"

"Yes, I see them."

"They are trying to catch fish over there."

"Are there fish in the pond?"

"Not many," William answered. He then shouted over to the boys, "Any luck?"

At that, the boys pulled their fishing lines out of the water and turned and walked away.

"Why did they leave?" Grace asked.

"They recognized me. Those boys know I saw them throwing things into the big meeting tent during the closing prayer the other day. I was the first to notice round objects flying through the air."

"What kind of objects?"

"Green apples—lots of green apples were being hurled in at us. I lifted the tent flap and got a good look at the boys making their escape, and they saw me. The boys that were fishing over there are the same ones that threw the apples."

"That was wrong! They shouldn't have been disturbing the meeting."

"They were just having fun," William said, laughing. He added, "I know boys. I have hundreds of them in my Corona Church Sunday School."

When the conference ended, the same drivers—who had brought the people from the Northfield railroad station two weeks before—were lined up to take them back to the station for the trip home.

One of the drivers mentioned, "Too bad about James Crawford."

"They say he died in the field."

No one said anything else for a while.

At the station, the families climbed down from the carriages, bag and baggage, and hurried to the station platform to watch for the train. Grace, Clara, and Liza found a place next to the track.

"Be careful there. Don't get too close," Otis called out to them.

Liza looked back and waved. Then she poked Grace's arm and pointed over to where William was lifting small children up onto a baggage cart.

"The youngsters will be able to see the train coming in from up there," Grace said. "How kind he is."

"I hear the train whistle," Liza said. Many leaned forward.

Suddenly, a small girl pushed past them excitedly and stepped out onto the tracks. It was then that her shoe got stuck under one of the tracks.

"I can't get my foot out! Someone help me!" she cried.

Immediately, Clara went out onto the track, calling for the others to stay back. Then Clara bent over and tugged hard at the shoe, which finally came loose. The little girl ran back into the crowd to her family. Grace and Liza congratulated Clara on her quick action.

The train whistle was heard again, and some of the people started shouting, "Here she comes!"

Now the train could be seen. It slowed down as it approached the station with the brakes screeching. When it stopped, the conductors jumped down from the passenger cars and lowered the steps. Then the people began boarding the train. Some pushed in front of others, hoping to get window seats. After the first excited passengers had climbed on, William and Otis helped Grace, Clara, and Liza onto the rear car of the train, where there were many empty seats.

"Are these all right?" William asked Clara.

"Oh yes!" she said. "Grace and I will sit here together, and Liza can sit opposite us. She doesn't mind riding backwards."

Grace looked up at her uncle.

"Don't worry," Otis said. "William and I will take these seats right behind you."

Soon the train began to move. It was then that William told Otis quietly that he planned to marry Grace. Otis shook his hand. "I know you'll be good to Grace and hold her dear."

"You can depend on it," William said.

Both men smiled broadly as the train began to pick up speed.

The Northfield drivers left their carriages and stood and watched as the train pulled out.

"Well, that's the end of the noise and confusion for a while," one said.

"What do those people get out of all that praying and preaching?" said another.

"Most of them are ministers, and they like to get together and be with each other."

"They do bring some money into town, which is a good thing," said one.

"Yeah, but not much. And how long do they stay?"

"Not long!" another one said.

Then one of the younger men asked in a loud voice, "Who's bringing the rum to the Grange dance at the town hall tonight?"

They all laughed. "Zeke Potter always brings the rum. Now let's get these rigs back to the barns."

Chapter 13

THAT EVENING, THE light from the kerosene lamps shone from the windows of the town hall. It was a warm summer night, and many of the townspeople had begun to gather for the Grange square dance. Most of the people walked from their homes to the dance, but some came in buggies and others in farm wagons. There was a hitch rack in front of the town hall, to which the horses were tied.

The town hall was a two-story building located in the center of town. There were wide wooden steps that led up to the door. The large main room had a high ceiling and three long windows on each side. There were chairs along the wall, and at the far end, there was a raised platform.

On the platform, Zeke Potter and his sons, Rob and Ben, were tuning up their fiddles. Zeke was getting ready to call the squares and start the dance. The hall was filling up quickly.

The older farmers were the first to get out on the floor and set up the squares—something they had been doing for years.

Their partners were their wives, their daughters, a neighbor, and sometimes a stranger.

Albert Bowman sat at a small table in the vestibule by the front door. As president of the Grange, it was his duty to collect a few coins from each person that was attending.

Three elderly women sat on chairs by the wall. They held tight to the shawls wrapped around their shoulders, and they kept their hats and gloves on.

The Potters started playing, and Zeke began calling. "Bow to your partner. Bow to your corner. All take hands and circle around."

The tempo was slow at first but gradually grew faster. The dancers knew the steps well, so there was no hesitation. The old women along the wall clapped their hands in time to the music and tapped their feet. They would nudge each other when a man was holding his partner too close. The square dancing continued on for some time until Zeke noticed a commotion at the front door.

Al Bowman signaled to Zeke, and the music stopped abruptly. The women by the wall looked toward the door.

"That is the rich man, standing there," she said.

"What is he doing here?" asked one of the others. "And who's that big man with him?"

"That's the German, Otto Kirschheimer. He is the boss of the workers who are building a mansion."

Then a man said loudly, "Look who is trying to come in behind them. It's that immigrant from across the river, and he's carrying a child."

Albert Bowman ignored what the man said and started talking with the rich man. Soon some of the farmers began to gather around to listen in.

Then he spoke up so that all could hear him, "I'm sorry to interrupt the dancing, but there is a wagon that has overturned in the street outside, and my carriage cannot get past."

"We will certainly help you," Bowman said, as the others shook their heads in agreement.

Then one of the farmers pointed to the short man with the child and said, "No outsiders are allowed in here. That child probably has diphtheria. I hear a lot of them have it. We should get him out of town before we all come down with it."

Then the rich man said again, "We need some men to right the wagon so we can be on our way."

Four men stepped forward and started out the door. Two of them hustled the man with the child down the steps, who said in broken English, "I need medicine." But none of the men paid any attention.

Before leaving, the carriage owner turned to Al Bowman and asked him if Kirschheimer could make an announcement to the people. Bowman agreed. Otto walked across the floor to the platform. The Potter men made room for him, and he began to speak.

The old ladies leaned forward so they could hear.

"What is he talking about?" one asked.

"He is asking if any of the men here want jobs helping to build the mansion."

"I thought those foreign men who came in on the train do that work."

"He says he needs more workers."

"I doubt if any Northfield men would want to work with those foreigners."

"You may be right because no one is raising their hands or going forward. It looks like Mr. Kirschheimer is giving up."

Kirschheimer stepped down from the platform and left the town hall. As he did, he passed the four men who had righted the wagon.

One said, "We chased the other guy away."

After the interruption, the squares formed again and the fiddling began. And Zeke called out loud and strong, "Round and round and up and down, and give your partner a hefty pound. Now over across and back you go, swing her fast then swing her low."

The dancing went on for another hour. The old women on the side amused themselves by watching some of the young men duck into the coat closet for a swig of rum.

"There goes another one in there," one said, and they laughed.

Then they turned their attention to the squares.

"Do you see the girl that's dancing with Bowman's son? She can't be more than thirteen."

"No! She's fourteen!"

"No! She's thirteen!"

"She's a pretty thing though, isn't she?"

They smiled knowingly at each other when Bowman's son and the young girl slipped out the side door and down the steps into the darkness.

The dance finally ended, and the people left the hall. Outside, some climbed into the horse-drawn buggies and wagons; and others walked home, chatting and laughing.

Soon all was quiet on Main Street until a few hours later, when the cocks began to crow in the barnyards across the valley.

Chapter 14

Corona, Long Island, New York
1884

TEN MONTHS LATER, on a Sunday morning, Charles Levering stepped out of his carriage in front of the Congregational Church in Corona, Long Island, New York. He gave his driver orders to return for him at noon.

Suddenly, he heard his name called out, and he saw Clara Lovett and her daughter, Liza, coming toward him.

"Have you heard anything from Pastor Ford?" Clara asked.

"Yes, I have. Pastor Ford married Ms. Grace White a few days ago in a church in Boonton, New Jersey. They are having a brief honeymoon at the Kittatinny Hotel at the Delaware Water Gap. But they will be back here next Sunday. I will be announcing that in church this morning."

"You are good to fill in for him at church this morning. Also, I have heard you have bought a house for them at the top of the hill," Clara said.

"I would rather not have that spoken about," Charles said firmly.

"Of course not, but did I tell you that Liza and I became well acquainted with Grace White last summer at the Northfield conference? She is a quiet, well-brought-up girl nineteen years of age. Some wonder if she is old enough to take on the many duties that will be expected of her here. But I am sure it will all work out well," Clara said. She added, "We all know that you are indispensible to Pastor Ford."

"He's a fine man. During my wife's last illness, he called at the house every day," Charles said. And he then told her, "You know, I will not be preaching a sermon this morning. I will just make some announcements and mention a few facts about the church's financial condition."

Then Charles surprised them by inviting them to dinner at his house after church.

Clara answered quickly, "Of course, we will come."

Then Liza smiled and added, "Yes, thank you very much!"

William and his young wife, Grace, moved into the house at the top of the hill. Grace brought cheerfulness into William's life and helped him in every way.

They were both glad when the news came that Charles Levering had asked Clara Lovett to marry him. The people of Corona talked of little more for weeks.

They were married in Charles's large house on Main Street by Pastor Ford, and when asked why they weren't married in the church, Clara said they were too old to make a fuss.

Chapter 15

A YEAR LATER, on a warm afternoon, Clara Levering came to visit Grace, who was now settled in the house at the top of the hill and was well liked by the church people. She and Clara had become good friends.

As they talked in the living room, they were suddenly interrupted and startled by a loud shout from the kitchen. The black maid named Huffy yelled out, "The reverend has been hurt!" Then rushing in from the kitchen, she said, "I seen him from the window. He is staggering up the hill with that Armenian man helping him!"

Grace and Clara hurried out to the front porch. William, with his arm around Boris Melikof's neck, stumbled up the front steps. Clara hurried to help Boris get William into the living room and onto the couch."

"You are bleeding," Grace said anxiously as she hurriedly placed a hand towel over the wound on his head.

"Who did this to you?" Clara asked angrily.

Boris answered, "A bad man did it down in town. He was punching the reverend over and over again and knocked him to the ground. Then he started kicking him and swearing at him. I rushed over to try and stop it, but when the man saw me coming, he ran off. Other people were there and saw what was happening."

"I'll be all right," William said weakly.

Clara turned to Huffy and said, "Go right down the hill and get Dr. Collier. He's in the house two doors from the church. Tell him to come at once."

"Yes, ma'am," Huffy said as she hurried back into the kitchen to get her hat. Then she went out the back door and down the hill as fast as she could.

After a few minutes, two policemen arrived at the door.

"I'm Patrolman Murphy, and this is Patrolman Ryan. We heard about the attack, and we have to know who did this to you, Reverend."

"Yes, we have to get the facts," the other policeman said.

"My husband shouldn't talk now," Grace pleaded. "He's in pain."

Then Patrolman Murphy said, looking at her, "I never thought I'd see the day when someone would assault a fine upstanding man of God like Reverend Ford."

William raised himself slightly, and Grace put a pillow behind his head. Then he began to speak. "Today, I was asked to call upon Mrs. Lewis, whose husband died two years ago. She wanted me to make arrangements for her second marriage. When I reached her home, there was another woman there. Her name was Mrs. Winters, whom I had never seen before. According to Mrs. Lewis, Mrs. Winters's husband had thrown her out of their house and threatened to kill her. So Mrs. Lewis had taken her in and offered her protection. I heard more about this and said I would do what I could.

"After I made arrangements with Mrs. Lewis about the wedding, I started out. As I left, a drunken man—whom I was to discover was the husband of the frightened woman—was standing at the bottom of the steps, waiting for me. Mrs. Winters called after me, 'Be careful! Try to calm him.' I walked down to him and attempted to speak to him in a quiet way, but I could see a burning hatred in his eyes. His fists were clenched, and he asked me angrily, 'What are you doing here with those women?' Then he saw my turnaround collar and recognized who I was and yelled out, 'Are you that man that preaches about Jesus? I don't like people that preach Jesus.' Then he hauled off and struck me in the face with his fist. Then, quickly, he hit me again with the other fist.

"I knew I could fight back and probably knock him out because he was shorter than me, and he was intoxicated. But something made me just take it, and I'm glad that I didn't touch him. When he saw that I wasn't going to fight him, he hit me again, and I fell down. Then he began to kick me.

"Boris was nearby and saw what was going on and came running towards us. Some other people came too. Then Winters ran off, cursing and riling against his wife, Mrs. Lewis, Boris, me, and the people who had gathered around. That is what happened. Then Boris helped me get home."

Patrolman Murphy spoke up, "Of course, you will press charges against this man."

"No," William answered weakly and closed his eyes.

"It was a vicious attack," Boris explained. "People that saw it will tell you how brutally that hothead went after him."

"William has to have quiet," Grace said.

Clara and Boris began to leave, both saying they would come back later to make sure he was all right.

Soon, the doctor arrived. After examining William, he confirmed that he had broken ribs and a possible concussion that would need time to heal.

Finally, the policemen left. Grace could hear Patrolman Murphy say loudly as he went down the front step, "People aren't supposed to beat up priests and ministers."

Chapter 16

New York City
1902

IT WAS SEVERAL years later when the first "Black Hand" letter came. Then more letters arrived. Each warned that Reverend Ford and his family would be hurt. By then, William and Grace had two children: Dudley, aged six, and Helen, aged four. The letters indicated that the children would be kidnapped and William would be killed if he didn't stop trying to keep the men from going into the saloons in Corona.

When Charles Levering heard about the threatening letters, he arranged for William to go with him to his bank in New York City.

"I want you to meet John Peterson, who owns a detective agency, and two of his men," Charles told William.

So the next day, they took the train to New York City. When they arrived, the streets outside Penn Station were crowded. Men in black coats and derby hats rushed about in all directions. Charles hailed a hansom cab, and they got in. The cabdriver maneuvered carefully out from the curb so as not to run over the people who swarmed around in front of him.

Charles began to speak seriously to William as they drove along. "At the office, you will meet John Peterson and two of his detectives. You will have to show them the Black Hand letters and explain the details."

"In each letter, the warning was the same," William said. "They write they will kidnap the children and kill me if I don't stay away from their saloons."

"You know, William, I have been told that you stand outside the bars on Main Street late Friday afternoons and try to stop the men from going in for a drink. Naturally, the man that owns the place gets angry. You are disrupting his business."

Then William reminded Charles that there are many wives and children that have the bread taken out of their mouths because the men spend their pitifully small wages on whiskey and beer.

The cabdriver had stopped short of the bank, as numerous pushcarts and throngs of people with bundles and baskets blocked the street. Finally, the driver, urging the horse forward, was able to park at the front door; and Charles and William got out.

As the driver attempted to move away, the rear wheel of the cab hit a pushcart and tipped it over. The pushcart man was knocked down to the ground. His load of potatoes rolled onto the street. Neighborhood children standing nearby saw what happened and rushed to steal the potatoes. The pushcart man got to his feet and began shouting angrily at the cabdriver as he hurriedly drove away.

Turning back toward the bank, William noticed a badly crippled beggar squatting alongside the main door. Charles shook his head and said, "I told the police to keep him away from here. But as soon as they leave, he comes back."

William reached into his pocket for a coin.

"Don't do that!" Charles said. "These immigrants, who are overpopulating the city, should take care of their own."

William leaned down just the same and gave the beggar a coin.

"Get some food," he said to the beggar.

Charles Levering shrugged his shoulders and led William inside. The bank tellers in the barred enclosures stood up as the bank president passed with William following him. His large office was at the rear, and Levering's secretary stopped him briefly as they came near.

"Mr. John Peterson, of the Peterson Detective Agency, and two of his men are waiting for you inside."

Charles nodded to him, and they went into the office.

Chapter 17

JOHN PETERSON WAS sitting in a chair in front of the desk. The two detectives were standing at the back of the room. John got up when Charles and William came in, and he went over to shake their hands.

"It's good of you to come," Charles said, and then he introduced him to William.

"That's not necessary," John said. "We know each other from the summer conferences in Northfield, Massachusetts."

"Little did I think last summer that we would be meeting like this," William said.

"Charles has told me about your trouble. That is why I am here." Then pointing to the men in the back, John said, "These two men, Reily and O'Toole, are detectives in my agency."

"Let's sit down and discuss what can be done," Charles said.

So the three sat down and began to talk.

John Peterson looked directly at William and asked, "I want you to tell me everything about these threatening letters you have been receiving."

William began, "I have managed to make enemies of people in the liquor business in Corona. It has become a habit of mine to stand outside the main saloon in town on Friday nights. That is when the men on the construction jobs get paid. I wait for them there."

"Do you know them?" John asked.

"I know some of them, but not all. You may not be aware of it, but Corona is growing fast. You can see new foundations for houses and stores being built everywhere. The construction business is thriving, and there are jobs to be had by the new immigrants. However, the workers head right for the saloons on payday and get drunk. I try and convince them to go home to their families instead of drinking, but with little success.

"So, once, I decided it was time for me to actually go into the saloon myself. Inside, it was dark and crowded. I pushed my way up to the bar and began talking to the men about sobriety and temperance. The man who owned the place stood behind the bartender and looked at me angrily. Most of the men paid little attention to what I was saying, but I am used to that. But it was after I went inside the bar that the Black Hand letters started coming. They read: 'Your son will be kidnapped, and you will be killed.' However, the letter that came this morning was different. It read: 'Leave 200 dollars on the flat rock in the woods at nine o'clock tonight. If you don't, we will know what to do.'"

"This is a serious situation," Peterson said, and he got up from the chair and walked over to a large window. He dug his hands deep into the pockets of his trousers as he concentrated on the problem. The others watched him in silence. After a few minutes, he turned around.

"I have a plan!" he said. "Detectives Reily and O'Toole will accompany you back to Corona today. Then they will contact the local police and get one of them to go into the woods with them tonight. They will find a hiding place near the flat rock where the money is to be left. While they are waiting, it will be your job, William, to go into the woods carrying a bag. There won't be two hundred dollars in it—there will be some blank pieces of paper. You will put the bag on the rock and leave. Then when the man comes to pick it up, my detectives and the policeman will arrest him."

William agreed and mentioned, "It's only three miles from my house to that place in the woods. I will ride my bike."

"Do you own a gun?" Peterson asked.

"No, I have never owned one and never will."

"Ford!" Peterson shouted. "When someone tells you that they will kidnap your children and kill you, you need a gun."

Immediately, Charles opened a desk drawer and brought out a small pistol.

One of the detectives from the back of the room came forward and said, "I'll show you how to fire it."

"No! I will take my chances without it," William said. He added, "But I have to admit that my wife, Grace, is very upset about all this. It was difficult for her to send our daughter off to her grandparents' house in Boonton, New Jersey. Now she's worried that harm might come to our son, who is still at home."

"If you can arrange a place for Reily and O'Toole to stay in Corona, one of them can keep an eye on the boy," Peterson said.

There was a knock on the door, and the secretary looked in. "Mr. Levering, your stepdaughter, Liza Lovett, is in the outside office and would like to see you when you are free."

"We'll be finished here in a minute," Charles said. Then he walked over to Peterson and shook his hand.

William did the same and said, "This trouble will be over soon, I'm sure."

"Yes, I am confident it will be," Peterson said. And he added, "I will look forward to seeing you this summer in Northfield. You and your wife must visit us at our cottage."

"We'll be glad to, and thank you for your help."

When he and the two detectives left the office, William saw Liza sitting outside. He went right over to her. "It's good to see you, young lady. How nice you look in your nurse's uniform."

"I'm glad to see you, Pastor Ford."

"I have heard that you are working at one of the big hospitals here in New York."

"Yes, it is Bellevue Hospital, and it is very crowded. We take care of many poor people, and there are a lot of TB cases. Some of the patients have been moved to a sanitarium in Upstate New York." Then she looked at the men with William.

"This is Mr. Reily and Mr. O'Toole. They are going back to Corona with me, but I can't explain why now. Your stepfather might want to tell you about it."

He said good-bye to Liza, and they headed for the front door.

Out on the street, the two detectives pushed their way through the crowds, looking for a streetcar, with William attempting to keep up with them.

Suddenly, O'Toole shouted, "Hurry up. There's one coming!"

So they started running, dodging people and carts as they went. They reached the trolley just in time and jumped aboard for the ride to Penn Station.

Chapter 18

THAT NIGHT, DETECTIVES Reily and O'Toole—along with Patrolman Murphy, from the Corona Police Station—made their way into the woods that bordered the town. Murphy showed the others the path to the flat rock that had been designated in the Black Hand letter as the place to leave the money.

When they got to the rock, Murphy held up the lantern he was carrying and said, "See those bushes over there? That is where we will hide. Pastor Ford should be here before long."

"How can he get his bicycle over that rutted path?" O'Toole asked.

"He rides that bike everywhere. He will make it," Murphy assured them. He added, "The letter said the money would be picked up at 9:00 PM. So we will settle down over there and wait."

Later on, O'Toole slapped his own face and swore, "Damn these mosquitoes . . . they are swarming all around my head."

"A mosquito bite won't kill you," Reily said.

"Then I think I'll have a cigarette? The smoke will keep them away," O'Toole commented.

"No, you can't. We must not show any kind of light."

After a while, O'Toole spoke up again, "Where is Ford anyway?"

"He'll be here." Then Reily turned to Murphy, "O'Toole and I had dinner with Pastor Ford and his wife at their house tonight."

"That's interesting."

"Mrs. Ford fed us some boiled potatoes and Swiss chard and some kind of meat," Reily recalled.

"The meat was so full of fat that it was hard to chew," O'Toole complained.

"She did the best she could and she is a nice-looking woman, but she is very upset," Reily went on. "Her hands were shaking when she served the food, and I thought she might cry. Pastor Ford told us that she has been afraid that the bad men are going to kidnap their son."

"Don't the Fords have a woman working for them?" Murphy asked.

"Not now. She is with their little girl at the grandparents' in Boonton, New Jersey," Reily explained.

"I agree, Pastor Ford's wife is a nervous wreck," O'Toole said. "And no wonder. When Pastor Ford walks right into a saloon and starts preaching against the liquor business, he's asking for trouble."

"It's a matter of principle with him," Murphy said. "Crime is getting to be a big problem here in Corona, and nightly drinking doesn't help. These immigrants bring their secret societies and violent ways over here with them from Europe. A regular person takes a real risk if he bothers them or tells them what to do or tries to get close to them."

Suddenly, there was a light on the path.
"Here comes Pastor Ford now."
"He's got a paper bag."
"He's looking all around."
"Shall we call to him?"
"No! One of the gang may be hiding behind those trees."
"He's looking into the woods over there."
"Maybe he sees something."
"He is probably just seeing shadows."
"Is there money in the bag?"
"I told you there wasn't any."
"Keep quiet, will you?"
"He's putting the bag on the rock."
"He's getting ready to leave."
"There he goes."
"Well, he's done his part. Now we have to wait and see if anybody comes for the money, and then we will grab him."

Chapter 19

AN HOUR PASSED, and finally, O'Toole stood up from a crouched position and stretched. "I don't like the idea of spending the whole night here."

"Get down!" Reily said. "We're getting paid to do this."

After another fifteen minutes, Murphy spotted a man slip out from the trees and move toward the flat rock. The man looked around and then bent down and picked up the bag.

Immediately, Murphy jumped to his feet and shouted loudly, "Stop! It's the police! Drop that bag and stand still with your hands over your head!"

The dark figure paused a moment, then dropped the bag and started racing up the path. The three broke through the bushes and ran after him. They were gaining on him when he darted off the path and into the dense woods.

O'Toole rushed after him, pushing the tree limbs aside as he went. The others followed. Then suddenly, they heard

O'Toole cry out. They hurried forward and saw that he had tripped on some fallen branches and fell into a hole.

"Where is the man you were chasing?" Reily asked, coming up to him.

"I couldn't catch him because I fell."

"Which way did he go?"

O'Toole pointed ahead and then said anxiously, "Forget him, I'm in pain. I think I broke my ankle."

"Get up, it's probably nothing," Murphy shouted. "I'm going after that punk!" And he ran farther into the woods.

Reily reached down and pulled O'Toole out of the hole and helped him get to his feet, while listening to him complain about his ankle.

"If you had looked where you were going," Reily said, "we might have caught that man. There's little hope of finding him now."

In a few minutes, Murphy came back and said, "I couldn't catch him. He had too much of a head start. When we get back to the police station, I'll explain what happened to the chief. Someone else can look for him tomorrow. From what I saw of him back at the rock, he didn't look like the saloon owner. He was too short. Anyway, the gang leaders often get lackeys, just off the ship, to do their dirty work—like this."

"Shall we tell Pastor Ford that the man got away?" Reily asked.

"I suppose so. He has a right to know. He's not safe from the gang yet," Murphy said. "Let's get out of here!"

"What about my ankle?" O'Toole asked.

"It's probably only a sprain and you can just walk it off."

Then they turned around and made their way back to the path that led to town.

O'Toole lagged behind in order to light a cigarette. Then he hurried, still limping, to catch up with the others.

"Are we off duty now?" he asked.

"I guess so."

"Well then, how late does that saloon in Corona stay open?"

"Until midnight," Murphy said, not paying much attention to him as he watched the starlight make weird shadows on the tree trunks along the path.

"So you need a drink?" Reily asked sarcastically.

"You are damned right I do!" O'Toole answered.

As they came out of the woods, they could dimly see in front of them the rows of darkened houses on Main Street.

O'Toole left them and limped in the direction of the saloon.

Murphy, with Reily, walked directly to the police station to make a report.

Chapter 20

THE NEXT DAY was sunny and warm in Corona. In the late afternoon, Liza Lovett hurried up the steps of the front porch of the Leverings' large house on Main Street. Her mother, Clara, rushed out to meet her. "Liza, at last you have two days off from the hospital," she said. They hugged each other. "Let's sit down here," Clara said, pointing to the rocking chairs.

"It's good to get out of the hospital, Mother," Liza said, settling back and relaxing. "The coughing of the patients never stops."

Then Clara said in a concerned tone, "I worry about you being there. You might catch a disease yourself."

"I'm careful," Liza replied and then sighed. "I'm glad to be back in peaceful Corona."

"Not so peaceful," Clara said. "The cleaning woman told me this morning that Patrolman Murphy was trying to chase a criminal in the woods last night. People think that he was after one of the men who have been threatening Pastor Ford."

"Oh no, somebody is really threatening him?"

"Yes, that's what they say. It's been hard for them. But they will be able to get away from the problem soon. Your stepfather has rented a cottage in Northfield for the Fords for the whole summer, and they will be able to attend the conferences there. Grace is happy about going. They leave in two weeks."

"When will you and Charles be going to Northfield?"

"We will go up about the same time," Clara said. "You will certainly come and visit us for a few weeks."

"I'll try!"

Then suddenly, Liza jumped up from the chair and ran to the railing of the porch. She began calling and waving to a man who was passing by.

"Liza, what are you doing?" her mother asked in surprise.

"That's Boris Melikof—you remember him! I had a chat with him coming out on the train today. He is in charge of the East Side settlement house in Manhattan. Can I ask him to come up onto the porch?"

"I suppose so."

"Boris," Liza shouted, "come up and say hello."

He turned and came toward them.

"Since when do you call that man by his first name?" Clara asked.

"He is a friend, and many patients at the hospital know him and call him by his first name. I see him when he visits them. He is well thought of, Mother. He is a truly good man, and he has been lonely since his wife died."

"I know that Pastor Ford talks well of him," Clara admitted.

Boris came up the steps and said in his thick European accent, "Good afternoon, Mrs. Levering. I am glad to see you again."

"Yes, I remember that we have met before," Clara said.

"Your daughter is an angel to those sick people at the hospital. I have heard that many of them arrive in this country with diseases they get in the crowded steerage part of the ships from Europe."

"That's probably true," Clara said. "I was hesitant when Liza told me some years ago that she wanted to be a nurse and work in a hospital. It's a hard life, but she was determined."

"She's well respected," Boris said. He added, "I'm living permanently at the settlement house in New York City, but I come to Corona often to see my friends."

"Mother, Boris mentioned to me on the train that he would be glad if you and I would attend the International Dinner tomorrow night at the settlement house. The dinners they have there are very interesting and are mostly attended by the new immigrants. Boris tells me that the newcomers wear their native costumes, and they serve food that is like the food in their home countries. Also, he wants you to meet a certain young man who will be there. His name is Martin Hall. He is a social worker and has an office at the hospital where I work. He's married to a young girl from Eastern Europe who helps Boris. They will be there at the dinner. Can we go, Mother?"

"You want me to go to an International Dinner on the Lower East Side of New York to eat strange food and where everyone will be speaking in foreign languages. Do you have any idea what your stepfather would say about that?"

"But, Mother, Charles is in Chicago on business, so he won't know about this!"

Clara shook her head and said, "Really, Liza, I'm not sure."

"Madam, I guarantee you a pleasant time and excellent food! And there will be music. Everyone is very friendly, and you will enjoy yourself," Boris said with a broad smile.

"All right, I'll go with you on one condition. The condition is that you don't mention this to your stepfather," Clara said. Then she turned to Boris, "If you will excuse me now, I have something to do in the house." And then she went inside.

Liza smiled at Boris and exclaimed happily, "So we will be there!"

"Excellent," Boris said, and he came closer and took Liza's hand briefly and kissed it. Then he went down the steps and out onto Main Street. Liza watched him go and waved when he turned and looked back at her.

Chapter 21

New York City
1912

THE INTERNATIONAL DINNER was held in the basement room of the Eastside settlement house in New York City. Long wooden tables had been set up, on which different kinds of food had been spread out. There were chairs and benches along the walls; and through the high narrow windows near the ceiling, the feet of people walking on the street above could be seen.

Late in the afternoon, many of the new immigrants from Europe began to descend the steps to the basement. The sound of foreign languages being spoken grew louder as the room filled up. Soon there were women standing behind the tables, dressed in the brightly colored costumes of their homelands. In front of them on the tables were bowls of fruit, baskets of bread, plates of meat, and other exotic food.

Two women from Czechoslovakia sat on wooden boxes at the bottom of the stairs and watched as people arrived.

One said to the other, "See that woman coming in? I know her. She told me she was bringing a kettle of *hrzlik* over."

"What's that?"

"It's a soup. It's made of calves' brains. Of course, you have to wash and skin the brains first, and then you add the flour and vegetables."

Then looking up the steps, the other asked, "Who are these people coming in now?"

"They are Hungarians. The fancy clothes they have on are the ones they wear at festival time in the old country."

"All of this makes me homesick for Europe."

"So, why did you and your husband leave?"

"There was no work to be had there, so we came here. A few days after we landed, my man found work in the needle trade."

"So, you are here. So you stay!"

"So, we stay." Then she asked, pointing, "Who is that handsome man over there?"

"That's Martin Hall. He used to work here at the settlement house, but now he has gotten a social-work job at a hospital. However, he and his wife, Mabel, still have a room here . . . look, here comes Mabel now."

Mabel was short with curly blond hair. She walked with a quick step, and she had a bright smile. She asked the two women if they were having a good time.

"Oh yes. It's very nice," said one.

"So how's the little bride?" asked the other.

"Fine, but Martin and I have been married six months, so I'm hardly a bride."

"You got a good man! Everyone likes him, but I was told he's not Hungarian like you."

"No, he is not. But that doesn't matter here. The main thing is that we both wanted to help poor immigrants," Mabel said. And then she laughed. "Poor people like me . . . but he does like his new job at the hospital now."

"He'll go places!"

Just then, Mabel saw Clara and Liza coming down the steps, so she went over to welcome them. Martin Hall and Boris Melikof, who were standing across the room, also noticed them coming in.

Martin asked Boris, "You know Liza Lovett from Corona—don't you, Boris?"

"Yes, I do. I like her very much."

"Did you know she is a nurse and works near me at the hospital? I see her often. But who is that older woman with her?" Martin asked.

"That's her mother, Mrs. Levering. She's the wife of a banker. If you are nice to her, she might give you a charitable donation, someday."

"Maybe so, but she doesn't look like she belongs with this crowd here tonight."

Mabel helped Clara and Liza select food as they moved from one table to the next.

"You have your choice of beef or pork goulash from the Yugoslavia table, or pork pie from the Romanian table over there."

"We will take the beef goulash," Clara said.

So they filled their plates, and then they found a seat on a bench along the wall where they could eat.

It was then that the band members began to arrive, carrying their banjoes, accordions, and drums. Some of the crowd shouted out when they saw the musicians come in because many were eager for the dancing to start.

Chapter 22

SOON THE BAND began to play, and Mabel took Martin by the hand and led him out to the dance floor. Others were quick to follow them. Martin had his own Western style of dancing that amused those who were watching. Some clapped their hands and stomped their feet.

The two women seated by the stairs looked on with the others.

"See, how Mabel looks at Martin! She's crazy about him," said one.

"Well, why not! He's handsome and intelligent . . . but I just hope he sticks by her."

"What do you mean 'stick by her'? That's not a nice thing to say!"

"Time will tell."

"It's still not a nice thing to say."

They stopped talking for a while and just listened to the music.

Suddenly, four men who came from the Ukraine went out onto the floor and began to do their native dance. They stooped down low, keeping their backs straight, and kicked their legs out in front of them in time to the music. They circled around several times, and the people cheered and applauded.

Later in the evening, the musicians took a break. Then, suddenly, all eyes turned toward the steps as Otto Kirschheimer came down into the room and shouted out, "Boris Melikof! Where are you, you old Armenian bandit?"

Immediately, Boris answered, "Here!" And he hurried forward and gave his old friend a firm handshake. Otto was tall and well built, with a handsome face and a deep resounding voice.

"And I hope you saved some *rostenky videnske* for me," Otto said.

"Oh yes, and there is plenty of the Viennese beefsteak left too, and some liver sausage," Boris said. And he added, "Are you off to Northfield, Massachusetts, again?"

"Yes, I am. And I was able to hire some strong Italian workers off the dock this time. I tell you, those construction-worker brokers on the New York waterfront are tough, but I got a good gang of men despite them. The Northfield school needs two more stone dormitories, and there's a rich man that's planning to build a French château there. That means plenty of work. I'll take the men up in the boxcar of the train tomorrow . . . But I'm hungry now. How about some food for me, you old Bedouin desert rat."

Boris led him over to the German food table, and Otto served himself and began eating standing up. Then Boris introduced him to Martin and Mabel, saying, "This big German and I came over on the same boat from Europe. Since then, he has been stopping at the settlement house to see me every time he's in New York. He meets the incoming ships from Europe and hires workers right off the dock."

Mabel spoke up, "You mentioned that the men ride in a train boxcar. It seems cruel to have them all crowded in like cattle. Aren't there regulations about that sort of thing?"

Otto looked at Mabel in surprise and then asked Boris, "Well now, where did this little Bohemian do-gooder come from?" Then he turned to Mabel and said, "Frankly, young lady, you don't know what you're talking about. The men I hire are glad to get the jobs. Mainly, they come from Italy. When the work is finished here, most of them go back to Italy with money in their pockets to help their families. Is there something wrong with that?"

Then he turned and looked at Boris. "What kind of place are you running here when young women like her are turning into hotheaded liberals? That can be dangerous in this day and age."

"She's nothing like that!" Boris said. "She works here. She is just softhearted and wants to help everybody."

Then Otto changed the subject and asked, "Where do you get a drink around here?"

"I have a few bottles of whiskey in a corner behind the furnace," Boris said.

"Well, let's get some," Otto offered, and they walked to the back of the room.

Meanwhile, Clara and Liza had finished eating and began talking about leaving.

"I'm tired now, dear," Clara said.

"Yes, let's go."

"It has been interesting here at the International Dinner, but it is getting late."

They climbed the stairs without anyone noticing they were going. The music started up again, and the clapping and laughing in the basement of the settlement house grew loud again.

Clara and Liza could still hear the music when they were on the sidewalk outside of the building. There were few people to be seen on the dark street due to the late hour.

They hailed a passing cab that took them to Penn Station, where they boarded a train for the ride back to Corona.

Chapter 23

Northfield
1917

BY THE SUMMER of 1917, a Northfield carpenter had built a small cottage for Reverend Ford's family on the ridge above the girls' school campus and conference center. It was located near John Peterson's much larger summer home. The Leverings' cottage was on the highest ridge and was also very large, with a wide screened-in porch.

Spending three months in the newly built cottage meant peace, rest, and enjoyment for the Ford family. In Northfield, William Ford was far removed from the obligations and responsibilities of the Corona church. He was free from the sudden parish tragedies, from the worries about money for the church, and from unseen enemies.

At the cottage, he enjoyed lying in the porch hammock and losing himself in a book about the cowboys of the Old

West. Also, he found great pleasure in the comradeship of other ministers he would meet at the conference meetings.

Although William never played golf himself, his friends John Peterson and Charles Levering played each day at the Northfield Hotel golf course. It was there that the two of them met E. B. Thompson, a wealthy manufacturer from New Jersey. He and his wife and their large family stayed each summer at the hotel.

One hot afternoon in early July, the three men were resting on a bench at the ninth tee before finishing their round of golf for the day.

"How many summers have you been staying at the hotel, EB?" James asked.

"Five years now. We take over the whole north wing of the hotel, which is out of the way. That keeps my six noisy children from disturbing the regular guests," EB answered. And then he said seriously, "However, I think this war with Germany will shorten our vacations here in the next few years."

"I didn't think that President Wilson would declare war," Levering said.

"He had to. The Germans are sinking our ships," Peterson explained.

"My stepdaughter, Liza, joined the Army Nurse Corps and is already in France," Levering told them.

"That is a coincidence," EB said, "because my son, Bob, has volunteered to join the Army Medical Corps. He'll be in uniform by September, and then he will go over. I wonder if they will meet."

"Speaking of the war," Peterson remarked. "My detective agency has a contract with the government to track down enemy agents in this country. There are dozens of German spies in New York City alone. The government wants my agency to help track them down and keep tabs on them. As a matter of fact, I am getting suspicious of that big German, Otto Kirschheimer, who is in charge of the golf house."

"He seems harmless to me," Levering said.

Suddenly, he noticed Ben Potter on a tractor, mowing the fairway. "Let's call Potter over here and see what he has to say about the German. These Northfield townspeople know everything."

So the three called out loudly and waved. Ben Potter heard them and slowly got off the tractor and walked over to them.

E. B. Thompson stepped out to meet him. "Hello, Ben, you remember me? I helped design this golf course. You do a fine job of keeping the fairways and greens in good condition."

Potter didn't answer but pulled a red bandana out of his pocket and wiped the sweat off his face.

"We asked you over to find out what you know about Otto Kirschheimer, who works at the golf house and who lives across the river," Peterson said.

Potter squinted, as the lowering sun shone in his eyes. He put his hand to his forehead and answered, "He's hiding some men in his barn."

"What!" Peterson shouted. "How do you know that?"

"The farmer that lives next to him told me some men showed up last week. They looked shabby and were badly sunburned. He said that Otto hides them in the barn during the day, and they sneak over to the farmhouse at night."

"Are you sure about this?" Peterson asked.

"Yes, but that is all I know," Potter said and quickly turned around and walked back to his tractor.

"When we finish the game, I'll go into the golf house and talk to Kirschheimer. If you two don't mind, I'll question him by myself since I am experienced in this kind of thing," said Peterson.

"Of course," they agreed.

Then they each teed off on the last hole.

Chapter 24

E. B. THOMPSON made a good putt on the ninth green, and the others complimented him.

"That settles it. You won!" Levering said. "But remember, you have an unfair advantage since you helped design this golf course."

EB smiled and told him, "I didn't do much. I just made a few suggestions to the real designer when he came to the hotel and started planning it."

"Last year, you told us you laid out the whole course!"

"I don't remember that."

They all laughed and walked off the green. Then Peterson suggested, "Why don't you two wait over there in the gazebo, while I go in and have a talk with this man."

"That sounds fine!" Levering said. So he and EB made themselves comfortable on the rustic chairs inside the small wooden gazebo that was located between the ninth green and the golf house.

When Peterson went inside, Otto was counting the money from the register. Hearing him, he looked up and asked, "Did you have a good round?"

"Fair," he said, and then he asked Otto how long he had been working at the hotel.

"Two years," he answered.

"I have heard that there are some men hiding in your barn!"

"What are you talking about? Who told you that? Whoever told you that was lying!" Otto said angrily. Then noticing the hard look in Peterson's eye, he said more calmly, "Sure, my cousin and two of his friends are staying with me. They are not hiding. They have been helping me around the farm while they are here. Why do you care about that?"

"Listen to me," Peterson said. "I care because those men may have come off a German warship that was seen in the water off Boston Harbor two weeks ago. Some of the crew got on shore, but they haven't all been found yet."

"What, are you crazy?" Otto shouted.

"No, I am not crazy! Suppose I come over to your place. I'd like to meet your cousin and his two friends! Expect me!" Peterson warned.

Otto glared at him as Peterson turned around and left.

Otto went to the window of the golf house and watched as the three men outside stood talking to each other. Then he saw EB start up the hill toward the hotel. After that, Peterson and Levering walked over to where Peterson's car was parked. The black chauffeur, Saunders—who had been asleep behind the wheel—woke up as soon as he heard the men's voices. He jumped out of the car and opened the rear door for them.

"You can take us back to the cottage on the Ridge," Peterson said as they got into the car.

Then Saunders hurriedly took his place behind the wheel of the car. Then he adjusted his uniform hat and started up the engine.

Otto watched them go. Then he took some money out of the cash register, explaining to himself that after two years on the job, he could take an advance. Then he proceeded to close the golf house for the day. He locked the door and went over to his Model T Ford car. He cranked the engine until it started and then got in. It didn't take him long to drive down Main Street and then over the bridge to his farm. His farmhouse and barn were located on a hill that sloped down to the Connecticut River.

As Otto got out of his car, he could see one of his cousin's friends picking ears of corn off the cornstalks in the field. He called out to him, "Where are the others?"

"They are in the barn."

"Will you go and get them out here? I need to talk to you all."

Then Otto sat down on the wooden steps of the side porch of the house and waited. When the three came over to him, he said seriously, "Somebody knows you are here."

"How can that be?" one said in German.

"I don't know, but you'll have to leave."

"Where can we go?" another asked anxiously.

"I have money for you. You will get into that canoe that is tied up on the riverbank and then paddle south until you see the tobacco fields on the left. Pull over there, get out, and secure the canoe. Then you will hide for the night in one of the tobacco drying sheds you will see. Tomorrow morning, look for the boss and ask for a job working there. Mention my name. He knows me. He will help you."

Soon, the three made their way down the hill to the river and got into the canoe. Otto could see them as they paddled out into the middle. He watched until the canoe disappeared around the far bend in the river. Then he went into the barn to see if they had left anything behind.

Later that night, after the conference service on the campus of the school ended, Peterson went to the hotel to send a telegram. He addressed it to detectives Reily and O'Toole at the office in New York City. It told them to get the train to Northfield the next day because he had a job for them.

After sending the telegram, he came out of the hotel and told Saunders that he wanted him to meet the afternoon train from New York the next day. "Look for Reily and O'Toole and bring them up to the cottage."

"Yes, sir, Mr. Peterson. I knows those two!"

Chapter 25

THE NEXT AFTERNOON, Saunders was waiting as Reily and O'Toole got off the train at the Northfield railroad station. He waved to them.

"Mr. Peterson's waiting for you," Saunders said.

"Do you know what this is about?" they asked as they got into the car.

"I just know the boss is waiting for you!"

When they arrived at the cottage, Peterson was practicing his golf swing in the side yard. Seeing them, he went over and smiled. "Well, you made it!"

"Yes, sir!" Reily replied.

"But that was a long train ride," O'Toole mentioned.

Peterson pointed to a small building behind the main cottage. "You will sleep in there while you are here. The cook will bring your meals out to you. Now about the job—we will be investigating a German here. I have reason to believe, on good authority, that he has been hiding enemy aliens in his barn. I'll give you more details later. Right now, I have things to do inside, so you two just make yourselves at home. I'm glad you are here." Then he turned and went into the cottage, with the screen door slamming closed behind him.

The two men looked out at the view. They could see woods and mountains to the west and rolling hills to the east.

"What a view," Reily said.

"Yes, but who would want to come to such an isolated place?" O'Toole asked.

"I have been told that people come here in the summer and attend the religious conferences."

"How dull, give me the city any time!"

"But it's still a great view."

"I bet there's no bar in this town."

"Not on your life, this town is completely dry. So is the hotel."

"What a backwater dump! It's good I brought my flask."

"Don't let the boss see it," Reily warned. "Now let's look at the place where we are supposed to sleep."

They walked up to the small building and went inside. There was only one room and one window and unfinished walls. There were two cots and two straight chairs—and a washbasin.

"How luxurious!" O'Toole said sarcastically.

"Let's move these chairs outside," Reily suggested. "We can relax."

So each of them picked up a chair and went outside and sat on the front lawn.

"You got a cigarette?" O'Toole asked.

"Yes," Reily answered, handing him one and taking one for himself.

At the same time, Clara Levering was walking down the long narrow path that went between her cottage and the Ford cottage. There were tall pine trees on both sides. When she arrived at the front step, she called out loudly, "Anyone home?"

Grace came out on the porch, smiling; she asked Clara to come in.

"I'm glad to find you at home."

"Oh yes, but I must look a sight," Grace said as she fumbled to remove her apron.

"You look fine."

"Let's sit here in the rockers," Grace said. She continued, "William and my daughter, Helen, are up in the woods cutting off birch branches that will be used to make a railing here on the edge of the porch."

"That's good. It will be safer," Clara said and then began talking more seriously to Grace. "I have a plan. Your daughter, Helen, is seventeen now—isn't she? So I thought it would be nice for her to meet young Bob Thompson. I mean for them to be properly introduced. Bob's family stays at the hotel. His father, E. B. Thompson, is a rich mill owner and plays golf with my husband, James, and John Peterson. You must have seen the Thompson family at church in the auditorium. They take up a whole row. My idea is for you and Helen to come to my cottage for tea tomorrow. I will invite Mrs. Thompson and Bob for tea also."

"Wonderful," said Grace. "You are so thoughtful. Of course we will come. I believe I know the young man you are talking about. He is handsome and tall and has a nice smile. He was standing near us outside the auditorium after the service last Sunday," Grace remembered.

"Well, that settles it. Come at four!"

Suddenly, there was a noise on the side of the cottage.

"Look, William and Helen are back. They are piling the birch branches against the house," Grace said.

"Ask them to come up."

So Grace called out, "Clara's here. Come say hello."

William smiled at his daughter as she began brushing wood chips off her black skirt.

"Don't fuss! It's only Clara," William said.

"Only Clara!" Helen whispered in her father's ear, and they laughed.

Then they both came up onto the porch.

William greeted his old Corona friend and parishioner. "You are looking well, Clara."

"No wonder—it's so peaceful here in Northfield," Clara said.

He was holding a birch branch in his hand. "Soon we will have a good sturdy porch railing here." Then William looked over to the Peterson property and said, "John must be having visitors. See those two men sitting on the lawn? They look familiar."

"I know who they are," Clara said. "They are two detectives from the Peterson Agency. James told me this morning they are coming here to investigate that German who works at the golf house."

"I know those two men," William said. "They helped me once, but I don't understand why John thinks he needs them here. Otto Kirschheimer has been in Northfield for years. I have often talked to him. He's a good person and is a friend of Boris Melikof's from the settlement house in New York City. I think I'll go over and have a talk with John about this."

Suddenly, Grace jumped up. "Oh no, Will, don't go. The Petersons are our friends. Don't stir things up!"

"I won't stir things up. I will just talk to him."

"You can't go over there looking like that. Your overalls are dirty," Grace pleaded.

"He's seen me in overalls before. I'm on vacation," Will said and left the porch. He walked across the side yard in the direction of the Peterson property.

Clara consoled Grace, "Don't worry. John Peterson likes your husband. It will be all right."

Then Clara turned and put her arm around Helen's shoulder. "Helen, you are coming to tea at my cottage tomorrow. And I am going to introduce you to a fine young man. His name is Bob Thompson."

"I think I know who you mean. I've seen him off and on around the conference ground," Helen said. "The only problem is that my one good dress has a tear in it. I put the heel of my shoe through the hem climbing up to the sleeping loft the other night."

"I'll mend it," Grace said. "You'll look fine."

Then Clara said good-bye and left. She walked slowly up the path that led to her cottage on the highest ridge. She enjoyed looking at the ferns bordering the path and felt a strange sense of protection that the tall pine trees seemed to provide on each side.

Chapter 26

AS WILLIAM APPROACHED the Peterson cottage, he saw Reily and O'Toole sitting on the front lawn talking, and they saw him.

"That's Pastor Ford from Corona coming towards us," O'Toole said. "I have never seen him out of his black suit and turnaround collar before. You would hardly recognize him."

"You know, there is something about that man that I like," Reily mentioned. "Look at him now. He's stopping to talk to Peterson's black chauffeur, who is trimming those trees over there. He is never too busy to be friendly."

Then William came up to them. They both stood up and shook hands with him.

"It's good to see you two again. I was never able to thank you for the help you gave me in Corona," he said.

"The police never found the man that wanted money from you."

Then William asked if John Peterson was in the cottage.

"The cook told us that he always takes a nap before dinner."

"Well then, I won't disturb him," William said and started to leave. Then he stopped and turned back. "Do you mind if I ask you why you are here? I heard it has something to do with a German man, Otto Kirschheimer, who lives here."

"Mr. Peterson hasn't made that clear yet," Reily said.

"I just want you to know that Otto has a good reputation here in Northfield. He's well thought of. People like him."

"Listen, Pastor, we don't know for sure what is involved or why Mr. Peterson asked us to come here—but whatever it is, I am sure it is confidential," Reily stated.

"Still, I will speak to John about this soon," William said. And then he started walking back to his cottage, pausing again to exchange a few more words with Saunders, who was still trimming the trees.

Not far from the Otto Kirschheimer's place, across the river, was a dairy farm. The next afternoon, the farmer and his son were herding their cows in from the pasture to the barn for milking. Suddenly, they notice a black car coming up the road.

"It's stopping over there at Kirschheimer's," he said to his son. "That car belongs to the summer man—Peterson. He is some kind of detective."

"Who are those other men with him?" asked the boy.

"A couple of his henchmen, I guess. I bet they are going to question Otto about those foreign men who are staying there."

"I think they left," his son said. "I was down by the river today and saw men getting into a canoe that was tied up down there. So I think they are gone."

Suddenly, one of the cows broke away from the herd. They ran after it and forced it back with the rest, shouting "Hey! Hey!" and using their sticks.

When the last cow was put inside the barn, the farmer came out and glanced over at his neighbor's barn. He saw three men standing in front of the house and decided to go over to talk to them. Peterson saw him coming, and they waited for him.

"If you were looking for those three strangers that were staying here, my son saw them getting into a canoe and paddling south on the river. They were staying here at Kirschheimer's for about a week, but I don't know what they were doing here," he said.

Peterson thanked him and watched him turn and leave. Then he and Reily knocked on the kitchen door of the farmhouse as O'Toole went into the barn.

Otto opened the door, and when he saw the men standing there, he said angrily, "I saw that other guy go into my barn. What's going on?"

"We are here to ask a few questions."

"My cousin and two friends were here but were just passing through. Anyway, they have gone now."

"Just passing through, you say . . ." Peterson said. "I've been doing some investigating. There is a chance those men are German sailors who survived the sinking of an enemy warship off of Boston, and they came here."

"That's a lie!"

"Step aside!" Reily said as he pushed his way into the house.

Peterson followed him in and said, "You check upstairs, and I'll look around down here."

"You have no right!" Otto fumed.

Soon, Reily returned and reported there was nothing suspicious upstairs. Suddenly, they heard tapping at the window. O'Toole beckoned to them to come out on the side porch, which they did.

"Look at what I found in the barn. It's a sextant!"

"Let me see it," Peterson asked, taking it into his hands and examining it. "It's got German writing on it."

Otto stood behind them in the doorway.

"Did your friends leave this?" Peterson asked, holding up the sextant.

"That's mine. It was my father's."

O'Toole said loudly, "I found it in the hayloft. And it looks like people have been sleeping up there."

"If it was your father's, how come it looks so new?" Peterson asked.

"Give it to me, it's mine," Otto said.

"No, we'll keep it."

"Then you get off my property right now and don't come back. I don't see why you come here and upset the peace and quiet of the town."

"If you ask me, your cousin and his friends are the troublesome ones."

At that, Otto slammed the door closed.

"We might as well go," Peterson said to the others.

As they walked away, O'Toole commented, "I'd like to give that big hinny a punch in the nose."

"Yes, and he'd give you one right back—and harder, I suspect."

So the three of them got into the car, and Saunders started up the engine. They drove slowly across the bridge to Main Street and then back to the cottage.

On the way, Reily asked if they would still be needed.

"I think I would like Saunders to drive you two down to the tobacco farms south of here and ask the owner if three men with German accents have come looking for work in the last few days. Report back to me. If there is nothing, then you can get the train back to New York tomorrow."

Chapter 27

THE NEXT AFTERNOON, Grace and Helen left their cottage and walked up the path that led to the Leverings' cottage on the seventh ridge.

Clara, who was waiting for them in the screened-in porch, saw them coming and called out, "Hello, you are right on time. Come up. Mrs. Thompson and her son, Bob, should be here soon."

As they climbed the steps to the porch, Helen looked back to the dirt road below in hopes of seeing the Thompsons' car coming, but there was no sign of it. Soon, the three were settled in the rockers on the porch. Clara noticed that Helen had been watching the road, and she patted her on the knee and said, "Don't worry, he's coming."

"Did I hear that this young man, Bob Thompson, will be in uniform soon?" Grace asked.

"That's true. There are hundreds of young men being drafted into the army and sent to France to fight the Germans.

Mr. E. B. Thompson told James that his son, Bob, is supposed to leave for France in September. He will be in the Army Medical Corps. It is a coincidence that my daughter, Liza, who you know, is already serving in France as a nurse with the Army Medical Corps."

"You must be very concerned about her?" Grace said.

"She left four weeks ago. We went to New York to see her off. Yes, I was worried, but there was no stopping her."

"I wonder if Liza and Bob will meet over there," Grace asked.

"It's possible," Clara answered as she got up and peered through the screens. "I wonder where Bob and Mrs. Thompson are."

Helen moved restlessly in her chair and stared down at the porch floor, murmuring to herself, "He probably won't come!"

Then they heard a noise coming from the side of the cottage. It sounded like twigs snapping. Suddenly, they saw Bob Thompson looking at them through the screen at the far end of the porch. He was grinning but said nothing.

"Come around and join us," Clara said.

"I wasn't sure this was the right cottage," Bob said as he came around to the front and onto the porch. He was six feet tall, with broad shoulders and a handsome face. He wore a starched white shirt and white flannel trousers.

"Let me introduce you to Mrs. Ford and her daughter, Helen," Clara said. And she added, "Although you might have seen them here and there in Northfield by now."

"Yes, I have."

"But where is your mother?" Clara asked.

Bob reached into his pocket and handed a note to Clara. "Mother asked me to give this to you."

"Thank you," said Clara, and she read it out loud.

Dear Mrs. Levering,

I am sorry I am unable to come to your tea party. I have hired a car to take some of the ladies who are guests at the hotel for a drive along the river. My son, Bob, will join you.

Cordially,
Mrs. E. B. Thompson

Then Grace said quietly, "I would have liked to have met her."

Suddenly, Bob spoke up enthusiastically, "There's a donkey baseball game at five o'clock at the field near the Northfield Hotel. Would you all like to go?"

Clara and Grace looked at each other in surprise. "Maybe Helen would like to go," Clara said.

"Yes, why don't you young people go along to the game," Grace agreed.

"Everybody in town will be there," Bob said, looking at Helen.

"I would like to go," Helen said, getting up.

Clara smiled and mentioned to Bob that he hadn't had any tea yet.

"The game starts in a half an hour, and it will take time to walk down there, so we better leave now."

"Before you go," Clara said, looking at Bob. "I have heard you will be going to France with the Army Medical Corps soon. My daughter, Liza, is an army nurse and is already there. Perhaps you will see her."

Bob thought for a minute. "I leave in September. I will be stationed in whatever field hospital I am assigned to. You never know ahead of time."

"I thought with both being in the Army Medical Corps, there's a chance—"

"I'm sorry, I just don't know."

Then Bob opened the screen door and said to Helen, "We better hurry. We don't want to miss the first pitch."

Clara and Grace watched them disappear down the path in the woods that led to a road that would take them to the hotel property, and the game.

Clara surprised Grace by saying, "Why don't we go to the game too? Charles will be there. He mentioned that he would be coming over to watch it after he finished his golf game."

"And William will be there. He never misses anything that's going on. Yes, let's go!" agreed Grace.

Chapter 28

BY FIVE O'CLOCK that afternoon, the townspeople, the summer people, and the hotel guests began converging on the large field to watch the donkey baseball game.

Bob Thompson and Helen Ford were among the first to arrive at the game, with Helen pausing to catch her breath after the fast walking, as she tried to keep up with him.

Bob pointed to a temporary grandstand that the groundskeepers had put up for the hotel guests and said, "That grandstand is for the older people. Let's stand behind first base, that's a good spot," Bob said.

"All right," Helen agreed, walking close behind him.

"Did I tell you that the game is between the Northfield farmers' team and the hotel employees' team? When a batter gets a hit, he must jump on the back of a donkey and get to first base."

"I thought donkeys were stubborn animals—hard to move," Helen said.

"If the donkeys refuse to move at all, there are some young town boys who are assigned to drag them towards first base. Also, if someone gets a good hit, the outfielder has to get on a donkey and ride to where the ball landed. Then he gets off and throws the ball to the infield. Anything can happen!" Bob explained and laughed.

The grandstand soon filled up, and many stood along the baselines. Soon, the players and donkeys were in position. A farmer from across the river was the pitcher for the farm team. The umpire was one of the town fathers. He stood behind the pitcher and called the balls and strikes. The game started, and at the first crack of the bat, the crowd cheered loudly.

An older hotel employee came to bat and got a hit. Then he climbed on a donkey's back and tried to get it to move. When it did move, it moved backward, much to the delight of the spectators. Then a young boy grabbed a rope around the donkey's neck and pulled it hard to first base.

Helen saw her father nearby, talking to some of the boys who were in charge of the donkeys. He was making them laugh. Then William, who was dressed in his black suit and clerical collar, climbed into the grandstand and sat with Charles Levering, John Peterson, and E. B. Thompson.

Turning back toward the field, Helen noticed that Bob was no longer standing next to her. "Why would he leave me here alone?" Helen said to herself. She looked around and then saw him over by the entrance to the hotel garage. He was talking to the garage mechanic.

When Bob returned, she asked him, "Where were you?"

"I was talking to the garage man. He was telling me how to fix a truck engine when it breaks down. Knowing something about truck repair may help me where I'm going."

"Why?"

"Because I'll be in the Army Medical Corps, and when I get to France, they may need me to drive an ambulance. Although I have been told that my main job will be carrying stretchers from the battlefield to the base hospitals—and also, I am to assist the surgeons during operations. I still might have to drive an ambulance."

"It sounds dangerous!" Helen said.

"No, I'll be all right," he said. And then he looked down at her and asked, "Will you write to me while I'm away?"

"Oh yes, I will."

"That's good. You know, Mrs. Levering didn't have to introduce us at her cottage this afternoon because I have known who you were since we were in the children's choir here at the conference a few years ago. And to tell the truth, I have always noticed you every summer when we all were swimming at Wanamaker Lake."

Helen cringed and frowned as she remembered. Back then, she had to wear a thin moth-eaten woolen bathing suit that didn't fit her right. "I don't remember you," she lied.

Suddenly in the grandstand, Pastor Ford stood up and called out, "Here comes Grace and Clara!" The others stood up and waved.

"Who are those two men coming along behind them?" Charles asked.

"It looks like Boris Melikof from the settlement house in New York City," William answered.

"That's Otto Kirschheimer with him," Peterson said.

"Yes, it is. Boris and Otto are friends. Boris must be visiting him," William told them.

"What is that German doing here at the game?" Peterson inquired.

"Otto has worked at the hotel golf house for two years. He's here to cheer on the hotel team."

Clara called out to them as they hurried toward the grandstand, "Are you surprised to see us? Grace and I didn't want to miss the fun, and look who is with us!"

William and Charles greeted Boris warmly and shook hands with Otto. Peterson turned his back on Otto and spoke to other people in the stands.

"Let's watch the game from over there behind third base," Will said.

They found a spot there just in time to see a donkey, with a player on his back, rear up and throw the player to the ground. The crowd laughed as the donkey got away and ran off the field to the road beyond, with the young boys chasing after it.

The game went on until dark. The farmers' team beat the hotel employees' team with a score of 5–1. Someone remarked that it was a simple fact that farmers knew how to handle donkeys better than hotel help.

Then the crowd began to disperse. Some went back to the hotel. Some went to the conference center. Some went to the cottages on the Ridge and some to their houses on Main Street. But the victorious farm team was proud of their win and weren't in a hurry to rush off. They finally left reluctantly and returned to their farms.

Chapter 29

France
1917

BY THE FALL of 1917, the war in Europe was in its third year. The Americans had joined the British forces in their battle against Germany. Army transport ships were leaving regularly from New York Harbor and steaming across the Atlantic Ocean to England. Hundreds of soldiers were on board along with some of the medical corpsmen as well. Bob and his college friend, Nat Fuller, were among the medics. They had had their training at a large army camp on Long Island, New York—after which they were shipped out with the rest of the troops. The crossing to England was to take fourteen days, and they were to land in Liverpool.

On the second night aboard, as Bob and Nat waited in a long food line. Nat, who had been noticed for his good humor, called out loud so all could hear, "Anyone know what's in that stew we're supposed to eat?"

"Don't ask," someone said.

Soon, he and Bob were at the place where the stew was being served. There, they pulled their metal bowls out of their knapsacks and pushed them toward the crewman who was doling out the stew.

Nat persisted, "What is in that stuff, anyway?"

"It's rabbit stew," responded the man as he was ladling out some into their bowls.

Then Bob and Nat found an empty space on the deck to sit and began to eat.

"This was some tough rabbit!" Bob said, chewing hard.

"Who are they trying to kid?" Nat said and got up and called out to the soldiers around him. "If you ask me, this mess on the top is hiding something underneath that is not rabbit meat! What is it?"

"Not rabbit!" one of the soldiers responded, laughing.

"Well, what then?"

"It's horsemeat, stupid!" said one of the older soldiers. "One hundred percent horsemeat. And you better get used to it because that's all you'll get to eat while we are on the ship."

Two weeks later, they arrived in Liverpool and were taken by train to Southampton. From there, the troops were transported in boats across the English Channel to Le Havre, France.

For several nights, Bob and Nat slept with the others on the floor of a large French barrack. There was a hole in the corner of the wooden floor that was used for sanitary purposes. On the wall above the hole were many sets of three brown finger marks.

"This place makes me sick," Nat complained.

"Didn't you ever go camping in the woods and have to sleep on the ground?" Bob asked.

"Yes, I went camping, but it wasn't like this. I'm surprised that you are not more put off by these lousy conditions, considering all the servants your rich family has at home."

"This isn't so bad," Bob said. "I have a feeling that this will seem like nothing when we get to the front and the real fighting, and when we start carrying the wounded from the field to the base hospitals."

Soon, the army was sent by overnight train from Le Havre to within three miles of the front. Bob and Nat's medical unit was assigned to a mobile hospital that was used as an advance dressing station behind the trenches.*

When they arrived, they heard from others that the Germans were preparing for a huge offensive. With hundreds of American soldiers arriving in France, the Germans knew it was time to attack. Within a day of their arrival, the battle of the Belleau Woods began.*

By the end of the week, the number of casualties had begun to increase. Bob and Nat carried more and more of the wounded in from the trenches and battlefields.

When there was a lull in the fighting, they would assist the surgeons. The operations were usually performed in an empty barn or a tent.

One night during an operation in a barn under lantern light, Bob noticed that the middle-aged nurse across the operating table was staring at him. When the surgeon finished and the patient was taken away, the nurse came over to Bob and called him by name.

"You are Bob Thompson, aren't you?" the nurse asked. "I'm Liza Lovett, Clara Levering's daughter. I'm a friend of Helen Ford. Her father is a minister in our church in Corona, and I have seen you in Northfield."

Bob looked a little bewildered and then said, "Oh yes, Helen's been writing to me and has mentioned you." But they had to stop talking as another casualty was lifted onto the operating table.

The first time Bob had been called in to help one of the doctors, he had nearly fainted when he looked down at a horribly wounded soldier lying on the table in front of him. He had suddenly become lightheaded and felt himself sway, but he steadied himself by staring up at the rough ceiling of the barn for several minutes. That seemed to calm him. Soon, he was ready to do whatever the doctor asked him to do.

Many of the wounded had to wait for hours to be treated because there weren't enough doctors.

In March of 1918, the Germans started their last major offensive. They used powerful cannon fire, Maxim machine guns, and they increased the use of gas warfare. The town of Nurlu was overrun. This action took them to within forty-five miles of Paris, and the British, French, and American armies were forced to retreat.

However, the Allies fought back. President Woodrow Wilson ordered thousands of US troops to France. The new troops arrived over a four-month period, and as a result, the German advance was stopped.

Chapter 30

BY OCTOBER 10, 1918, most of the Germans had been driven from the Argonne. As a result, many of the American and English soldiers were granted leave and headed for Paris.

Bob and Nat, with two other medical corpsmen and three nurses, were able to commandeer a military truck and follow the others to Paris. Liza Lovett was one of the nurses that went with them.

It was late in the afternoon when they arrived at the Champs-Élysées in Paris and saw that the boulevard was filled with excited shouting people as the news spread that the Germans were about to surrender. Bob and Nat's group left the truck and found seats at a sidewalk café and soon joined in with the general hilariousness that surrounded them.

Suddenly, a young Frenchwoman ran over to Nat and put her arms around him. Nat pulled her onto his lap and kissed her. Then the other corpsmen beckoned to the woman's friends to come over too.

Then Liza said loudly, "Nat, I hope you realize that there are thousands of prostitutes in Paris. If you want to return to the base hospital with a venereal disease, you can encourage these women, but I wouldn't advise it."

Then she turned to Bob and said, "I've heard that some of the medics will have to stay on here in France longer than some others. President Wilson has ordered that no soldier with VD can return to the United States until he is cured. If you are delayed here, Bob, taking care of them—when I get back home, I will go and see Helen Ford and tell her about what you are doing."

"In her last letter," Bob said, "she told me she had gotten a job at a publishing house that specializes in children's books. So she goes to New York City from Corona every day."

The noise of the celebrating crowd around them grew louder and soon drowned out everything else. Liza stood up and told the other nurses that it was time to go to the Red Cross headquarters, where they could find a bed for the night.

The men stayed where they were and mentioned something about the Folies Bergére. "Well, that's not for us," Liza said firmly, and she and the other nurses left.

Chapter 31

IT WAS SEVERAL weeks after Bob and Nat had returned to the base hospital, that the Germans finally signed the armistice with France, Britain, and the United States, along with the other countries that fought with them. The date was November 10, 1918. As Peter Bosco described the last day of the war in his book *World War I*:

Suddenly, across the entire western front, everything stopped. The soldiers, with mouths wide open, stared at "No Man's Land," dumbstruck by the wonderful quiet that now reigned.

A few minutes later, the men began to laugh, cry, shake hands, and slap each other on the back and cheer. For the first time, men stood up in their foxholes. They walked in the open with nothing to fear. They built campfires for the first time. They took off their boots, dried their socks, and warmed their chilled fingers.

Almost immediately, Yanks and Germans got together in the middle ground. Most left their rifles in the trenches. Active bartering sprang up. Doughboys gave Germans cigarettes, food rations, and soap in exchange for buckles and even a few iron crosses (German Army medals).

Most of the fighting men were too dazed to think much about the future. Relief and joy was all they felt. "No more bombs," said one Yank. "No more mangled bodies, no more exposure to terrifying shell fire in the rain and mud."

Later, on November 10, 1918, the news of the armistice reached the United States. In Corona, Pastor Ford climbed on his bicycle and rode down the hill to Main Street with hundreds of others to celebrate the end of the war. Grace walked hurriedly behind him. Soon, most of the townspeople were gathered together there, and they cheered and greeted each other. Patrolman Murphy looked the other way when some youngsters began stealing food from the outside markets and trying to push over lampposts.

Clara Levering saw Grace in the crowd and called to her to come up on her porch. As Grace joined her, she said triumphantly, "This means the soldiers will be coming home! And Helen's Bob Thompson will be with them."

When the people of Northfield heard that the armistice was signed, some of the men gathered at the old horse-watering trough at the center of Main Street to talk about it. The names of the Northfield boys who had been killed in France were mentioned respectfully.

Ernest Nelson said, "I am glad the war is over, but I don't see why we had to get into it in the first place. I believe in taking care of our own country and not getting mixed up in foreigners' battles."

Then one of the other men said, "I hope we get plenty of snow in the next few months so the hotel will fill up with people coming for the winter sports. You know, the ones that come for skiing."

"It will snow."

Chapter 32

New York City
1919

IT WAS A cold day in December of 1919 when, inside the Union Club in New York City, the manager was giving instructions to a new front-desk employee.

"Look into the dining room," he said. "Do you see those four men at the table by the window?"

"Yes."

"Three of them are important longtime members of the club. They come regularly. I want to make sure you know their names and make no mistake. From left to right, they are John Peterson, of the detective agency; E. B. Thompson, a textile manufacturer; and Charles Levering, a city bank president. The clergyman sitting next to Mr. Levering is Reverend Ford, who comes quite often with the others but who is not a member."

"I have written down their names now. I'll be especially attentive to them," the new man said, and the manager left.

At the table, John Peterson smiled and said to William Ford, "It's good to have you with us. We all have shared so many nice times each summer in Northfield, attending the conferences and enjoying our vacation cottages. I like reminiscing about it. And of course, we look forward to next summer. You know, EB spends most of his time on the golf course when there—"

"Playing with you and Levering," EB added, and they both laughed.

William looked behind him and remarked, "This is a magnificent dining room. I assume the large gold-framed portraits on the wall are of the former club presidents?"

"That's correct," Levering said. "Some of the presidents appear more somber in their portraits than the others. But it is a great honor to be chosen as president of the Union Club."

"Yes, this is a great room," EB said. "The heavy drapes and the thick carpets add to the elegance."

"And don't miss the good view we get of Park Avenue from the window of this table," Peterson said.

Then the waiter came and took their orders.

While they were eating, Pastor Ford turned to EB and mentioned that he was glad to know that his son, Bob, had returned safely from France.

"Yes, I met the troopship that brought him back in Norfolk, Virginia, a month ago. It was quite a sight to see those soldiers rushing down the gangways to get their feet on home soil. Bob would have come back sooner, but his medical unit was needed to care for the wounded and sick that remained in the French hospitals."

"Has he been discharged yet?"

"No. Right now, he is assigned to the mental ward at Bellevue Hospital, just downtown from here."

"I suppose he's caring for some of the shell-shocked soldiers," Levering said.

"That is correct. Bob has always been calm and easygoing by nature, which is an asset when you are dealing with the mentally disturbed. Also, he is big and strong and can control the violent cases," EB explained before turning toward Pastor Ford. "I hear my son, Bob, has been visiting your daughter at your home in Corona."

"Yes, we have had the pleasure of seeing him several times. Also, Helen has a job at a children's magazine here in the city. I believe they meet occasionally after work."

"Bob isn't sure what he wants to do after he gets out of the army. Before the war, he thought that he'd like to be a doctor. But after months on the battlefield in France, taking care of the wounded and dying, he has decided not to do that."

Peterson changed the subject and asked the others, "Were any of you active in getting the Prohibition law passed?"

"As a minister, I avoid politics. I am no friend of the saloonkeepers in Corona because excessive drinking can ruin lives."

"Well, if you ask me, there are two reasons why the Prohibition bill passed," Peterson said. "First, there were thousands of young men fighting in France. Since they were out of the country, they were unable to vote against Prohibition. And secondly, most of the breweries have

German names—such as Pabst, Busch, and Anheuser. And some of the 'Drys' have been saying that 'Prohibition spells Patriotism.'"

"One of the leading ministers in New York proclaimed that the liquor consumed by the doughboys in France was the Kaiser's best ally," Levering mentioned.

"Prohibition has closed some of the bars, but liquor is available regardless of the Prohibition law," Ford mentioned.

Peterson agreed. "A great deal of my detective-agency work is assisting the police in tracking down gangsters who are smuggling whiskey into Long Island from ships offshore and selling it to the 'speakeasies.'" Then turning to Ford, Peterson asked, "Do you remember my two top detectives, O'Toole and Reily?"

"I remember them well," Ford replied.

"They were both sent to France, but they are back now. Reily returned in good shape, but O'Toole came back badly shell-shocked. I believe he is a patient at the mental ward at Bellevue where your son, Bob, works. I think I might stop over there and ask Bob if I can see him."

"You know my wife's daughter, Liza, is a head nurse at Bellevue now. She may be able to give you that information."

"No, I will let Bob Thompson tell me about O'Toole."

"He'll be glad to, I'm sure," said E. B. Thompson. He then added, "Whatever became of the German fellow in Northfield who was under suspicion of spying?"

"My wife, Clara, tells me that Boris Melikof—who runs the settlement house here in New York—keeps in touch with the German, Otto Kirschheimer," Levering said. "Boris often travels to Northfield to see Otto. Evidently, besides farming,

Otto is doing some loom work—making household items that he tries to sell."

"Speaking of textiles, you might be interested to know that I have purchased a textile mill in Philadelphia," EB informed them.

"What about the paint business?" Peterson asked. "Weren't you running that company?"

"My younger brother has taken it over with the backing of most of the family, and now he is in full charge. I'm still on the board, but that wasn't enough to do, so I bought a textile mill in the Kensington section of Philadelphia. It should do well."

"We will miss seeing you," Levering said.

"No, I will only be in Philadelphia on weekdays. I will take the train home on the weekends. My wife didn't want to leave the house in Elizabeth, New Jersey, or the apartment in New York City."

"And of course, we'll be seeing you next summer in Northfield," the reverend commented.

"Yes, by all means," EB answered.

"We will all be there!" Peterson and Levering agreed.

Chapter 33

A FEW DAYS later, Mabel Hall hurried down a long corridor of Bellevue Hospital in New York City. At the end of the hall was the administration office of the Heart and Lung Association that her husband was in charge of. Martin hadn't left her enough money when he walked out on her and the child a week ago, and the rent collector had come to the small apartment and insisted that the rent had to be paid that day.

As she walked along the corridors with offices on both sides, she noticed a familiar name on one of the doors. It read: Liza Lovett, RN, Supervisor of Nurses. Mabel had heard Boris Melikof speak of Liza many times, and she remembered being told that she went to Northfield every summer, and she also remembered meeting her at one of the International Dinners at the settlement house. But she let that thought go as she concentrated on seeing Martin and getting the money from him that she needed.

The door to the office was unlocked, so she let herself into the small reception room. She expected to see the secretary sitting at her desk, but there was no one there. Mabel saw that the door to the main office was partially open, so she moved toward it. From there, she had a plain view of Martin and the secretary inside. They were locked in each other's arms and were kissing and whispering.

Mabel continued to peer through the opening in the door and heard the secretary say, "I can hardly breathe. You make me feel so—" Then he kissed her again.

Then Martin said, "It's going to be you and me from now on."

"But what about your wife?"

"Oh, her—that's dead! There's nothing there anymore—nothing. It's over, and I'm not going to let you go!"

As Mabel watched them and heard what they were saying to each other, a strong feeling of loss and humiliation swept over her; but also, she feared that if she suddenly interrupted them, Martin might give her a final ultimatum that she feared would be coming soon.

So Mabel backed up quietly and reached behind her for the outer doorknob. She let herself out and walked unsteadily as she retraced her steps down the long hallway.

Suddenly, to Mabel's surprise, she was standing face to face with Liza Lovett, who had just come out of her office. There was a middle-aged man with her.

"You're Martin Hall's wife, aren't you?" Liza asked cheerfully.

"Yes," she said and tried to smile.

"And this is John Peterson," Liza continued.

"How do you do?" Mabel answered, trying to calm herself.

"I'm showing him the way to the mental ward of the hospital. He wants to visit a patient there that was a former employee of Mr. Peterson's detective agency."

"Forgive me, but I'm in a hurry," Mabel said and rushed by them.

"I wonder what's wrong with her," Liza said to John, watching her go. "She is always so friendly, although I've heard her husband doesn't treat her very well."

"Yes, but how do we get to the mental ward?" John asked impatiently.

"Oh, of course. Yes, it's this way. I'll show you," Liza said, and they walked off together.

A hospital security guard sat by the door of the psychiatric wing. Across from him was a visitor's bench. A young woman was sitting there, and Liza recognized her right away.

"It's Helen Ford, Pastor Ford's daughter," Liza said and hurried over to her. "What are you doing here?"

"I am waiting for Bob Thompson. He's going to take me out to dinner when he's through work."

The guard across from them laughed. "He should have been through an hour ago, but he's having trouble with one of the patients."

"I don't mind waiting," Helen said. Then she held out her hand and showed Liza a small diamond ring she was wearing. "Did you know Bob and I are going to be married in April?"

"I have heard rumors about that from my mother, Clara. She talks to your mother all the time. Congratulations," Liza said. Then turning around, Liza said, "You remember Mr. Peterson from Northfield"?

"Yes, I do." Helen got up from the bench and shook his hand.

Then Liza turned to the guard and explained that Mr. Peterson wanted to see a patient and that there should be no trouble about it. So the guard got up and unlocked the door, and John went in. Liza smiled again at Helen and left.

When Peterson entered O'Toole's room, he was surprised to see Bob sleeping in a comfortable chair next to the empty bed. O'Toole sat on a stool in the corner of the room.

Bob opened his eyes to see who had come in. When he recognized Peterson, he got up quickly and came over. "I heard you might be coming. It must be two and a half years since I saw you at the donkey baseball game in Northfield," Bob said. "I've been to France and back since then. I understand you are here to say hello to your former employee, O'Toole," he said, pointing toward the corner.

"Yes, that is right," Peterson said and walked over to O'Toole.

O'Toole sat with his head down, and suddenly, he looked up and shouted, "The barrage has started! Don't you hear it? Get down or a red-hot piece of shrapnel will cut into you."

Bob quickly moved toward him and put his hand on his shoulder. "You're not in the trenches anymore, old man. We are safe in New York," he said in a low, calm voice. "Don't you want to say hello to your old boss?"

"No!" was the answer.

"Are they taking good care of you here?" Peterson asked him quietly.

"That guy is always around," O'Toole said, looking at Bob. "He keeps the devil from coming into the room."

Peterson attempted to laugh. "I never can tell when you are serious and when you are joking. Your old partner, Detective Reily, speaks of you often and hopes you will be able to come back to the agency and work with him again."

Suddenly, O'Toole darted to the open window and thrust his head and shoulders through it. Then he violently jerked his hips and legs forward.

"Grab his left leg. I'll get the other," Bob shouted. "It's eighteen floors down."

Together, they pulled him back from the window; and Bob tackled him down to the floor, where he held him. "Push that red button on the wall there," Bob yelled at Peterson, who did it.

A loud sound could be heard going off in the hall. Soon, two hospital orderlies rushed through the door and wrestled O'Toole into a straitjacket. With Bob's help, they laid him down on the bed.

"You'll have to get a doctor in here to give him a shot," Bob informed one of the men.

O'Toole kept muttering, "I got to get outta here."

Peterson and Bob looked at each other and shook their heads sympathetically. Then Peterson said, "There's a young lady waiting for you outside."

"I know, because I'm taking her out to dinner."

With O'Toole secured in the bed, they both left. Peterson said good-bye as they signed out with a guard at the door. Then seeing Helen on the bench waiting for him, Bob immediately went over to her, grabbed her hand, and said "Let's go."

In minutes, they were away from the hospital and out on the streets of New York City, breathing in deeply as hundreds of people rushed around them, going in all different directions as they hurried to get home from work.

Chapter 34

SPRING CAME EARLY that year. So it was a warm day when Boris Melikof and Mabel Hall—along with her small son, Tom—left the settlement house and walked down Twenty-Eighth Street toward the waterfront. The little boy tried to run ahead of them, but Mabel had tied a rope around his waist and held the other end of it in her hand. People passing by stopped and smiled to see the child attempting to pull his mother along.

"How old is Tom now?" Boris asked.

"He is three years old."

"It's hard for me to believe that Martin has left you, but I'm glad you decided to stay on at the settlement house."

"I'm glad for that too. It's difficult for me to talk about Martin!" Mabel said. And then she asked Boris, "It won't be easy to find Otto Kirschheimer on the dock. It's always so crowded before a ship leaves."

"No, the plan is for Otto to meet me at the end of the pier after the Italian workers are safely on board the ship for their trip home."

"Will he stay with you tonight at the settlement house?"

"Yes, I'll take him back for supper and a bed. Then he will return to Northfield tomorrow . . . but, Mabel, you must be very lonely now."

"I have little Tom, and I'm expecting another baby. I told Martin about it, but he doesn't seem to care."

"No, that's not right!"

Then Mabel changed the subject. "Do you think I'll have any trouble trying to say good-bye to my friends Sophie and Gaby on the dock before they are deported?"

"They are the two radical friends you know, aren't they? You will probably see them because the police will be escorting them."

"It's a disgrace to deport these women just because they were encouraging the garment workers to strike. I went to their trial and felt so sorry for them."

"I heard they made quite a ruckus in the courtroom. Some say they were shouting out their communist slogans and swearing at the judge."

"They had a right to speak out against the factory bosses that are hard on the poor workers."

At that point, Boris was concentrating on getting the three of them across the busy street safely and into the entrance of the pier building.

Inside, there were a great number of people in line, waiting to get aboard the ship. Also, many relatives and friends were there to see them off.

Mabel and the boy were guided by Boris to a narrow gangway that stretched from the dock to the ship's steerage section. "If you wait here, you might to able to see your friends," Boris told her.

"Thank you," she said and watched as he disappeared into the crowd.

Tom pulled on the rope and looked down at the water between the seawall and ship. Mabel pulled him back and told him to stand quietly beside her. She was not surprised to see members of the radical groups from her neighborhood that had also come. Soon, she saw Sophie and Gaby being led through the crowd by two policemen. Newspaper reporters and more police followed them. Cheers went up from the radical groups when the two women appeared. Some rushed forward, but the police pushed them back.

Mabel picked up Tom and moved ahead until she blocked the gangway. Suddenly, Sophie and Gaby stood before her.

"Don't worry, we will keep working on what you started," Mabel said firmly.

Immediately, a policeman elbowed her to the side, using less force than usual because of the boy in her arms.

Then Sophie said loudly to Mabel, "Be careful or you will be the next to get thrown out of the country!" Then Gaby looked back at the city and shook her fist.

Chapter 35

IT WAS APRIL 22, 1922. It was the day that Robert Thompson, son of E. B. Thompson, and Helen Ford, daughter of Rev. William J. Ford, would be married in the Congregational Church in Corona, Long Island, New York.

Very early that morning, a light showed from Pastor Ford's study window. Inside, Grace stood, looking down at her husband who sat at his desk.

"Today, they will be married!" Grace said.

"You are glad about it, aren't you?" William asked.

"Oh yes, but I am worried about the wedding going off all right. It's so expensive . . . and there are so many bills that have to be paid. I'm getting desperate about it."

"I told you I borrowed a little money from the bank to take care of those things."

"A little money—that's right! And how will we pay it back? Why have we always been so poor? It never changes. I thought it would get better eventually, but it's always the same! There's never enough money!"

"Be calm, Grace," William said, looking up at her. "Today, Helen will marry a fine young man from a well-established family. You must not be so nervous."

"I guess you are right. But you don't know everything. The food is one thing. Mrs. McCarty had agreed to make all the sandwiches and bake the wedding cake, and then she died suddenly last week."

"I'm sure she didn't plan to let you down. Anyway, now, Clara Levering has promised to bring all the food that's needed."

"Well, yes, but what is she bringing? The whole Thompson family and the Petersons are coming, and they are used to the best. They may not like what Clara has chosen."

"Grace, stop worrying. You don't want Helen to see that you are upset."

"Also, when you were out yesterday, the violinist came here and said he wouldn't play at the reception because we couldn't pay him in advance."

"I saw him. But there will be music!"

"What music?"

"I have arranged for some music."

By the middle of the afternoon, the Leverings' car had arrived at the Ford house. Clara got out and hurried in. Levering waited in the car and reminded the chauffeur that they would be taking the ladies to the church.

Clara found Grace in the living room and told her that the food for the reception was already in the church basement. "My cook and two maids are taking care of everything."

"Thank you, Clara. Oh, look. Helen is coming down the stairs."

Clara sang out "Here comes the bride!" and walked over to her.

"You look beautiful," she said and then paused. "Now wait a second. I just need to straighten your headpiece a little." Which she did. "Now you are perfect."

Then Grace called up the stairs to Helen's friend, who was to be the maid of honor, "Hurry up. Mr. Levering's car is waiting to take us to the church."

All the parishioners and many of the townspeople had been invited to the pastor's daughter's wedding. The guests began to arrive from all directions. The front doors of the church were wide open, and the church filled up fast.

Pastor Ford and Bob were having a talk on the back lawn, just outside the rear door of the church.

"Well, Bob, today's the day. And thank you for getting here on time. I have had plenty of anxious moments waiting for grooms to show up. Only once did I wait in vain—not a good situation," William said, and they both laughed.

"Yes, I am on time, but it's more likely that my family will be late."

"Helen tells me you have bought a house in Philadelphia."

"Yes, we have. It's a small row house, and it's not too far from the Kensington section of the city where I'll be working at my father's textile mill."

Just as he said that, they heard some giggling coming from the bushes. Looking around, they saw three small Negro boys.

"Who are they?" Bob asked.

"They are children from the mission church," William said. And then, turning toward them, he asked, "Why are you here?"

Slowly the children emerged from the bushes with eager faces. Their clothes were torn, and their feet were bare. "Mr. Armstrong, at our church, told us to come over and ask what time you wanted the band to come," answered one of them.

"You tell him that I want you all here at five o'clock."

When the children heard what he had said, they quickly ran from the churchyard and out onto Main Street, and then south to the other side of town.

William explained, "I started a mission church for the Negro families here in Corona several years ago. I preach and officiate there as much as possible. They have put together some kind of band, and I asked them to come play here at the wedding reception."

"That will be fine," Bob said in his good-natured way.

Then William took out his pocket watch and looked at it. "It's time for us to go in," he said to Bob.

He answered with a big smile, "I'm ready."

Chapter 36

AT THE SAME time, the car had arrived at the church, bringing the bride, the bridesmaid, the bride's mother, and the Leverings. An old friend saw the car and hurried over to it. He leaned into a window to tell Grace that the Thompson family had not arrived yet.

"But it's four o'clock already," Grace said anxiously.

"They'll be here in a few minutes," Clara said.

Then Grace announced firmly, "Everyone stay just where they are! We will wait in the car until we see that the Thompsons are here. Then we will get out."

Helen's maid of honor, who was perched on a jump seat in the car, looked over at Helen and giggled. Helen smiled back but remained calm because she knew that Bob had arrived earlier, as planned, and was probably in the church already.

Ten minutes passed before they heard the honking of a horn. They all looked out and saw the Thompsons' car pull up behind them. Then they watched as Bob's brother jumped out, followed by his three sisters. Mr. and Mrs. Thompson were assisted out of the car by the chauffeur.

Clara touched Grace's shoulder and said, "Look at Mrs. Thompson! Isn't she the picture of the grand lady in her long white lace dress and black velvet hat? See how the string of pearls she is wearing hangs all the way down to her waist. And notice how she walks. She has a queenly manner."

Then Levering spoke up, impatiently, "It's time for us to go in!"

Helen stood in the back of the church next to her father. When she heard the strains of the wedding march, she took her father's arm, and they began the walk down the aisle.

Helen could feel everyone's eyes on her, and she gripped her father's arm tightly. But when she saw Bob standing up ahead, smiling at her, she felt a sense of relief. He had never wavered in his decision to marry her, even though she had heard that his mother had said she would be a millstone around his neck. She immediately dismissed that thought from her mind and kept her eyes on Bob.

As the bride and her father came to the front, Pastor Ford went around the rail and faced the congregation. "My role of father has temporarily ended. And my role as minister has begun."

There was laughter and then quiet. Bob stepped up and stood next to Helen, and the marriage ceremony began: "Dearly beloved. We are gathered here in the sight of God . . ."

All the responses went well, but when Pastor Ford said the words "until death do you part," there was a loud sound of crashing pots and pans coming from the church's basement.

Clara, in the front row, shook her head, knowing it was her cook and maids that had caused the noise.

As soon as the couple was pronounced "man and wife," Bob looked out at the congregation and smiled and waved. Helen tugged at his coat and whispered, "You are supposed to kiss me!"

Bob leaned down and kissed her and then waved again to the people. As they walked out onto the side lawn for the reception, the wedding guests descended upon them, to wish them happiness.

Quickly Clara arranged chairs for Mrs. Thompson and Mrs. Peterson, so they wouldn't be left standing among strangers.

Clara's cook and maids had prepared gallons of lemonade and had made dozens of sandwiches and a wedding cake, all of which were set out on a long table.

Then Clara asked Mrs. Thompson cheerfully, "Will we see you in Northfield this summer?"

"I am not sure. We may have cousins visiting from Scotland, so our plans are indefinite, but we usually go there for a time."

"I understand that Helen and Bob will go to the Northfield Hotel for their honeymoon."

"Yes, that is true," Mrs. Thompson said. And then she stopped suddenly and exclaimed, "What is that awful racket?"

"Oh, that's the Mission Band coming in," Clara said and hurried on to talk to someone else.

Into the church grounds marched the Negro Mission Church Band, twenty strong and of all ages. They were playing trumpets, banjos, drums, and some homemade instruments, such as washboards and broom handles.

"What are they doing here?" Mrs. Peterson asked.

Detective Reily, who had accompanied them to the wedding, asked John Peterson if he should stop them.

Pastor Ford, who overheard him, said, "Absolutely not!" Then he quickly stood up on a chair and got everyone's attention. "I want to welcome this fine band from the Corona Mission Church. I personally invited them to play at my daughter's wedding reception, so give them a big hand."

There was clapping and whistling.

Soon afterward, Mrs. Thompson rose and went over to Grace and thanked her and said good-bye. She walked regally to her car, and EB and the children knew that it was time to leave.

The parishioners and other guests quickly made the band players feel at home. Many sat down on the grass and listened to the music. Bob and Helen sat down with them. Some of the children from the band did a dance for them, and everyone cheered.

Meanwhile, Bob was thinking of the long overnight ride in the Pullman sleeping car from New York City to Northfield. As he thought about it, he took Helen's hand in his, and she smiled up at him.

When it was time for them to leave, they walked to the car that would take them to Penn Station in the city. Helen looked back at the church. It was then that she realized that she was saying good-bye to a familiar scene she had known all her life. She was also saying good-bye to her parents and old acquaintances, and she sensed that her life would never be exactly the same again.

Momentarily, a feeling of sadness gripped her heart as she stepped into the car. But the feeling vanished completely by the time she and Bob rushed across Penn Station to catch the train that would take them to Northfield.

Chapter 37

May 1922
Corona, Long Island, New York

ONE MONTH LATER, Pastor Ford walked down the hill from the house to the main street of Corona. He was on his way to Cedar Grove Cemetery in the neighboring town of Flushing. He was going to officiate at a burial service there. It was a four-mile walk, and the hot sun shone down on him. He reached up to loosen his clerical collar and then kept going.

Suddenly, he heard a horn and looked around to see Charles Levering's car pulling up alongside of him. Charles got out, and they greeted each other cheerfully.

"I suppose you're on your way to Mrs. Winter's burial," Levering said. "Clara mentioned it to me this morning. Let me drive you to the cemetery. It is quite a trek from here."

"If you have time, I'll be glad to get a lift."

"When we get there, I'll wait in the car. After the service, I'll have Murphy drive us back," Levering said, looking at his chauffeur, who quickly opened the door for them.

"You're Peter Murphy," William said, looking at the driver.

"You remember me?"

"Oh yes."

Then Levering said, "When Murphy retired from the police force, he became my chauffeur, and he's a good one."

"I guess I did hear about that," said William vaguely.

Then Murphy spoke up, "I wonder if you remember when two of Mr. Peterson's detectives and I were hiding in the woods, waiting for you, Pastor? We were there that night because one of the Black Hand mob was coming to collect hush money. You were gone by the time the scoundrel showed up. We chased him through the woods, but he got away!"

"I had almost forgotten about that, but thank you for what you did."

With Levering and the pastor in the back of the car, Murphy drove slowly down Main Street and out onto the highway. Soon, they arrived at the large, open iron gates of Cedar Grove Cemetery.

"There won't be many at the grave site," William said. "I believe a few cousins and a niece said they would come. The widow was very poor and lived alone, but she was faithful to the church. She was there every time the door opened."

When they were inside the cemetery, William got out of the car. Levering and Murphy watched him walk through the myriad of tombstones.

Many of the stones had names on them of people William had known well. Soon he came to the place where a plain pine casket lay by an open grave. A small group of women stood nearby. Levering could see Pastor Ford greeting each one of them. Then he took his place at one end of the casket, and taking a black book from his suit pocket, he began to read.

"I wonder how many funerals he has officiated over the last forty years," Levering mumbled to himself as he relaxed in the car. Then he closed his eyes and rested his head against the back of the seat.

Only a short time had passed when, suddenly, Murphy shouted, "Mr. Levering, Pastor Ford has fallen down!"

At that, he opened his eyes wide and looked out the car window. He could see that William was lying down on the ground. Both men rushed from the car to help him. They tried to get him to his feet. The women huddled together, and some began to cry.

Three gravediggers, who had been sitting under a large tree some distance away, saw what had happened and stood up. Levering, seeing them, called out, "You, men, come over here and help me carry this man to my car."

Two of them lifted William up and brought him to the car, where they laid him on the backseat.

It was then that Levering bent over him and asked, "Can you hear me? What happened?"

William opened his eyes, and seeing his friend, he said in a low voice, "Everything will be all right."

One of the gravediggers said to another, "That man has had a stroke."

The second said, "We will be burying him . . ."

Then a third one interrupted him, "Don't say that! I like that preacher. I have watched him conduct burial services here for years, and he never failed to come over and talk to us in a friendly way after the mourners had left . . . never!"

By the time they got him home, Pastor Ford was dead.

Chapter 38

OVER TWO THOUSAND people came to the funeral. They crowded into the church in Corona, and some stood in the street outside. Those who watched the rich and the poor, the Catholics and the Protestants, the politicians and the shopkeepers, who filed past his casket, began to realize the number of lives Pastor Ford had touched. That day, the flags on the schools and the Jewish synagogues were at half-mast, and the Roman Catholics prayed for him at mass.

It came to many that day, what a life truly dedicated to God could mean to a community. Some already heard that a memorial to Pastor Ford was being planned. It would be a full-length stained-glass window at the church, depicting a shepherd and his sheep.

Several distinguished ministers came to officiate at the service. All agreed that Charles Levering should give the main eulogy. Hymns were sung, and prayers were said. Then Charles climbed the steps to the pulpit and began to speak.

"William, our pastor, wrote me a letter some years ago when I was away. I would like to share it with you now. The words in this letter portray vividly his dedication to his church and the people. He wrote:

Dear Charles,

I would like to tell you that I have been unable to dismiss from my mind the pathetic side of life I see in the struggles of my parishioners each day. Recently, I was called out at two in the morning to see a brave sea captain pass away in his home after he had faced the storms of forty winters in the Atlantic. Many times, I have witnessed the last inevitable struggle of a beloved relative in someone's home. As I pass many of these homes today, I still see the breasted crossed hands of the departed. It would take a long list to record the appearance in the homes of the 'stranger'—suicide. I see the inebriate's struggle with delirium. I have seen the sorrow in the wake of sudden accidents when I am the one to break the news. I have come to know the scene worse than death when love has died in the home, where the fireside was cold and the heart beats only in hate.

I remember the scene when there were three caskets at the church altar after a fire in a home. I have listened sympathetically to the heartbreaking confidences of mothers whose daughters were in trouble, and sons were mixed up with the police. I have tried to help when destitute men who can't find work come to me. In the life of any minister, grievous occurrences sadden him, but there are times of great joy. Such as marrying a loving young couple, baptizing a healthy baby, preaching a sermon that is well received, listening to laughter at a well-phrased joke, and being enthusiastic as each new day dawns.

"He signs the letter, 'Looking forward to seeing you again, Charles. Your pastor and friend, W. J. Ford.'"

The service ended with the singing of the hymn "Abide With Me."

Then the doors of the church were flung open. The pallbearers carried the casket out of the church and down the steps to the hearse, with Grace following close behind. Then the hundreds who had attended the service filed out. It was decided that Grace would ride with the Leverings to the cemetery. Their chauffeur, Murphy, assisted Grace to the car and put a robe over her knees. Saunders, the Petersons' chauffeur, bowed as they approached and settled themselves into their car. The Thompson family's Packard was next in line. Then the automobiles started up and followed the hearse. Many of the parishioners and townspeople also went to the cemetery.

More words and prayers were said, and finally, the casket was lowered into the open grave.

A black woman from the Corona Mission Church, standing in the back, suddenly cried out loudly, "I just saw an angel come down and take the pastor up." Saunders hurried over to her in order to quiet the woman.

Grace stood rigid by the grave, staring straight ahead. Helen looked at her mother and became concerned. She turned to Liza and asked if she thought her mother was all right.

"She's in shock!" Liza said sympathetically. "It is natural. The shock will pass eventually, but sometimes it takes many months or even years."

Another thought was bothering Helen. "What will happen to my mother Grace now? What will she do? The house belongs to the church, and a new minister will come. Of course, there is the cottage in Northfield, but it is not a permanent, year-round home."

Helen glanced over her shoulder. There was Bob—tall, handsome, and always with a good-natured expression on his face. He had never said no to her about anything. So, immediately, she was sure that he would agree to let her mother live with them in Philadelphia.

Suddenly, there was a loud noise as a strong gust of wind blew down and passed over the grave.

"Where did that wind come from?" someone asked.

"That's strange," said another, looking up.

"Why would a blast of wind whirl down on us like that when there isn't a cloud in the sky?" another asked.

Then it was still again, and gradually, the people began to leave the cemetery.

Chapter 39

New York City, New York
1925

TEN YEARS LATER, as the sun began to set over the Lower East Side of New York City and the last streams of light filtered through the tenement-lined streets, the neighborhood had a more respectable look than it had had under the harsh noon sun.

It was on this evening that Boris hurried down the steps of the settlement house. He was wearing an old tuxedo. He stopped when he saw children playing ball in the street. When the children saw Boris, they ran toward him.

"You look funny," one said.

"Are you in a play or something?" asked another.

Boris looked down at them and explained, "I am wearing this tuxedo because I have been invited to a big affair, uptown."

Suddenly, there was a loud voice coming from across the street. One of the boys pulled on Boris's sleeve and said, "Fatty Smith is yelling to you."

Boris walked over to where the woman was sitting on her front steps. Her huge size hid all but one of the steps. Her nose was lined with small red veins, and her face was puffy. She gave Boris a toothless smile and asked, "Where did you get that monkey suit?"

"The tailor on the corner lent it to me. It belonged to a man that died," Boris answered.

"And where might you be going dressed like that?"

"I am going to a charity ball at the Waldorf Astoria Hotel for the benefit of the Bellevue Hospital."

"And who would be asking you to a fancy ball?"

"I have a friend who works at the hospital. She got me a ticket."

"Well, ain't you the one!" she said, and they both laughed. Then he turned and left.

After walking a few blocks, he heard footsteps behind him. He turned and saw Mabel Hall following him. When she caught up to him, she said, "Fatty Smith told me you were going uptown to a ball at the Waldorf Astoria Hotel."

"That's right. Liza invited me to go. We will be sitting with the Leverings and the Petersons."

"I think my husband, Martin, may be there too," Mabel said. "He goes to all the big events now."

"But you're not going?"

"Oh, no!"

Then Boris asked her, smiling, "So, why are you chasing me?"

"Well, I thought you should know that there might be a protest riot in front of the hotel tonight. I heard about it this afternoon. The radicals are recruiting a lot of workers for a demonstration."

"You mean the Communists?"

"Yes, some of them are Communists, but others are just people that are jobless and hungry, or who work long hours for pennies."

"Mabel, you must know that those hotheads will always be planning to riot here and protest there, and to bomb this or to bomb that. You must not take them seriously."

"They sounded determined this time."

"Don't get mixed up with them. I'm telling you this for your own good."

Then Boris stepped toward her and put his arm around her shoulders. "Is Martin living with you and the boy now?"

"No, he isn't. We tried to start over and make it work, but it wasn't any good, so he's gone now. There is someone else, a woman. But I am worried because I will have his second child in six months."

"Did you tell him?"

"Yes."

"And he left anyway?" Boris said. "Martin is acting very badly. I'm disappointed in him."

"He's changed, but I don't want you to worry about this," she said insistently. "You go to your party." And she added that she thought Liza would like the way he looked in the tuxedo.

"Good-bye, my friend," Boris said affectionately, and he watched her turn and walk slowly away.

Chapter 40

AS BORIS ENTERED the Waldorf Hotel, he was struck by the grandeur of the main lobby. It was brightly lit, with golden light fixtures on the wall and crystal chandeliers hanging from the ceiling. The floor was covered with thick green carpeting, and the overstuffed furniture was upholstered in red velvet. He noticed that the sofas and chairs were arranged in a way that would encourage conversation. Tall palm plants had been placed to soften the corners, and large framed mirrors on all sides added elegance to the surroundings.

The hotel manager and a uniformed employee, who were standing behind the front desk, saw Boris come in.

"What have we here?" the manager asked. "What a head of hair and what a beard!"

"His tuxedo is too small for him," the other said, "and the pants are too short!"

"He's definitely not one of the smart set!" the manager commented. "But I guess we have to let him in."

They watched him carefully as he walked across the lobby.

Ahead of him was the entrance to the large ballroom. The steady beat of the orchestra's drums and the din of people talking grew louder as he came into the room and began looking for the Levering table.

A tall, middle-aged man in white tie and tails, who appeared to have an official position of some sort, walked up to Boris and asked, "What group are you with?"

"Mr. Charles Levering's group."

"Of course. Mr. Levering, the banker. You will find his table in the middle, just to the right of the dance floor.

The room was very crowded, but as Boris made his way around the dance floor, he saw Liza waving enthusiastically to him from their table, and he hurried over to her and the others.

Suddenly, he stopped short as he saw Martin Hall standing behind Clara Levering's chair, talking to her. Martin appeared to be ingratiating himself to everyone at the table. Liza pointed to the empty chair next to her, and Boris moved toward it, but Martin blocked his way. "Boris, old man, I've been telling these people about my work at the Heart and Lung Health Agency."

Boris managed to squeeze past Martin—without speaking—and quickly sat down next to Liza.

Clara then announced that Martin had just come over to say hello and that he is sitting next to the mayor at the head table.

Then John Peterson added, "I see there are many important city officials at the mayor's table tonight. I know most of them. Some are reputable citizens, while others need watching."

Martin bent down closer to Clara. "This affair is far more grand than the old International Dinner at the settlement house, where I first met you."

"Yes, it is," Clara agreed. Then she turned to her daughter, "Liza, you remember when Boris invited us to the settlement house dinner?"

"I remember it well. The people were all dressed in the native costumes of their countries. It was very colorful and interesting. And we ate different kinds of foreign food."

"You won't have any Hungarian goulash here tonight," Martin said, laughing.

"No," Peterson remarked. "I believe we have been promised a good steak dinner."

Then Levering spoke up, "Martin, you used to work at the settlement house, didn't you?"

"Yes, I did. When I first came to New York from the Midwest, I met some people who had told me about it, so I got a job there for eight dollars a week. I was a starry-eyed idealist in those days. I wanted to help the poor immigrants get started up in the city. I learned a lot about poverty by working there. I feel my job at the health agency is a continuation of what I tried to do there."

Boris looked up at Martin and said in a voice loud enough for everyone at the table to hear, "I saw your wife, Mabel, this evening. She told me I might be seeing you here tonight. I believe she would have liked to attend a charity ball such as this one."

Martin looked away from Boris and said to the others, "I have one of these charity or political fund-raisers practically every night. It's hard for me to get to all of them." Then he excused himself, saying that he had better get back to the mayor's table.

After Martin left, Mrs. Peterson mentioned that she thought that Martin was a very charming and good-looking man.

"And he is very ambitious and clever," her husband added.

Then Liza said, "I heard at the hospital that Martin will soon be divorcing his wife, Mabel, and he will be marrying his secretary."

No one remarked on what she said.

Then Levering announced cheerfully, "Look, the orchestra has come back!"

Chapter 41

AS THE BAND began to play and the strains of the "Flower Waltz" filled the room, Boris asked Liza to dance. She got up and took Boris's hand.

"I'm not a very good dancer," she said as they walked onto the dance floor.

"It's easy. You just follow me."

Clara, watching from the table, said, "Boris is light on his feet. He knows the steps well, and Liza is keeping up with him. They make a nice-looking couple."

"Now, don't get ideas!" Levering said, looking directly at his wife, Clara, and then turning to the others, he mentioned that his wife was known as the world's most active matchmaker.

"No, I won't get ideas," she answered. "But Liza does like him."

Then they noticed Boris swinging Liza in the opposite direction when Martin Hall, who was dancing with the mayor's wife, came near them.

John Peterson turned his head away from the dancing and mentioned, "Soon, we will all be together in Northfield. We plan to stay longer this year. How about you and Clara?"

"We are usually at the cottage for two months. Northfield is a welcome change from the city in the hot weather," Levering said. "And the conference meetings are very worthwhile."

Clara then reminded everyone that she and Liza had been going to the conferences at Northfield for many years, long before she married Charles.

When the band stopped playing, Boris and Liza returned to the table.

The dinner was served, and as they ate, John Peterson said to Boris, "I understand that you know the German, Otto Kirschheimer, who has a farm across the river from Northfield?"

"Yes, we are friends. We met when we shared a steerage cabin on a ship coming to this country. That was a long time ago. But we've kept in touch."

"What is that German up to these days?"

"He had a job at the golf house at the hotel for a while. Now he works on the farm, and also, he weaves cloth and makes dish towels and the like to sell. But interestingly enough, I have heard that a young nephew of his named Fritz has come from Germany to work at the new youth hostel in Northfield, and Otto is often there to help him."

Mrs. Peterson asked innocently, "Will those two be attending the religious conferences?"

"No, I don't think so," Boris answered. "Their interest is in the youth hostel. As you know, it is a place where young people can spend the night while they are biking through

New England in the summers. They are fixing up a large old house on Main Street in Northfield, which has a barn attached to it. I believe there are some rich German businessmen in New York City who are financing it. Youth hosteling is very popular in Europe."

"Bicycling sounds like a very healthy activity for young students in the summer," Clara said.

"I'm sure there are plenty of parents who are delighted to get their youngsters out of the house and onto the road during the summer," Levering said, laughing.

"Now wait a minute," Peterson said seriously. "There could be a pink tinge to this."

"What do you mean, 'pink tinge'?" Liza asked.

"This youth hosteling could have a questionable side. Think about it. You have young people traveling in groups together, interrelated and interdependent. They ride around with little money. And they sleep in barns and lofts at the hostels, which are managed by recent immigrants. All that has a Socialist ring to it."

"It sounds innocent enough to me," Clara said.

"Think what you like," Peterson continued. "But I am going to look into this youth-hostel business when I get to Northfield. Northfield is important to all of us because we have been going there each summer for years and own property there, so it doesn't hurt to be aware of what's going on in town."

Chapter 42

LATER IN THE evening, the mayor of New York stood up at the head table and began to speak to the charity-ball patrons. He praised the good work that was being done at the Bellevue Hospital, and he expounded on the need for financial assistance. He had begun to enumerate the duties of the devoted doctors and nurses when, suddenly, the sound of breaking glass was heard as the huge glass window crashed to the floor behind the mayor. Bricks and stones were thrown into the room.

Then men in work clothes climbed in through the window, brandishing long sticks in their hands. They began tipping over tables and breaking the china and crystal, which caused some of the people in the room to panic.

Many immediately got to their feet and struggled unceremoniously to reach the door at the far end of the ballroom that led to the lobby. Some of the younger dinner guests and the waiters made an attempt to subdue the rioters, but they were no match for the rowdy gang that kept pushing their way in.

The mayor shouted to Martin Hall to go outside and get the police. Martin elbowed his way through the crowd and ran through the lobby and out onto the street. Standing outside were hundreds of demonstrators, holding up signs and shouting. They waved with clenched fists, and anger was etched on their faces. Martin was relieved to hear the sound of the police wagons approaching.

A young ruffian recognized Martin and approached him. When he saw that Martin was dressed in evening clothes, he stopped and spit out the words "Traitor! So you crossed over to the enemy!"

"What enemy?" Martin asked angrily.

"The landlords, the bankers, the dishonest politicians—that's the enemy."

"Listen to me," said Martin excitedly. "I worked for five years at the settlement house, helping the poor get jobs and decent places to live."

"What jobs? You mean men working fourteen hours a day for practically nothing!"

Suddenly, two policemen grabbed the man who was shouting at Martin and threw him bodily toward the others, who were being pushed into the police wagons.

The man shouted again at Martin, "Traitor!"

Martin called back, "You are wrong to call me that. I am on your side and always have been."

"You go to hell!" was the last shout he heard.

By this time, some of the charity-ball patrons had come out of the hotel and were standing on the sidewalk, watching the police make arrests. The Petersons, the Leverings, and Liza and Boris saw the rioters being jammed into paddy wagons.

Levering shook his head and remarked, "Some of them will go to jail, for sure. They shouldn't have smashed that big window and come in like that. Peaceful demonstrations are one thing, but not this."

"What are they so angry about?" Clara asked with concern.

"It's a number of things," he said. "Working long hours for little pay is one thing they object to. Living on top of each other in crowded, unheated tenements is another—both of which promote misery and disease. Also, they bring their radical political ideas over with them from Europe. Then it is a great surprise to them when they run into people who have been here for generations and are more reticent and accept life as it is."

"It's sad," Clara said.

"Don't sympathize with these troublemakers. They are dangerous and desperate and a threat to public safety," Peterson stated loudly.

After the last police wagon left the scene, Boris stepped forward and thanked Liza and Clara for inviting him to the banquet, and said that he better get back to the settlement house.

Then the Levering car, with Murphy at the wheel, pulled up to the curb. Levering asked Boris if he could drop him off. Boris thanked him but explained the walking would do him good, so he said goodnight with a special wave to Liza. Then he turned and started the long trek back to the Lower East Side.

When the Leverings arrived at their house in Corona, they got out and climbed the front steps to the porch. It was then that Liza asked her mother and stepfather if she could have a talk with them in the living room. When they were inside, Liza announced that Boris had asked her to marry him when they were dancing.

There was a sudden long silence in the room.

Then Clara said thoughtfully, "You and Boris are both middle-aged now. Do you think it is wise to get married?"

"I love him, Mother. And he loves me."

"He's a lot older than you, and do you think you know him well enough?" Clara asked.

"Yes, I do. We have been meeting frequently after work in the city."

"He is so foreign, Liza. His accent and his European ways make him seem different from our friends and acquaintances."

Levering moved uneasily in his chair and said, "I'd go slow on this if I was you—but I guess it's not my place to give advice."

Then Liza looked from one to the other and said firmly, "I'm going to marry him!"

No one said anything for a few minutes, and then Clara said, "You go ahead and do it, Liza. I'll be happy for you."

"If your mother is for it, I am for it too."

"Strange how it has turned out," Clara said. "It all started years ago when Liza and I went to Northfield for the religious conferences with Pastor Ford. I remember it well. Pastor Ford was on the train with us. Do you remember, Liza?"

"Yes, Mother."

"On the train going to Northfield, Pastor Ford told us then about how kind and helpful young Boris Melikof from Armenia had been to him when he was attacked by a drunken man. He always had a good word to say about Boris. He considered him a close friend."

Liza got up and kissed her mother and smiled at Charles.

A few weeks later, Boris and Liza were married at the chapel room at the Bellevue Hospital. When people asked Liza why she wasn't married in the Corona church, she said, "It was simpler to do it at the hospital."

They traveled to Northfield for their honeymoon and spent the next month at the Leverings' cottage on Rustic Ridge. There, they were surrounded by tall pine trees; and in the late afternoon, they had a view from the porch of the setting sun going down behind the green mountains.

Chapter 43

The 1930s
Northfield, Massachusetts

DURING THE 1930S, the townspeople and farmers of Northfield struggled to survive in the long-lasting economic depression. The Depression was hard on people who wanted to work, and there were few jobs to be had.

The arrival of the summer people in Northfield brought some money into the town, but not much. The religious conferences on the school property were still well attended. Ministers and Christian church people still found their way to the beautiful Northfield school campus. Many now spent the summers in the simple cottages they had built on the Rustic Ridge. They welcomed the poor Northfield farm boys who brought fresh vegetables to their back doors to sell, and they smiled at their younger brothers who sold gladiolas at the front door for a nickel a bunch.

The Town and the Troublesome Strangers, 1880-1980

The farmers worked hard—plowing, planting, and harvesting—but many needed to take other part-time jobs to earn enough money. Some did maintenance work at the school and at the conference grounds during the summer. Others took jobs at the Tap and Die Mill in Greenfield. Some young men got jobs in forestry and went around in trucks, which carried large ladders and cleared land for the County and State. As always, the people of Northfield stoically accepted the burdens of the times. They faced each day with perseverance and with their usual sense of dry humor.

On one hot summer afternoon in July, Boris left the cottage on the Ridge and drove his car down Main Street. The backseat of the car was filled with overflowing trash cans. He was on his way to the dump. The dump was located at the foot of Parker Street, near the river. When Boris drove in, he saw Otto Kirschheimer's pickup truck parked there. Then he saw Otto standing on the edge of the garbage pit, heaving some debris into it.

"Otto, what luck to meet you here!" Boris said, getting out of his car.

"Ah, my friend," Otto said cheerfully. "How have you been?"

"Fine!"

Then Otto—looking toward the car—said, "Let me help you get that stuff out of the back of the car."

"It's mostly tin cans, corncobs, old newspapers, and tree slash."

The two men got rid of all the trash. And when they were through, Boris lit his pipe, and they sat down on an old wooden bench and began to talk.

"How are you, Otto?" Boris asked.

"Things are the same—not bad! I do my farm work and some loom work too, and I have been helping my nephew, Fritz, at the youth hostel on Main Street. He came over from Germany recently. I cut the lawn and do odd jobs for him. But tell me, how are things up on the Ridge?" Otto asked.

"Quiet, for the most part, although I did hear some disturbing news from a neighbor this morning. It seems some children found a local young man hanging from a tree in the woods. Evidently, he lived with his mother year-round in one of the empty summer cottages."

"He hung himself, you say? That's not good! Who was he?"

"It was Chuck Higgins."

"Oh, the Widow Higgins's oldest son—that's sad," Otto said. "I have heard that the poor woman has had to live on one relief check a month, and she has four younger children. It seems that Chuck has been trying to get a job around town, but there was no job to be had."

"My neighbor said Chuck left Northfield for a while, looking for work elsewhere, but he had no luck. Then he came back to Northfield—disappointed, broke, and hungry. He was a big, awkward kind of fella, but not a bad kid," Boris said.

"I don't know how that family survived in the winter in that three-room shack with no heat and little money for food. I remember when Chuck once begged me for a dollar. I gave it to him. He seemed so desperate. Even back then, things seemed to be closing in on the boy," Otto remembered.

"Well, he couldn't take it anymore, I guess. So he hung himself in the woods."

Then they started talking about the old days, when they came to America on the same ship. After a while, Boris explained that Liza wanted him to meet her and some others for a swim at the lake. So they said good-bye and left.

Chapter 44

THAT AFTERNOON, SOME of the summer people and a few of the town youngsters had gathered at a small lake situated down a steep hill from the school. It was known as Wanamaker Lake in honor of a rich department-store owner who had donated a great deal of money to the Northfield Seminary School and the religious conference.

A dam had been built across a fast-moving stream. The dam forced the water back and enabled a deep lake to form. A wooden raft was placed in the middle of the lake, and sand was brought in to make a beach area. A shack had been put up for changing clothes—one side for the men and one side for the women.

Grace Ford, Helen Thompson, Clara Levering, and Liza Melikof sat on blankets under a tree and watched the young people splash and swim in the water. A few girls were sunning themselves on the sand. Boris, who had just arrived, sat on a concrete slab of the dam and began writing in a notebook. He was wearing the same loose-fitting shirt and trousers that he had been seen in every day for weeks, and his bare feet were immersed in the water.

Suddenly, a cloud of sand and dust descended on the four ladies.

"What was that?" asked Grace, shaking off the sand.

"Are you all right, Mother?" Helen asked.

"Oh yes, but what was it?" asked Grace again.

"It is those boys over there, wrestling in the sand," Clara said.

"Who are those boys?" Helen asked indignantly.

"That good-looking one with curly brown hair is Mabel Hall's younger son, Dave—and the other one is Georgie Mitchell."

"So that's Mabel's younger son, Dave," Liza said.

"He is only about fourteen or fifteen years old," Clara said.

"I was surprised to hear that Mabel had moved to Northfield from New York City. Of course, I knew her slightly from the settlement house there," Liza said.

"Well, I guess she decided to move away after her husband left her," Clara said. She then mentioned, "My husband tells me that Martin Hall has become well known in political circles, and he has now been given a job in Washington, DC."

"Boris and I worry that Mabel doesn't get enough money from him to support herself and the two boys," Liza said.

"Besides that, how does Mabel like living in Northfield?" Helen asked. "I hear she is making friends."

"She's very outgoing and pleasant, and you are right to say that she is making friends. Also, I hear she has been helpful to that young German, Fritz, who works at the youth hostel.

Their European backgrounds are similar, you know," Clara explained.

Another cloud of sand went up as Dave and Georgie continued wrestling, grabbing at each other and turning over and over.

Helen asked in a concerned tone, "Did more sand get on you, Mother?"

"Oh no, I'm fine!" Grace answered calmly. "I believe all the wrestling is just to show off in front of your daughter, Diane, and your niece, Jenny—our pretty sunbathers!"

The boys finally stopped and got up and moved closer to the girls. The girls got up and smiled at them. Then they all laughed, and Diane and Jenny ran off to the changing shack, muttering, "It must be getting late."

Back under the tree, the others heard Helen say, "I'm afraid my daughter, Diane, is becoming boy-crazy. Sometimes I worry about her."

"She's awfully pretty," Clara said. "And she's being brought up well by you and Bob, so you shouldn't be concerned about her."

Then Dave and Georgie climbed up a steep bank at the far end of the lake, and they sat on the edge of a stone-walled bridge that spanned the stream as it flowed into the lake. They watched as Diane and Jenny finally came out of the changing shack. The girls were wearing thin summer dresses and carrying their bathing suits wrapped in towels under their arms. They walked slowly up to the stone bridge, where the boys were sitting with their legs dangling over the edge.

When Dave saw the girls approaching, he immediately stood up on the wall and shouted to them, "Would you like to see me do a swan dive or a jackknife?"

Diane looked down at the water below and saw how shallow it was, with big rocks showing just below the surface. She looked up at Dave in shocked disbelief that he would try anything that dangerous.

Jenny, who briefly glanced over the wall, covered her face with her hands and said, "Don't do it!"

Clara Levering, still on the beach, saw what Dave was planning to do and waved to him to get down. Boris also saw the danger of the situation from where he was sitting on the dam and threw his notebook down and ran toward the bridge. "Don't dive!" he shouted. "The water's too shallow there!"

Diane watched with her face frozen with fear and amazement. Georgie, who was still seated on the stone wall, smiled confidently up at his friend and said, "Do a good dive! Everyone is watching!"

"Here I go," Dave called out. He bent his knees and jumped high and out. His strong young body sailed up and then down toward the shallow water. He somehow managed to dive into a slightly deeper part of the water, just inches beyond the submerged rocks. He surfaced unscathed and stood up in the knee-deep water with a devilish smile on his face. Then he waded ashore.

"Let's see you do it again, Dave," Georgie said, laughing.

Diane rushed over to Georgie and said, "He could have broken his neck. Don't you dare tell him to try it again! I thought you were his friend."

Georgie looked up at her blankly and said nothing.

Boris confronted Dave as he came up on the bridge. "You could have been killed! I'm glad your mother wasn't here. Never try to dive from here again. It is one thing to take a slight chance once in a while, but another to be a complete idiot. You could have been killed on those rocks."

Dave looked at Boris with a degree of respect and couldn't think of anything to say.

The sandy beach of the lake was soon deserted as the evening shadows gathered, but Dave Hall's reckless dive from the stone bridge into the rock-filled shallow water was talked about in Northfield for some time.

Chapter 45

A FEW DAYS later, Anne Mitchell and Minnie Johnson were walking down Main Street. They stopped to look at a newly posted sign on the front lawn of a large gray house.

"The First American Youth Hostel," Anne read out loud.

"It's a nice-looking sign, but what is a youth hostel?" Minnie asked.

"Haven't you seen young people riding their bikes into town? Well, this is a place where they will spend the night. Then they go on, riding north, and stop each night in a different youth hostel. They usually sleep in the barns. This house here is the main one," answered Anne. And she said, "I remember when I was growing up, and this house belonged to old George Fielding. He lived in it for eighty years, and before that, his father and grandfather lived in it. It was one of the first houses built here in Northfield," Anne said.

"Some of the bikers I've seen look like hoodlums, and that young German man who works here doesn't mingle much with the town people," Minnie commented.

Just then, they saw Fritz and Otto Kirschheimer come out of the side door of the house. Otto was carrying a saw, and Fritz was pointing to some tree limbs that needed to be trimmed. The two women, seeing them, turned and continued walking along Main Street.

Suddenly, there was the sound of a train whistle coming from the direction of the railroad station.

"It sounds like the train is arriving," Fritz said.

"Does that mean a new group of hostelers will be here soon?" Otto asked.

"Yes, that's right. It will take a while for them to get their bikes out of the baggage car, but then they will ride directly here."

"How many are coming?"

"I heard there will be fourteen in this group: ten Americans and four Germans. The main youth-hostel organizer in New York City called to tell me they are on their way. Some have been here before, but not all. I will have to make sure they sign the registration book."

Then looking toward the river, they noticed Boris Melikoff coming across the back field from the river. Fritz called out to Boris and laughed when he saw Boris was carrying a fishing rod. "I have seen him go down to the river many times. He's trying to catch fish, but I've never seen him bring any back."

As Boris approached, he called to them, "What are you two up to?"

"We're waiting for a new group of hostelers to arrive. Their train just got in. Why don't you stay and help us welcome them?"

"I wish I could," Boris answered. "But I promised my wife, Liza, I'd meet her at the church's antique auction. The things to be sold are all set up on the side lawn of the church. I think I'm late already. But I'll try and come back. I'd like to talk to the bikers that stop here. I think it is great for them to get out in the open air and go from town to town and enjoy nature. But I have to go now."

So he turned and began walking up Main Street toward the church. Otto started cutting back some of the overgrown tree limbs. Fritz propped open the main door of the youth hostel and then went inside and put the registration book in a prominent place.

Chapter 46

THAT AFTERNOON, AS the sun shone down, the monthly antique auction was getting under way on the side lawn of the Northfield Congregational Church. More than forty people were seated in rows of chairs, facing a podium where the auctioneer began describing the latest antique for sale in a loud voice.

Dozens of other antiques were displayed behind him. There were tables, bureaus, desks, cedar chests, chairs, trunks, old baby carriages, all spread out to be viewed. Some older town boys stood by, ready to hold up each item so it could be seen clearly when it came up for sale.

When Boris arrived, he stood in the back. He smiled when he saw that Clara, Liza, Helen, and John Peterson's wife had found front-row seats. John Peterson saw Boris and joined him in the back of the crowd. They exchanged remarks about the senselessness of passing old junk back and forth from house to house, whether it was needed or not. And they laughed as they talked about it.

Then John called out loudly, "Look at all those bikers riding down Main Street." Heads turned as people watched the bikers going by swiftly in single file, on their way to the youth hostel.

Then Boris commented, "They look like boys between the age of fourteen and eighteen. How sunburned they look. I've been told these hostelers travel light. They never have more than one pair of shorts, two shirts, and sturdy shoes with them—and always a penknife."

"I hope you noticed the last four in line. They have German flags attached to the back of their bikes," John said.

"No, I didn't see that."

"Well, I've been making inquiries about how the youth hostel got started here in Northfield. It seems several wealthy German businessmen in New York City got together and decided to promote youth hosteling in the United States, since it has been such a great success in Germany for many years."

"Isn't the idea mostly for young people to see new places and enjoy the great outdoors?" Boris asked.

"Frankly, I don't see the good of it," John said.

Boris looked away, and then they both heard the loud chanting of the auctioneer again. "Do I hear fifty? Do I hear fifty?" he shouted out as the helpers held up a gate-leg table for all to see. Suddenly, a hand went up. "Sold for fifty!" the auctioneer finally shouted as he banged down the gavel.

"That auctioneer is the best one around. He comes from Putney, Vermont," Boris said. But Peterson didn't hear him because he had moved on and was talking with some of the other summer people.

Diane Thompson and her cousin, Jenny Ford, were standing nearby. Jenny said quietly, "This isn't too interesting when you don't have any money to buy things!"

"No, I like it. I like to look at all the old antiques," Diane said.

Then Georgie Mitchell began circling the girls again and again, which made them laugh. Finally, Diane asked him, "Where is Dave?"

"He's caddying at the hotel golf course."

"He must get tired carrying those heavy golf bags?"

Then Georgie mimicked her: "He must get tired carrying those heavy bags."

"I'm not talking to you," Diane said, losing her temper. "Go away!"

Then Georgie said, "Listen, Dave has to caddy. He needs the tip money!"

Diane frowned at him and turned away. So Georgie left and went and stood with the town boys that were helping the auctioneer.

Chapter 47

Northfield, Massachusetts
August 1938

AT THE END of August 1938, a formal dance for the summer employees was being planned by the religious conference leaders and the hotel manager. It was to be held at the French château near the hotel. The employees who had worked all season as waitresses, busboys, cooks, caddies, chambermaids, lifeguards, and grounds keepers looked forward to the special night. Some would soon be going back to college.

Tom Hall, Mabel's eighteen-year-old son, was sitting at the kitchen table in the house they rented off Main Street. He was writing down names on a piece of paper. His mother entered the kitchen and asked, "What are you doing, Tom?"

"I'm making a list of my friends and their perspective dates who will be coming to the dance tomorrow night."

"Why can't your friends find their own dates?"

"Somebody has to organize things in this town, or nothing will happen. I talked to most of the gang about this. It's settled now that Ted Burton will take the minister's daughter from the ridge to the dance. And my friend Ed Fisher, who drives the campus truck, said he would ask one of the other summer girls. And Gregg Lockwood, the farm manager's son, will bring his regular town girlfriend, and his brother is taking that blond curly haired waitress from the hotel. I'm just making sure that everybody has somebody to go with."

"I think I know who you will be taking," Mabel said, smiling.

"Kathy Curtis, of course," Tom said. "Kathy's the best looking of the summer girls, and the smartest and most fun."

"I saw young Diane Thompson recently, and she is very pretty," Mabel mentioned.

"Sure, she's pretty, but she's too young. She's only thirteen," Tom said, looking over his notes.

Suddenly, they heard footsteps on the back porch. The door opened, and Dave, Tom's younger brother, walked in.

"How was the caddying?" his mother asked.

"It was hot out there, but I made two dollars. You know some of those old ministers can hardly play golf. They are nice, but they can't afford to tip much."

Tom looked up at Dave and then asked, "Would you like to go to a formal dance at the Château tomorrow night?"

Dave looked at him in surprise and said loudly, "No, I wouldn't. Anyway, I don't know how to dance. And besides that, I didn't think they let kids in."

"You're old enough to go to a nice dance like that," Mabel said encouragingly.

"Of course, you would have to have a date," Tom told him.

"A date!" Dave shouted out and then grinned sheepishly and began to laugh.

"I have heard you say you like that cute summer girl, Diane Thompson," Tom said.

"I'd never have the nerve to ask her."

"Don't worry. I'll get word to her that she is going with you."

Dave gave Tom a bewildered look and then went over and got a Coke out of the refrigerator.

"I suppose that handsome lifeguard will be going," Mabel said.

"I asked him about it, and he said that he would try and look in. He's older than the rest of us, and all he talks about these days is how worried he is that there will be a war in Europe. And if there is," he said, "the US will be dragged into it. He tells everybody that if that happens, he's not going to let himself be drafted into the army. He says that he'd be a conscientious objector and go and live in Canada."

Mabel spoke up, "That reminds me. I called your father in Washington today and urged him to not forget Dave's fifteenth birthday next week, and he mentioned that there is talk in the capital about a possible war in Europe."

"What else did Dad say?" Tom asked, hoping for a special word from his father to him.

"Not much, he is very busy."

Then Tom reminded his mother that she and Liza and Boris were to be chaperones at the dance. "We talked about it and will be glad to do it," Mabel said. And she added, "The Château is a perfect place for a dance. It used to be called the Castle in the old days. I was told about the Château history when I first came here and was visiting at the Mitchells' house. The Château was built in 1902 as a summer residence for a wealthy businessman of Dutch ancestry, who was from New York City. It was constructed to look like a French château. The architect thought that it would be very interesting to have an Old World–type castle in the middle of a New England farm environment. It has forty rooms and four towers. From the tower windows, you can see the hotel and golf course, the village of Northfield, and the two campuses—Northfield School for Girls and Mount Herman School for Boys. And also, you can see the distant mountain ranges in all directions."**

Then Dave informed them that the best part of the Château is the dungeon in the basement. "Georgie and I go down there and explore sometimes when nobody is around."

"Don't get caught for trespassing," Mabel said seriously.

At that, Dave got up and went toward the door.

"Remember, you are taking Diane Thompson to the dance tomorrow night," Tom said.

"You said you would tell her!"

"I will, don't worry!"

Dave went out the door and down the front steps. Then, as was his custom, he started up the street toward Georgie Mitchell's house to see if anything was going on.

When he got there, he saw Georgie mowing the lawn. He stopped and went over to his friend.

Then Dave told him, "You wouldn't believe what my brother got me into."

"Who, Tom? What?"

"He is fixing me up with a date for the employees' dance Saturday night at the Château."

"Who?"

"Diane Thompson."

"No kidding. I hear that she lets guys hold her hand. She's the youngest of the summer girls that guys notice . . ."

"Hey, why don't you ask Joan Brownell to the dance? You have had a crush on her since the fourth grade."

Georgie said, "Me ask her? One, she hates me. Two, she can't stand the sight of me—"

"OK, forget that!" Dave said.

"Anyway, her grandfather, Andrew Brownell, has funny ideas. He thinks everyone should share their money with everyone else. And she is like him."

They sat down on the grass and talked about what they would do the rest of the day.

Chapter 48

THE EMPLOYEES' DANCE was held the last Saturday night of August 1938 in the large château, which was ablaze with lights. As the young couples arrived, they walked up the thirty granite steps to the massive open doors. Beyond, there was a large entry hall that led to the Grand Ballroom.

In the ballroom, crystal chandeliers glistened from above. There were long gilt-edged mirrors on each side of the fireplace. The rich family's crest could be seen in the center of each stained-glass window that faced west. The orchestra was practicing at the far end of the room. Boris and Liza Melikoff and Mabel Hall, acting as chaperones, stood inside the ballroom and welcomed the young people as they came in.

There were several smaller rooms off the ballroom. One was called the Gold Room. There were many small gold-painted chairs there; and there were two life-size portraits of the owner and his wife on the wall, all in heavy gold frames.

There was another room adjacent to the ballroom. It was the billiard room.

Dave Hall, with Diane Thompson beside him, noticed the billiard room and said, "Hey, there is nobody in that room. Let's go in there."

"Don't you want to dance?" Diane asked, following him.

"I hope Tom told you I never danced before. Can you dance?"

"Oh yes, I go to dancing class in the winter at home. I think I'm supposed to put my left hand on your shoulder and you take my—"

Looking at an open door in the billiard room that led to the outside balcony, Dave interrupted her. "Let's go out there," he said, grabbing her hand and pulling her out onto the dark balcony. Diane caught her breath and smoothed down the skirt of her white brocade evening gown, wondering what he would think up next.

As their eyes got used to the darkness, Dave pointed to a long flight of stone steps that led down from the balcony. "Those steps go down to the sunken garden," he said. "It's a long way down."

Then Diane suggested softly, "Why don't we just sit here at the top step for a while."

So they sat down together and listened as the dance music and the sound of laughter and talking drifted out from the ballroom.

Inside, Boris was having an argument with a college student who had been working as a lifeguard at the lake all summer. Boris was saying, "I'm afraid there will be a war in Europe. Germany is arming. I know there are many pacifists and isolationists that don't like to hear about that. Some college professors lecture in the colleges against any kind of military buildup here and any kind of national mobilization."

The young man answered quickly, "Well, I can tell you right now, I am a conscientious objector. No one is ever going to draft me into the army and tell me to go out and kill complete strangers. I'd leave the country if I thought that was going to happen. I hate war, and it's always young men my age that are sacrificed."

"We are a long way from that yet," Boris said, raising his hand in a quieting gesture. "Some of what you said is true, but this is a party, and we don't want to ruin it for others by arguing."

The orchestra began to play a polka, and Boris saw a chance to end the conversation with the young man, so he said, "How would you like to see how a real polka should be danced?" But there was no answer because the other one had hurried away.

Boris turned to Mabel and asked her to dance. She agreed, so he took her by the arm and led her to the middle of the floor, and they began to dance the polka. All the others stepped back to watch the old couple and clap their hands.

Boris swung Mabel around and around. Then he stomped with his left foot first and then with his right foot, back and forth, in time to the beat of the music. Mabel followed him well. The crowd began to laugh and cheer as the couple danced faster and faster. When the polka ended, Boris put his two strong hands around Mabel's waist and lifted her high off the floor to the delight of everyone. After the performance, Mabel hurried to a chair, exhausted.

To Dave and Diane sitting in the darkness on the top step of the stone stairs of the balcony, the music and gaiety inside the Château seemed to have little meaning. They looked down at the shadows in the sunken garden below and whispered off and on about everyday things, but they were mostly silent. They stayed there for a couple of hours.

Much later on, they heard the sound of a car horn. Dave jumped up and again grabbed Diane by the hand. They ran down the steps, past the sunken garden; and then Dave, with his strong arms, dragged Diane up the steep grass embankment in front of the Château to the waiting cars.

"Aha!" Tom said. "Where have you two been?"

Another shouted out, "What were you two doing all this time?" And the others laughed as they got into the cars.

Diane, bewildered, let go of Dave's hand and hurried to a car she knew would return her to the Ridge. Dave joined his brother.

So ended the end-of-the-season dance at the Château in Northfield.

Chapter 49

BY JUNE 1939, the worst of the Great Depression was over. There were more jobs to be had. There were more automobiles on the roads, and business at the stores was increasing.

In New York City, Boris Melikof was still the manager of the Eastside settlement house. As always, new immigrants went there to discuss their problems, and to socialize with each other. The Saturday Night International Dinners were still well attended. Boris and his staff were available and helpful to people who were looking for jobs and housing.

But Boris began to see a new type of immigrant coming to the settlement house in the late thirties. These people left Europe because they were afraid there would be an all-out war. Some came because they were being persecuted by the Nazis in Germany. These refugees were often not as poor as the ones who had come in the 1920s, but they were just as anxious to make a place for themselves here.

One morning, a man came to Boris's office to tell him there was a Greek ship in New York Harbor with a thousand Jewish refugees on it. And the Immigration officers wouldn't let the ship dock. He asked Boris if he could do anything to help the refugees to get into the country.

"I'll think about it," Boris said, and the man left.

As he thought it over, Boris looked out the front window of the settlement house to the street below. Suddenly, he saw Fritz Kirschheimer hurrying up the street with a bundle under his arm. Boris smiled as he watched Fritz bound up the front steps of the building. He walked out to the entrance hall to meet him.

Boris laughed as he said, "I thought you were your uncle Otto when I saw you coming along. There's a strong family resemblance. Especially the way you walk."

"Many people have mentioned that."

"And how is Otto?"

"He is getting older but still farming and doing loom work. As you can see, I brought some samples for you."

"That's what you have there in that bundle?"

"Yes, Otto is grateful to you for trying to sell them."

"I'm glad to do it."

"I can't stay long," Fritz told him. "I'm taking a group of American youth hostelers to Germany. Our ship, the *Bremen*, leaves the pier at six o'clock."

"So you're off to Germany with some more young bikers. How many are in this group?" Boris asked.

"There are eight in all. I have three young women this time, and another fellow they call Shorty. But the strongest and most eager guys in the group are two brothers, Dick and Carl Newberg, and a neighbor of theirs, Hank Snyder. Dick and Carl's father grew up in Germany and is keen on having his sons spend six weeks bicycling through his former homeland."

"I read in the paper that Germany is in the process of raising a huge army and manufacturing guns and tanks. Doesn't that worry you at all?" Boris asked.

"No one is going to bother eight student bikers who go from one youth hostel to the next, minding their own business. They will simply be seen as young enthusiastic tourists while they are there. Also, the press exaggerates a lot about the degree to which Germany is arming."

They talked for a few more minutes, but soon, it was time for Fritz to leave. "I promise to see you when I return in six weeks. You will probably be in Northfield by then," Fritz said.

"That's right," said Boris, who wished him well on his trip, shaking his hand.

Then Boris went to his desk and began to think again about the Jewish refugees stranded on the ship in the harbor. So he wrote down a list of names of social workers he knew, and he began to plan how to contact them. His idea was for them all to go and confront the Custom officials and convince them they should let the Jewish refugees' ship land.

Within a week, the ship was permitted to dock, and the refugees were free to enter the country. Later, many heard about Boris and what he did and came to thank him.

Chapter 50

FRITZ AND THE young people in his group boarded the SS *Bremen*, and soon, the ship was steaming eastward across the Atlantic Ocean. The ship would make a stop at Southampton, England, and then continue on to Bremerhaven, Germany.

On the second day of the voyage, Dick Newberg woke up early and quickly jumped down from the top-tier bunk in the third-class cabin. He yanked on his shirt, shorts, and shoes. He left the cabin quietly so as not to wake up the others, and he went up on deck.

The upper deck was mostly deserted, and Dick began to look around. He was fourteen years old and the youngest of the youth-hostel group, although he was already six feet tall. He had brown hair and eyes, and a square German-type jaw. His shoulders were broad, and his body strong. He accredited his good health to his long summer bike rides through New England that always started in Northfield. Sometimes he appeared to be immature and naïve. Some of the group found that engaging, while others laughed at him.

After a quick run around the decks, he leaned on the ship's railing and looked out and watched the sun come up. Then he stared down at the ocean, hoping to catch a glimpse of a porpoise or a flying fish or the fin of a shark, but he only saw bluish-green water. The thought that a submarine could be cruising below the surface would never have crossed his mind.

Dick was always the first one in the dining room for breakfast. Later, his older brother, Carl, and their friend Hank joined him. After they ate, Dick talked them into playing a game of shuffleboard. The game didn't last long because there was an American Youth Hostel meeting in one of the lounges at 9:00 AM, led by Fritz. The meeting started with singing. There were two favorite songs they all liked. One was "There's a Long, Long Trail A-Winding" and "Frère Jacques."

Fritz handed out the itinerary and maps of places they would be biking through in Germany. The maps showed where each overnight hostel was located. Fritz went over the routes, emphasizing where the mountainous terrain would be found and which rivers they would cross. The group was grateful for all the information they received from Fritz and spoke enthusiastically about the adventures that were ahead of them.

After the meeting, the group separated. Some went swimming in the ship's pool, while others played quoits and Ping-Pong. Some just walked around the decks. None of the group ever missed a meal or four o'clock tea. In the evenings, they listened to the Seamen Choir, and sometimes there was a movie or a dance.

Early one morning, Dick, Carl, Hank, and Shorty decided to go up to the first-class section of the ship to play deck tennis. They had learned from one of the crew that the third-class passengers could use the first-class court from 7:30 AM to 8:45 AM. Fritz decided to go along with them to make sure they kept out of trouble and didn't disturb the first-class passengers.

The four laughed and joked as they played, enjoying their hour and fifteen minutes of deck tennis.

"It's great to be up here on the big open deck and breathe in the sea air," Shorty said.

"Take a last breath," Hank said. "Here comes a steward to shoo us away."

"It's time!" the steward said. "You will have to go below."

Dick came up to him and asked, "When we stop at Southampton, England, tomorrow, can we go ashore for a few hours?"

"I've been told that only passengers disembarking at Southampton will be able to leave the ship. All others will remain aboard. That is a new regulation issued by the British Custom officers. The rules have become stricter lately."

Chapter 51

AFTER DOCKING AND then leaving Southampton, England, it took the SS *Bremen* twenty-four hours to reach the port of Bremerhaven, Germany. The youth hostelers disembarked from the ship and boarded a train for the city of Hamburg.

The railroad station at Hamburg was very large. It was there that Dick, Carl, and Hank began to notice young German boys in uniform. They were dressed in green shirts, black shorts, and black neckties; and they were marching in close formation through the station.

"Who are they?" Dick asked Fritz.

"They are like our Boy Scouts," Fritz answered.

"But there are so many of them!"

Leaving the station, they saw the Hamburg harbor in front of them, where a large fleet of German warships were anchored.

They spent the night at the Hein Gogenwerde Hostel, just outside the city, and then returned to the Hamburg station the next day. There was a place where bicycles could be rented. They made their selections and put the bikes in the baggage car. Then they boarded the train to Kassel.

It was raining hard that evening when the train reached Kassel. The group biked through the downpour to the Yugend Heinburger Hostel. Immediately, they were told it would cost ten pfennig to shelter their bikes in the barn.

"Why do we have to pay for that?" Dick asked loudly.

"It is better that they are safe instead of being stolen," Fritz said.

"We never had to pay to park our bikes in Northfield!"

Then Carl, Dick's older brother, spoke up. "This isn't Northfield. This is Germany. Don't be such a baby!"

They soon began to realize that the hostel was crowded with Hitler Youths, who had arrived before them. They were milling around inside, and Fritz went over to one of them and began talking to him.

Later in the evening, the Americans and the Germans sat on the floor at opposite ends of the main room and ate their supper. "Those guys are in really good shape!" Hank said to Fritz.

"That's not surprising. I spoke to one of them. They had just completed a fifty-kilometer hike."

When the Germans had finished eating, one of the leaders shouted out "Achtung," and they all stood up as one. Then the leader gave another order.

"What's going on?" Hank asked.

"They are being ordered to form a single line and march up the stairs that lead to the sleeping loft."

After they left, Dick, Carl, Hank, Fritz, and the others lingered in front of the fireplace, where logs had been set and lit. Now, the fire burned brightly.

"When did all this Hitler Youth business get started?" Carl asked Fritz.

"The Hitler Youth program has been around for years," Fritz said. "Each summer, thousands of young boys travel on foot from their hometowns to Nurnberg. There, they participate in the annual Nazi Party Congress. They marched in front of the Führer and all the Nazi youth leaders. The pageantry of these ceremonies reaches dynamic proportions. As a result, the German youth develops an avid commitment to their government, and they are inspired with awe by the discipline of their leaders. They knew that when their time in the Hitler Youth program was over, they would be automatically taken into the SA or SS or the Nazi Motorized Transport Corps or become regular soldiers of the Third Reich, so their futures were secure."**

"You seem to know a lot about this, Fritz," Carl said.

"I do to some extent. I have a German cousin who sends me letters to Northfield often. She writes that some of the German parents object to having their sons indoctrinated and taken away from them for good at such a young age. But she believes that the regular German people will keep the new government from going to extremes."

The group was silent for a few minutes. Then Dick yawned and said, "I'm tired."

"Yes, let's hit the sack," Fritz suggested. "Tomorrow, we ride from Kassel to the hostel in Eisenach."

Chapter 52

July 1939
Eisenach, Germany

AT 6:30 AM the next morning, the group retrieved their bikes from the barn and was ready to go.

"It's fifty-four miles to Eisenach," Fritz told them. "And there is a long uphill ride into Eisenach at the end. You will pass through some villages. If you get lost, ask for directions."

"I'm supposed to ask directions in German?" asked Shorty.

"Most people speak English."

"I wonder if Shorty and the three girls can bike fifty-four miles," Carl asked Fritz.

"They must have known that there would be some hard biking when they signed up."

"Let's go!" Dick shouted, being the first in line. Fritz gave an encouraging smile to Shorty and the three girls, and soon, they were all on the main road out of Kassel.

Six hours later, the American group—except Shorty and the three girls—had arrived at Eisenach, which was a small-sized city nestled in wooded hills. They rode into the youth-hostel grounds and went inside to register. The German manager of the hostel spoke to them in English.

"Do you know that you have come to a place that has an enormous importance in the history of German civilization?" he asked in a friendly way. "This is because of its position at the foot of the spectacular hilltop castle known as Wartburg Castle, which was built in the eleventh century. It became an early center for music and poetry, immortalized by Richard Wagner's opera *Tannhäuser*. Two centuries later, the castle achieved a place in world history when it sheltered Martin Luther, who had been outlawed by the Roman Catholic Church for his 'heretical' views. During the year he spent here (1521–1522), he worked on his German translation of the Bible. Also, right here in town is the J. S. Bach House, commemorating the birthplace of Eisenach's most famous son."**

"You have an interesting history to be proud of here," Fritz said and then explained that they would wait outside for the rest of their group to arrive.

It was beginning to get dark when, suddenly, they saw an open truck drive in. In the back of the truck were Shorty and the three girls and their bikes. Fritz and Dick hurried over to help them get out and remove the bicycles. It was then they noticed a potent smell and knew there had been cattle in the truck. And one of the girls was holding her nose and looking disgusted.

Shorty asked Fritz nervously, "Will you thank the truck driver? I don't feel up to it, and I don't have any money."

Fritz walked around to the front of the truck and thanked the driver in his best German but didn't offer to pay him any money. The driver seemed pleased to have helped out and drove away laughing.

Fritz asked Shorty, "Is there anything wrong? You look pale, fella."

"There is plenty wrong," interrupted one of the girls. "We stopped in a small town a long way back to get some food, and Shorty fainted. He blacked out, and we had to pick him up off of the ground. Then we had to hail that truck and ask that driver to give us a lift to Eisenach—which he did, thank heavens. It wasn't until we started up that we noticed that there had been cattle in the truck, and we had to sit next to the smelly mess all the way."

Then one of the other girls spoke up and said emotionally, "I'd like to know whose idea it was for us to bike so far up those steep hills all in one day." Then she started to cry.

"Now don't worry," Fritz said. "We will get you settled in the hostel here, and you will feel better when you've had something to eat."

It was later on that night, when the Americans were together in the main room of the hostel, that Shorty and the girls said they were quitting.

"It's too hard," said one of the girls.

"We never realized there would be so many steep mountains to pump our bikes up," another said.

"And I don't like all these young boys in uniform crowding into the hostels," the third said. "And I don't like seeing all those trucks filled with soldiers speeding by us."

"I'm sorry to quit," Shorty muttered. "I'll miss you, but I never fainted before in my life. So I guess I'm not as strong as I thought I was."

"It's all right," Fritz said, knowing he couldn't convince them to go on. "I will buy your tickets for the train ride back to Bremerhaven tomorrow. Then you can go back home on the USS *New York*. I believe it sails sometime this week. Tomorrow, be sure you have all your belongings and especially your passports with you. Now get a good night's rest."

Chapter 53

August 1939
Nuremberg, Germany

SEVERAL DAYS LATER, those of the group that were left biked into Nuremberg. They had been told that Nuremberg was one of Germany's greatest surviving medieval cities. Kings and emperors had resided there for five hundred years. There were castles and gothic churches that dated back to the eleventh century. **

As the bikers came into the center of the city, they noticed a large crowd was gathering.

"What's going on?" Dick asked.

"I'll find out," Fritz said and walked over to a woman and asked what was happening.

The woman informed Fritz that the local people were organizing a parade. They would march to the carnival grounds outside the city, where they would have a Kinderfest.

"Hundreds of people will be marching with their children," the woman said. "When they get there, there will be games of all kinds and food and a free show to enjoy."

"It should be interesting! Shall we go?" Fritz asked the others.

"Yes, let's follow them. It will be fun," Dick said.

Carl and Hank agreed, so they went along with the crowd. As they left town, they noticed beer gardens and well-kept parks and old museums.

The games had already started by the time they arrived at the festival grounds.

"Look at those guys wrestling!" Hank exclaimed.

"Look at those kids lifting the heavy barbells," Carl said.

There were streamers and flags fluttering in the summer breeze. Refreshment booths had been set up. Signs had been posted, indicating where the various games were being played. Fritz had to hold Dick back when the start of a running race was announced. "Better not get involved," he said.

It was then that Fritz overheard a local man mention to another man that Hitler often held his rallies, called *Reichspartettag*, on these grounds. "It was here that he gave his speeches that inspired his followers," the man said.

Fritz didn't mention to the others what he had heard but simply joined them and watched the games and races. An hour passed, and Fritz began to worry about getting a place to sleep at the Nuremberg hostel, so he suggested they hurry back.

When they reached the hostel, the manager told them that the hostel was already filled for the night. But he added, "You may be able to get a place to sleep at the Catholic Home for the Poor. The nuns are very kind there."

And he gave them directions. "You go to the Saint Sebald Church with its twin towers near the Rathausplatz. There is a house in the back of the church, where the Catholic Home for the Poor is located."

They found the house and parked their bikes. Then they knocked on the door. A nun opened it and welcomed them. She showed them to a small room on the first floor where there were three cots.

"We are one cot short," Hank mentioned.

"I saw a small sofa in the main room," Carl said. "Dick can sleep out there."

"I saw it too. It's not big enough," Dick said.

"Too bad, it's just for one night," his brother answered, and the nun left them.

Then they decided to go to the center of town and get something to eat. Along the streets were timber-framed and gabled houses. Also, there were numerous bars, cafés, theaters, cabarets, and some quaint-looking secondhand shops. They stopped at one of the outdoor cafés and sat down at a table. It was then that Fritz gave them each a mark to pay for their food. They ordered the cheapest on the menu. As they ate, they watched the people passing by.**

Later, they returned to the Catholic Home and were soon asleep. The next morning, they woke early because the nuns had told them they would have breakfast at 7:00 AM. The nuns served them bread and hot milk, and one said, "You must see the Kaiserburg Castle before you leave Nuremberg."

The group agreed to go there, and after thanking the nuns and waving to the poor who were already lined up and waiting for food from the kitchen, they got on their bikes and rode to the Kaiserburg Castle. It was an enormous, majestic castle that dominated the center of the old town.

After propping their bikes against an iron fence, they climbed up the front steps.

"If you've seen one castle, you've seen them all," Hank said.

"How can you say that?" Fritz retorted as they went through the main entrance of the early Gothic castle. "Look around. Look at the stonework, the statues, and the collection of paintings and fine art."

"Yes, but there's something else here," Dick said. "Somebody told me there is a torture chamber in the basement. Come on, Hank, let's explore."

"That's a waste of time," Fritz said.

"No, it will be fun," Dick answered.

They soon found the old steps that led down to the cellar.

There were iron tables there. "I guess that's where they tied up the victims," Hank said.

"What's that for?" Dick asked, pointing to a strange-looking machine.

"I bet that is where they stretch people's limbs out," Hank said.

After some other gruesome discoveries—including a human skull found lying half-buried in a far corner—they decided they had seen enough. So they climbed up the stone steps and joined Fritz and Carl. Soon they were on their way to Ingolstadt, a five-hour ride to the south.

Chapter 54

AFTER INGOLSTADT, THE next two weeks were spent in Heidelberg, Manheim, and Munich.

On the last day in Munich, while biking through traffic toward the railroad station, they heard loud cries of someone in pain coming from an alleyway. They stopped and glanced into the alley, and they saw five men beating up a smaller man. They had him on the ground and were kicking him relentlessly as he screamed out in agony.

"Shall we try and stop them?" Dick asked Fritz.

"No, it's not wise for us to interfere," Fritz said, shaking his head. "Let's just continue on to the station."

"But that's not right, five against one," Dick insisted.

"No, let's just keep going."

And they started to move ahead.

"I feel guilty," Dick said, taking one more look back into the alley where the brutal beating continued.

From the Munich station, they took a train to Northern France, where they got off and once again were out on the open road.

They biked from the French border into Belgium. Riding through a city there, Hank began to complain, "Riding over these cobblestones is terrible! Why don't they flatten out these roads?"

"Hang on," Fritz said. "The roads in Holland are smoother and easier to ride on. They have wide, flat bike paths on each side of the streets there."

After several days of biking along the North Sea coast, they left Holland and were once again in Germany. They hoped there would be a hostel in Nordheim. When they biked into the town, Fritz asked a pretty young girl standing by if there was a youth hostel in this town.

"There is none here," the girl said. "But a mile south of town, there is an old abandoned schoolhouse that is sometimes used by bikers. It has a belfry."

"Can we sleep there?" Fritz asked.

"Oh yes. A group of Americans on bicycles passed here earlier today and were going there," she said.

Fritz was in no hurry to say good-bye to the girl. He stayed on to talk about the weather and places of interest. Then he asked her, "Are all the girls in Germany as pretty as you?"

Before she could answer, they heard a loud shout.

"It's time to get going!" Hank called out. And then he laughed, seeing Fritz with a girl, and added, "Remember, we are on a schedule!"

Fritz reluctantly got on his bike and gave the girl a parting smile, and she waved good-bye. As Fritz passed Hank, he mumbled to him, "I was just being courteous." Then he sped ahead of the others.

Soon they came to the century-old school building. Dozens of bicycles lay on the front lawn. From inside the building, they could hear the sound of many young people speaking English. They put their bikes down and went inside. The main room was filled with American youth hostelers like themselves.

"What a crowd!" Fritz said.

"What a mob scene!" Hank said under his breath.

"Old home week," Carl said.

Soon they learned that most of the others were high school students from the Midwest. Dick, always the consequential diplomat, was very friendly to those he met and immediately got out his notebook and wrote down their names and addresses.

An elderly German man came over to Fritz and introduced himself. He told him he was a teacher at the school but now managed the house and welcomed traveling young people. Then he informed Fritz that he and his group, being the last to arrive, would have to sleep in the hayloft of the barn because the schoolhouse was filled up.

Fritz agreed to this. Then the man urged them to stay on in the house with the others and have something to eat. Soon they were all singing songs and sharing food and swapping stories of their adventures on the road.

Finally, Fritz, Dick, Carl, and Hank went out into the dark night; and with the help of Fritz's flashlight, they were able to find the door of the barn. Soon they located a ladder and used it to climb up to the hayloft.

Hank explained in disgust, "What's next? I bet there are bats up here. And the hay is dusty!"

"This isn't so bad for one night," Fritz said. "And remember that in two days, we will be on the SS *Bremen* again going home."

"Always the man with the positive words," Carl said, looking at Fritz.

Soon, they all settled down into the hay and slept.

Chapter 55

IN LATE AUGUST of 1939, the SS *Bremen* was tied up at the dock at Bremerhaven, Germany. There were a large number of people waiting in line to go on board. When Fritz, Dick, Carl, and Hank got to the dock, they went to the end of the line. Fritz took this time to hand out the money to each one that was left over from the trip. When Dick got his share, he said he wanted to go back in town to the shops, where he could buy some souvenirs.

Fritz warned him, "If you are late and miss the boat, you'll have to swim home."

"The ship leaves at 6:00 PM," his brother reminded him.

They shook their heads in dismay as they watched him rush off, and then they laughed.

The line of the people waiting to get on the ship moved very slowly. Each passenger was stopped at the custom post at the foot of the gangway. The custom officers scrutinized each passport and identification card with great care. Some people were told to step aside and were not allowed to board the ship, which caused angry arguments and delays. Many in the line seemed especially anxious to get on the ship and out of Germany. Others waited patiently and watched the dockworkers loading luggage and crates of all sizes into the hold of the ship.

There was an elderly couple standing in the line directly in front of the Americans. The man wore a black suit and hat and had a long beard. He stood silently with his hands behind his back. The woman with him had on a well-worn dress and no hat. She was slightly bent over. Then the woman made a remark to the man she was with.

Hank, who was watching them, whispered to Fritz, "They are speaking English, but they look like Germans."

Fritz answered, "Plenty of people speak more than one language."

Suddenly, the large cloth bag that the woman was carrying slipped out of her hand and onto the dock, near where Carl and Fritz were standing. They hurried to help her retrieve the contents of the bag that were strewed about. Her husband looked away, letting the strangers pick up her scattered belongings.

"You shouldn't bother, but thank you," the woman said to them, reaching down and putting the last of the things back in the bag.

Then Fritz approached her husband and said casually, "The line moves slowly, doesn't it?"

"Why do you speak to me? Have I ever met you?" the man said suspiciously with a frown on his face.

Fritz, undisturbed, continued talking to him. "We are Americans, and we have just completed a six-week bicycle tour of Germany. We saw a great deal of beautiful country, interesting towns, and of course, the big cities. We learned a lot."

"Beautiful countryside?" the man repeated sarcastically. "Don't you know what is going on?" His face was flushed with anger.

"What do you mean?" Carl asked. "What's going on?"

Then he talked directly to the three of them. "Have you ever heard of the Viennese Emigration Plan? Last year, Jews in Vienna were told they had to emigrate out of Austria. They were told false tales of a better life elsewhere. This happened after the Germans invaded Austria in March of 1938. Thousands were quickly resettled in Poland after their homes, shops, and bank accounts were confiscated. My wife and I were fortunate because of the money sent to us by the American Jewish Joint Distribution Committee. Now we will board this ship and leave Europe, perhaps forever. But why am I wasting my time explaining this to you three nincompoops?" **

Then the man turned his back on them.

The line finally began to move faster. Suddenly, Carl saw Dick running along the dock. He watched him push his way past the crowd and force his way up the gangway to where they were. Then he told them loudly, "Someone stole my wallet with all my money in it. So I couldn't buy any souvenirs. I don't know how it happened. The wallet just disappeared."

"Too bad," said his brother. "If you had stayed with us, it wouldn't have been stolen. Now let's stick together."

"Tough luck," Fritz said to Dick. "I can lend you some money until we get home."

"No thank you. Carl has enough to share with me."

Later, as the ship got under way, the four stood on the deck and watched as Bremerhaven receded from view.

Suddenly, Hank exclaimed, "Clean bunks and regular meals, at last!"

Then Carl mentioned, "It's funny, but now that we are back on the ship, I can hardly remember all the different experiences we have had."

"The memory of all of them will come back to you," Fritz said. And he added, "I must admit that it is nice to relax."

"I can't wait to look around the ship again," Dick said. "I had forgotten how big the *Bremen* is."

Chapter 56

1940
Northfield, Massachusetts

THE LAST WEEK of December 1940, the Northfield Hotel was filled with guests who had come for the skiing and ice skating and to enjoy the snowy winter scenery and the good food in the hotel dining room. Bob and Helen Thompson—with their daughter, Diane, and their niece, Jenny Ford—were among the guests. They had taken a train up from Philadelphia to Northfield the day after Christmas.

The hotel was ready for the winter crowd. There were steep ski slopes on the snow-covered golf course and steeper ski trails on the downhill roads on Rustic Ridge. There were horse-drawn wagon rides available every day, and a toboggan run had been erected in front of the hotel that extended down to the frozen pond below. The pond provided good skating, which Diane and Jenny took advantage of right away.

Meanwhile, the American Youth Hostel was holding a year-end reunion. Dick Newberg, now a senior in high school, had persuaded his friend Hank Snyder, who was a freshman at Dartmouth College, to come with him to the reunion. They came up from their homes in Tarrytown, New York, to the youth hostel. Fritz, who was still the assistant manager there, welcomed them enthusiastically.

The first afternoon, Dick and Hank sat with the others on the floor in front of the fire in the main room. They took turns reminiscing about their many bike trips, and Dick spoke up and told them about his group's adventures when they biked through Germany the past summer.

After a while, Fritz stood up and informed everyone that there was good ice skating at the hotel pond. Dick grabbed Hank by the arm and yanked him up. "Let's go!" Dick said. Then they got their parkas and skates and hurried out the door.

The tall elm trees that bordered each side of Main Street had long since lost their leaves. Now the stark branches swayed back and forth in the cold winter wind. Several inches of snow-covered the ground. Also, long icicles hung from the edges of the roofs of the colonial-style houses that were set back from the street. In front of one of the houses, children were pulling their sleds and throwing snowballs.

Dick and Hank walked fast and soon came to the skating pond, where they could hear music coming from the warming hut. They could also hear the skaters laughing and calling back and forth to each other.

"Let's put on our skates here," Dick said, and they sat down on a wooded bench at the edge of the pond.

Hank looked up from lacing his skates and jabbed Dick in the ribs. "Hey, look at them!" he said.

Dick immediately saw two pretty young girls skating on the pond in front of them.

"I get the blonde!" Hank said hurriedly.

Dick—who was already up and out on the ice—called back, "That's what you think!" He came up fast behind the blond girl. He asked if he could skate with her, and before she could answer, he took her arm and guided her quickly over the ice.

Totally surprised and not wanting to lose her balance, Diane Thompson held tightly to Dick's arm.

Hank skated up behind Jenny and did the same thing. Wide-eyed and speechless, Jenny nodded her head to him and then tried to match his long skating stride.

On the edge of the pond, Diane's mother, Helen Thompson, who was wearing a long fur coat, stood talking to the hotel manager's wife. "Who are those young men skating with the girls?" Helen asked.

"I don't know them, but I am sure they are here in town for the youth hostel reunion."

"They look much older than Diane and Jenny," Helen said.

"Don't worry. Everyone skates with everyone else here." Then changing the subject, the manager's wife asked, "Why did you and Mr. Thompson decide to come to the hotel this winter? You never came before."

"Well, frankly, Bob and I had an ulterior motive. Our daughter, Diane, became quite infatuated with young Dave Hall last summer when we were here at our cottage on the

Ridge. She has received two letters from him this fall. We thought it would make her happy to be able to see him for a short time again, so we decided to come. When we arrived, we were disappointed to hear from one of the hotel staff that Dave and his brother were not here but had gone to New York City to visit their father."

"That's right, the boys left last week. And their mother, Mabel Hall, is also away at some other place. The divorce was hard on the boys, but here in Northfield, we are all very fond of Mabel. She's always cheerful, helpful, and fits in well."

They kept watching the skaters, and then Helen said, "Diane and Jenny seem to be enjoying themselves with those two boys. The attention Diane is getting right now might make her feel better. She was quite sad when we got here and she found out that she wasn't going to see Dave."

"We all think Dave is an unusually handsome boy and has quite a nice sense of humor. When he caddies at the golf course in the summer, he is always sought after by the best players. You might say that he is everyone's favorite."

"Look, they have stopped skating," Helen said.

Dick, Hank, Diane, and Jenny stood on the ice in a circle in the middle of the pond. "Will you give me your name and address?" Dick asked.

"I'm Diane Thompson," she said, and Dick quickly took a small notebook and pen out of his pocket. "Will you give me your home address?" he asked.

She slowly gave it to him, and he wrote it down.

"Who are you?" Diane asked, looking at him.

"I'm Dick Newberg from Tarrytown, New York. I will write to you."

Then Hank reminded Dick that supper would soon be served at the youth hostel, so the circle broke up, and they said good-bye. The boys quickly took off their skates and started across the crusty snow in the direction of the hostel.

Diane and Jenny sat down on the wooden bench outside the warming shed and began removing their skates. They were giggling and laughing, and Jenny asked, "Who was that one you were skating with?"

"He's Dick somebody, and he comes from Parrytown, New York . . . the boy from Parrytown," Diane said, laughing.

"No, he said 'Tarrytown,' not 'Parrytown,'" Jenny insisted. And they looked at each other, and both laughed louder.

Chapter 57

"I KNOW A shortcut back to the youth hostel," Dick told Hank. "You go behind the hotel and past the Château. Then there is a long hill down to a stone bridge that crosses a stream. I'll show it to you."

"Are you sure it's the shortest way back?" Hank asked suspiciously.

"It's much shorter!" Dick insisted.

So they turned off Highland Avenue and tramped through the ankle-deep snow until they came to the Château, where they stopped and looked up at it.

"Some wealthy man built this in 1895. Back in those days, Northfield had become famous because of the religious conferences held here. The preaching of the well-known evangelist, D. L. Moody, brought hundreds of people to Northfield each summer. One summer, thirty-six thousand people came to Northfield. The New York, New Haven, and

Hartford railroad trains stopped here in Northfield. And that's how most of them got here," Dick told him.

"That's some building!" Hank commented, looking up.

"Yes, they say there are forty rooms in there and a two-story basement. It has a chapel inside, and it has a ballroom where formal dances are held."

Then Hank said restlessly, "Okay, that's nice, but let's get going."

So they started down the steep hill. They had to struggle to keep from falling on the snow-and-ice-covered surface.

At the bottom of the hill, Hank asked, "Now, where do we go from here?"

"We go across that field," Dick said, pointing ahead. "It leads to Main Street."

As they walked along, Hank began to talk seriously to Dick. "My history professor at Dartmouth thinks that the US will soon get into the war. He says that people in our country are starting to shift away from isolationism and are becoming more aware of the war over there. The professor told us that our country has given sixty old US Navy destroyers to England. So if he is right, there is a good chance we might get into it."

Then Dick said, "Fritz keeps talking about the Neutrality Act of 1935. He believes in the importance of international understanding and diplomatic negotiations, not war."

"That sounds good. But the leaders in Washington are keen on helping the British defeat the Germans."

"Fritz doesn't believe that," Dick said.

"Naturally, he wouldn't—because he was brought up in Germany. Figure it out. He wouldn't want the US to declare war against Germany. He must have relatives there."

"Well, it's all beyond me!" Dick said, and he changed the subject. "You know I have sent in my application to Dartmouth. It would be great to be there with you and to ski all winter."

"I thought your father wanted you to try and get into the Naval Academy in Annapolis?"

"He does. Actually, he has made arrangements with my senior-class teachers to permit me to leave high school for two months this spring and attend a cram school in New York City to study for the entrance exam for the academy."

"What do you think about that?" Hank asked.

"I'd rather go to Dartmouth any day! But Dad has it all planned out. You know, he's not a rich man—and my older brother is in college, which is expensive for him. And since there is no tuition or room and board payment to worry about at the Naval Academy, that would take the pressure off of him. So I guess I have to go along with what he wants."

Soon, they came to Main Street; looking south, they could see the lights from the youth-hostel house shining out onto the snow. As they got closer, they could hear the laughter and talking coming from inside, and they hurried in.

Chapter 58

THE SUN WAS lowering in the sky and the shadows were lengthening as Helen and the two girls left the skating pond and started walking up toward the hotel.

Diane and Jenny were still talking about the two young men who suddenly appeared and began to skate with them.

"They seemed to come out of nowhere!" Jenny said.

"They did, didn't they?" Diane agreed. "Yours seemed much older than mine."

"When he took hold of my arm and said 'Let's skate double,' I nearly fainted," Jenny said. "Then I saw you sailing off across the ice with the other guy, and I recovered. But I still couldn't say anything, no matter what he asked me."

Helen heard what they were saying and said, "Those two are here for the reunion at the youth hostel. At least, that is what the hotel manager's wife told me."

Suddenly, they heard someone shouting, "Hello." Helen looked up and saw her husband, Bob, standing outside the main entrance of the hotel, waving to them. The three also noticed that there was a horse-drawn wagon parked there. As they came nearer, they saw that Bob was talking to the driver. The driver was holding on to the reins tightly as the horses stomped their hooves on the icy driveway.

"Hey, Dad!" Diane shouted.

"Hey, Uncle Bob!" Jenny called out.

"How was the ice skating?" he asked, smiling.

"Oh, fine!"

Then Bob said, "I have just been telling this man about the donkey baseball games they used to have here years ago." Then turning to the driver, he asked, "You must have heard about them."

"That was before my time, but I have heard they used to do things like that," was the driver's brief answer.

Then Helen put her hand on Diane's shoulder and said, "I had my first date with your father at a donkey baseball game, here. I had just met him on Mrs. Clara Levering's porch, and he asked me to go to the game with him. Of course, I said yes! So off we went."

"Those games were fun!" Bob said. "After a batter hit the ball, he had to climb on a donkey's back to go to first base. The outfielders were on donkeys too, and had to ride over to retrieve the ball."

"I remember that day well," Helen said.

Then she said, "Of course, Diane, that is when your grandfather—William Ford of Corona—was alive and took his summer vacations here. I remember also Boris Melikof showed up. He had come all the way from Corona to Northfield to see his friend, Otto Kirschheimer."

Suddenly, the front door of the hotel opened, and a group of guests came out, laughing and talking with each other. They were bundled up in warm clothing, and they began to climb into the back of the wagon.

"These people are going on a ride through the woods," Bob explained. And he added, "Shall we go with them?"

"No, the girls are tired from skating. It's best if we go back to our rooms," Helen said, and they went into the hotel. Bob stayed outside for a few minutes in order to wave good-bye to the group of wagon riders. He watched the horse and wagon move slowly down the snow-covered drive to the road that led to the woods.

Chapter 59

THEN BOB WENT inside and walked over to the front desk in order to buy a pack of cigarettes. He was surprised that there was no one on duty there. However, the door to the inner office behind the front desk was open. Bob could hear voices coming from there. As he looked closer, he could see the manager talking to an old man. Bob heard the manager say, "I'm sorry, but you will have to leave!"

"But the hotel is my home!" argued the old man.

"We need your room for paying guests. I know you claim that because you were part of the religious conferences here years ago, you were told you could have a free room at the hotel, always."

"That's true!"

"But that was years ago—and now, unfortunately, there have been complaints about you here at the hotel. I have been told that you stop the guests and talk incessantly to them, not letting them get away."

"Many here like me!" the old man answered, his voice quivering slightly.

"I've made some inquiries around Northfield," the manager said. "And there is a third-floor room available at Mrs. Mullen's boardinghouse on Main Street. We will send your things over there tomorrow, but I must ask you to leave now!"

The old man got up, turned, and walked unsteadily out of the office.

The manager, seeing Bob at the desk, came out. "Good evening, Mr. Thompson, how can I help you?"

"I need a pack of cigarettes."

The manager reached down to a cabinet below and handed him a pack.

"I couldn't help but overhear you talking to that old fellow. Is there anything that I can do to help?"

"Nothing at all!" the manager replied quickly.

Bob turned and watched the man go unsteadily down the inside steps to the main door of the hotel. A bellhop, sitting on a bench nearby, got up quickly and held the door open for him. The old man lifted his head and smiled at the boy, who smiled back. Then when he was out in the cold, the old man tripped on the concrete steps and fell down them and rolled to the driveway.

Bob rushed out to him, and the manager followed. Soon, Bob realized the man was struggling to breathe and had probably had a heart attack. Bob turned to the manager and said, "I know what to do. I was an army medic in France during the war."

So he knelt down and began giving the man mouth-to-mouth resuscitation. When that failed, he tried to revive him with hands-on pressure to his chest. Several of the hotel guests began to gather around. One had the foresight to run back inside and try to telephone for a doctor. But soon, the person returned and said, "There's no doctor in town right now!"

After ten minutes of trying to save him, Bob realized he couldn't get him to breathe again. The manager then asked the people who were standing around to return to the hotel lobby. He followed them inside and immediately called the town undertaker, who soon arrived and took the body away.

Later, when Bob was upstairs in their hotel room, he said to Helen, "Before he became unconscious, the man bit my tongue when I was trying to give him mouth-to-mouth resuscitation, but soon he was unconscious. The rhythmical pressure to his chest didn't help either. The man just slipped away. I felt sorry for the old fella, but I did what I could."

"I know that man from the past," Helen said. "Yesterday, he stopped me in the hall and started to tell me about his life. He had been part of this town for seventy years and had always worked at the conferences. He must have been very lonely."

"They should have an old men's home in Northfield, for people like him," Bob said.

"Actually, I think they had one once. It was located in a house on Main Street, and I remember seeing the old men rocking on the porch. But, gradually, they died off, and others didn't want to go there," Helen said. "Now that I think about it, I remember seeing that man who died tonight—almost every summer that I came to Northfield. When I was young,

I would see him on the conference grounds. He helped with the meetings and often sang solos at the services. He was tall, good-looking, and well respected then. But as years passed, things changed. New people began to take over the schools and the conferences. In recent summers, I would see him sitting alone on the steps of the town hall or walking up and down Main Street by himself. I was surprised to hear that he lived at the hotel. He liked to talk to everyone he came across. But in spite of that, I believe that the people of Northfield were always kind to him."

On the last day of December 1940, the Thompsons had left Northfield and returned to Philadelphia. Bob needed to get back to his work as president of the textile mill, and the girls were due back at school.

The youth-hostel reunion ended also. Dick and Hank were the last to leave because they wanted more time with Fritz so they could reminisce and laugh about their six-week bicycle ride through Germany in August of 1939. It was time for Hank to return to Dartmouth and for Dick to start studying hard to fulfill his father's wish: that he pass the entrance exam and get an appointment from a congressman that would secure him a place as a midshipman in the class of '45 at the US Naval Academy.

Chapter 60

A FEW DAYS later, Mabel Hall and her two sons returned to Northfield. Early the following Sunday, Dave left the house and stomped down the front steps on his way to the country store to get a newspaper for his mother. He breathed in the cold air and saw a white mist leave his mouth. He noticed the brightness of the sunshine glistening on the snow in all directions as he went along.

He was at the corner of Holton and Main Street, and he could see that cars were beginning to turn into the parking lot of the Congregational Church. It was then that he heard a loud whistle and saw Georgie Mitchel running toward him.

"Hey, you're back!" Georgie shouted.

"Yeah, we had a swell time with Dad in New York."

"I bet you don't know you missed your pretty girlfriend, Diane Thompson."

"Diane was here in Northfield?" Dave asked.

"The whole family came up for the winter sports. They stayed at the hotel. I think she hoped to see you."

"Boy, that's too bad. I should have written to her and told her that I wasn't going to be here. Did you see much of her?"

"I saw her ice skating with that skinny cousin of hers, Jenny, but that was about all. Now tell me about New York City."

"What a time Tom and I had with our dad. He took us to a nightclub in New York, and the girls in the floor show had practically nothing on, and one of them kept winking at me."

"What was she . . . blind?" Georgie joked.

"Very funny . . . and I drank my first martini. Actually, I drank two—or was it three?"

"Did you get drunk?"

"I got happy. I had a lot of fun. Dad saw some radio announcer at the nightclub that he knew. He was some famous guy. I forget his name, but I recognized him. He came over and sat down at our table and talked with us."

"I guess Northfield seems kind of slow to you after that."

"No, I'm glad to be back."

"Will you do me a favor, Dave?" Georgie asked.

"Sure."

"They are having a special service at the church this morning. It is forty years since Dwight L. Moody died, so they are having a special hymn sung during the service. My family has been insisting that I put in an appearance. How about coming in with me?"

Dave kicked at the snowbank that lined the sidewalk near him and said, "I'm supposed to be buying a newspaper for my mother." He hesitated slightly but finally agreed to go into the church with Georgie.

They noticed that the church was filled when they got inside. They sat in a pew in the back. People began to shout out the number of the hymn in the hymnbook that they wanted to be sung.

"Number 36! 'Trust and Obey,'" one called out.

So the organist began to play the hymn, and the congregation stood up and sang loudly.

"Trust and obey, for there's no other way," rang out, and they sang all four verses.

Dave, in a humorous way, threw back his head and sang especially loud; and Georgie tried to join in with him but ended up just laughing.

Then Georgie elbowed Dave. "Look, there is Joan Brownell sitting over there with two of her friends. I never saw her in church before."

"So you still like her," Dave said.

"Sure I do, but she always crosses to the other side of the street when she sees me coming."

Anne Mitchell, Georgie's mother, and her cousin Minnie Johnston began to notice Dave as he sang.

"He's putting his heart and soul into the singing," Anne said.

"He is just showing off," said Minnie with a snicker.

The next hymn number was called out, "Number 44! 'He Leadeth Me.'"

The boys found the place in the hymnbook; and again, Dave sang out, "He leadeth me. Oh, blessed thought."

Ann pointed to Dave again. "He sings like he really believes it," she said.

"He's just playacting," Minnie insisted. "He is known for making fun of things."

"He does have a nice way about him, and he's so handsome."

"If you ask me, he has the devil in him."

"You are wrong! I don't believe that."

"Well, if you don't—you don't," Minnie said.

Then they hurriedly looked through the pages of the hymnbook until Ann shouted out. "Number 67! 'All Hail the Power.'"

The organist began to play the hymn, and they all rose again and sang out in unison. Some noticed that the winter sun shining through the glass windows cast long golden streams of light that shimmered inside the Trinitarian Congregational Church that morning.

Chapter 61

IN LATE MARCH of that year, Mabel Hall climbed the steps of the old stone library on Main Street. She struggled to open the heavy wooden door and then went inside. Warm air came up through the grates in the floor from the basement furnace, and there was a smell of furniture polish and old books in the air. To the left were rows of shelves holding hundreds of volumes. To the right was a reading room, and it was there that Mabel saw Otto Kirschheimer sitting at a table. She hurried over and sat across from him.

He closed the atlas he was studying and smiled at Mabel. "You have something to tell me?" he asked, smiling.

"You won't believe it!"

"Yes, I will! What's the big news?"

"Martin telephoned me from Washington, DC, this morning. You know he is now head of a government agency there, and for the first time in his life, he has a decent salary. Martin wants to enroll Dave into a prestigious boys' school near Philadelphia: The Hill School. He said that many men in high government positions send their sons there. Also, before Dave starts school, Martin has arranged for him to spend a few weeks in New York City with his friend Nat Lieberman and his wife. Nat produces plays on Broadway and has agreed to introduce Dave to some interesting people."

"Does he need to meet these people?" Otto questioned. "Dave is a well-balanced youngster. He is intelligent and very good-looking. He should get along fine anywhere. I don't see what more he needs, but I am glad he is going to a good school."

"Well, it is what his father wants, so I just go along with that," she said. "There is something else. When Dave goes off to school, I am going to leave Northfield."

"Leave Northfield!"

"As you know, my older son, Tom, is in college now. And with Dave away, I think it is time for me to move on. I'd like to get a small apartment in Greenwich Village in New York City. I could get a social-work job there. Also, Boris Melikof is still manager at the settlement house, and he is encouraging me to do this."

"I will miss you and the boys," Otto said. "You three have brightened up life in Northfield over the past years."

"Thank you, Otto. But I have definitely decided to move away."

Mabel and Otto didn't realize that two of the older town women were behind the stacks and had heard what was said.

"Did you hear that?" one whispered to the other.

"Yes, I did!"

"I'm not surprised. I do like her, but I never thought that she would stay permanently in Northfield."

"Yes, but it has been nearly eight years that she has been here."

"Georgie Mitchell will miss her son Dave. They are great friends. They are always together."

"Well, it is like I always say: the outsiders never seem to be permanent. Sooner or later, they get up and leave."

Chapter 62

New York City
1941

ON AUGUST 1, Dave boarded the train at the Northfield Station that would take him to New York City. He sat back and watched the New England countryside go by out the window. But soon, his thoughts turned to what was ahead of him and the exciting times he was expecting to have in the big city.

After he arrived at Penn Station, he found a taxicab stand and waited in line for the next available cab. When it came, he got in. He asked the driver to take him to East Seventy-Third Street. On the way, he was amazed to see hundreds of people crowding the streets, and all were walking fast. In a short time, they arrived at the apartment house, and Dave reached forward and handed the cabdriver the exact cost for the ride and added a nickel tip. Then he stepped out of the cab, and he was surprised to see the driver get out and come around to him. The cabdriver confronted Dave with an angry look on his face.

"Listen, kid, you never give a nickel tip to a grown man!" he said angrily. "*Never* do that again!"

Dave, who only had one dollar left in his pocket, just backed away.

The doorman at the apartment house was pleasant and showed him where the elevators were located. Dave took one of them up to the top floor, where Nat and Sylvia Lieberman lived in a penthouse apartment.

Dave rang the bell, and Nat opened the door with Sylvia standing behind him.

"Come in, young man," Nat said.

"We are delighted to have you," Sylvia added.

"Any son of good old Martin Hall is OK with me."

"I hope I won't be any trouble," Dave said.

"Of course not. You come in, and first, I have to show you the view from here."

Dave put down his suitcase and followed Nat out to a large balcony.

"You can see the Verrazano Bridge from here, and the Empire State Building is over there," Nat said, pointing one way and then the other. "Wait till you see this view when the lights come on tonight."

"That's something!" Dave said.

"Your father wants me to show you the town. And as your father and I know, to show you the town means to show you the nightlife," Nat said. "Do you have a tuxedo?"

"Yes, I brought one. The students need a tuxedo to wear for the weekend dance parties at the school that I'm going to."

"OK, at eight o'clock tonight, we'll take you out to the Stork Club. There is a writer friend of mine that is out of town, so his cute wife can be your date. There will be other show-business men and their wives at our table. It should be interesting for you."

"Well, let's get you settled now," Sylvia said. "Just follow me." And she led the way down a hall to a bedroom.

Dave hurried after her, saying to himself, "This is great!"

Chapter 63

THAT NIGHT AT the Stork Club, the Lieberman party was seated at a table near the dance floor. Dave had a good view of the scantily dressed showgirls as they danced. There were several of Nat's theater friends at the table, and a blond-haired woman who had been seated next to Dave was acting very friendly.

"How about a bourbon old fashion to start with, Dave?" Nat suggested.

"Sure!" Dave answered, hardly believing his ears.

The woman next to him started leaning toward him, getting her head next to his as she said, "I'm glad they put me next to you."

"Nat tells me your husband is a writer," Dave said.

"Yes, but he's away. He's always away doing research for his books," she said and changed the subject. "You know, you are a very good-looking young man. How old are you?"

"I am almost seventeen!" Dave lied.

Dave wished that Georgie Mitchell was there to see him with this older woman. He remembered how he and Georgie used to talk about Diane Thompson in the summers in Northfield and laughed when he bragged to Georgie about how easy it was to get Diane to kiss him when they walked back to the cottage on the Ridge at night. Georgie would never believe that a grown woman was flirting with him now.

Then Sylvia called across the table. "Listen, Dave, to what is being said here, and you'll learn something about the theater business."

Nat Lieberman and one of his dinner guests were having an argument about a new play on Broadway.

"There is a mood of unpleasantness about that play," the man said.

"You are wrong. The show is funny. I admit that it is a bit arrogant in some scenes, but it is funny. It makes people laugh, and it makes them forget their troubles. That is what counts," Nat insisted.

"I tell you, the author is an old hack. He was washed up five years ago. His trouble is that he thinks he is always right about everything and everyone else is wrong," the man said.

"That playwright has had plenty of hits. I predict it that this new one will run for at least a year," Nat insisted.

"How wrong can a guy be?"

Nat gave up temporarily and turned to Dave. "Drink your bourbon, Dave. You don't want to get left behind."

"Sure," was Dave's reply. Then suddenly, he felt the blond woman next to him laying her hand on his knee.

Looking into Dave's eye, she asked, "Your dad is really famous, isn't he? I'd like my husband to get to know him better. Writers need important friends."

Dave suddenly began to feel some anger toward this complete stranger who was flirting with him. So he said, "Look, lady, I don't know much about what my father does. But I suppose it is important. Anyway, I wouldn't talk about his work to anyone if I didn't know them."

She took her hand off his knee and looked the other way.

Nat renewed the argument, praising the play they were discussing. "I still don't think there is a thing wrong with that new play."

Then Sylvia spoke up, "Well, the play removes the small amount of dignity that politicians may have and makes a laughingstock of them, using mostly four-letter words."

"Hey, you are supposed to be on my side," Nat grumbled, looking disapprovingly at his wife.

"You are right, Sylvia. Regardless of the four-letter words, the mood of the play is sour, and there is a smugness about it," the man said.

"I wish you would all stop knocking show business," insisted Nat. "Show business brings glamour and happiness into people's lives. Let's drop the subject."

Suddenly, the lights of the Stork Club dimmed, and the main show started with a dance routine first and then jokes from a stand-up comic, with the band playing in between each act.

After a third drink, Dave was beginning to feel very relaxed. Nat leaned across the table and said, "We will be going to other nightclubs while you are here, so you are sure to have a good time."

"Thanks," Dave said with a slur in his voice.

"Your dad is an old poker buddy of mine. I'm glad that he suggested you stay with us. You might call him in the morning and tell him what we did tonight."

"I will, if he's not too busy to talk," Dave said—and to himself, he remembered that his father had left his mother alone to bring up his brother and himself. She struggled to bring them up in Northfield; but in spite of that, Dave said to Nat, "Dad's been nice to me lately. He has enrolled me in a good prep school."

On the way back to the apartment in the cab, Sylvia said to Dave, "I guess you didn't have much in common with the author's wife. She must be at least ten years older than you."

"We didn't talk much," Dave said.

"Do you have a girlfriend?" Sylvia asked.

"There is a girl—Diane Thompson—that I like. She and her family come to Northfield every summer."

"Don't worry about meeting girls," Nat interrupted. "Your father told me that he has put your name on the list of several debutante coming-out parties that will be held this coming season. That is where you will meet wealthy girls, not country girls."

Dave looked over at Nat and said, "Diane is not a country girl. She lives in Philadelphia, and her father owns a textile mill. Actually, I'll probably invite her to the first dance weekend at my new school."

Soon they were at the apartment, and Dave went right to bed and slept until noon of the next day.

Chapter 64

Pottstown, Pennsylvania
1942

BY THE FALL of 1942, Europe was engulfed in World War II. It had started when Germany invaded Poland in September 1939. It was at this time that England and France declared war on Germany. After that, Holland, Belgium, and France were invaded by the Germans.

Then on December 7, 1941, the Japanese air force bombed the United States naval base at Pearl Harbor in Hawaii. The next day, President Franklin D. Roosevelt declared war on the Japanese Empire—and soon after, Germany and Italy declared war on the United States.

However, at the Hill School at Pottstown, Pennsylvania, few of the students were thinking about the war. The boys were getting ready for the house-party weekend. As the girls arrived on a bus from the train station, they rushed forward to welcome the girls they had invited.

Dave had invited Diane, from Philadelphia, for the weekend. Diane stood by the main gate of the school with the others, but she began to realize that Dave wasn't there.

Then an older boy drew her aside. "Are you Dave Hall's date?"

"Yes," Diane answered. "Where is he?"

"Well, Dave and I and two others who are on the House Party Committee were assigned to go to Philadelphia to ride back with the girls."

"I didn't see Dave on the train," Diane said.

"We had a half an hour to wait when we got there until it was time for the girls to arrive and board the train. It was then that Dave and another guy found a bar on Broad Street near the station. They went inside, and Dave ordered several straight whiskeys. When Dave started to stagger, his friend led him back to the station. When the train pulled in, we had to hide Dave in a rear car so nobody would notice he'd been drinking."

"I didn't know he was on the train."

"Also, we knew the headmaster would know he was drunk if he took you through the receiving line at school when we got back. So we managed to get him back into his dormitory room as soon as we arrived. Again, nobody saw us."

"Well, what do I do now?" Diane asked.

"If you simply walk behind me and my date through the receiving line, the headmaster won't realize that Dave is missing. There will be another couple close behind you. It will work out all right."

So Diane did just what the boy told her to do. She couldn't help feeling a kind of reverse admiration when she thought of Dave's outlandish behavior. Her mind flashed back to all the times that Dave and Georgie had played tricks on her in Northfield. They were always just funny tricks, nothing malicious. So she wasn't too surprised that this had happened. Actually, she thought that Georgie and the girl he liked (Joan, back there) would get a big laugh out of it.

Then the boys, with their dates, and Diane, alone, left the receiving line and walked to the guesthouse, where the girls would be staying. Diane noticed the school's large redbrick library, the gray stone chapel, and the huge science building as she passed by.

Along the way, one of the girls near her said, "That is an interesting hat you have on. I have never been able to wear that kind of hat myself."

Diane didn't say anything, but she immediately felt uneasy about her appearance. The black off-the-face hat with a small pheasant feather glued to it must have looked dowdy. The girl who had spoken to her didn't wear a hat at all, and neither did any of the other girls. She wished her mother would have helped her shop for becoming clothes for the weekend, but Helen was thrifty and watched how every penny was spent. Diane had bought the hat by herself at a small shop on Chestnut Street in Philadelphia with money from her small clothes allowance.

"What are you wearing to the dance tonight?" another girl asked in a friendly way.

"I have a long green satin dress that my grandmother bought for me. And for the dance tomorrow night, I will wear a strapless blue net dress that my girlfriend lent to me."

At seven o'clock that evening, the girls were picked up by their dates at the guesthouse. Dave appeared with the others. Diane could hardly say anything because of her deep feelings for him that had begun during the summer-night wanderings in Northfield.

"Hello," was all she could say, and Dave smiled and took her hand.

Chapter 65

THE COUPLES STARTED walking toward the main building—where dinner would be served, followed by dancing.

On the way, Diane heard one of the girls say to her date, "Do you like my perfume? Smell me!"

"Smell me? I'd never say anything like that," Diane thought to herself.

The older boy that had spoken to her when she arrived came up behind them and said to her, "Your date, Dave, is called Harpo here—after Harpo Marx in the movies. Harpo has curly hair and doesn't say much, just like your guy."

"But Dave's better looking!" Diane said quickly.

"You're right about that, and he's a big hero around here. He won the football game for us against Haverford last Saturday. The Haverford team was really fired up and attempted a field goal. But Dave was able to block the kick, grab the ball, and then run seventy yards for the winning touchdown."

"He did that!"

"Yes, he did."

Dave, who was listening, said, "OK, that's enough!"

His friend continued, "The team wanted Dave to be captain, but the headmaster said no because his grades were low."

Then Dave grumbled, "You know, you talk too much."

Soon, they entered the huge dining hall of the school. The high ceiling was supported by sturdy beams that crisscrossed each other above. Dark red velvet curtains hung at the windows. Along the walls were large oil paintings of former headmasters and famous alumni. Long oak tables and chairs were set up in rows. The students and their dates took their places at the tables. Throughout the dinner, there was the sound of cheerful talking and laughter, along with the clatter of dishes being put down and taken up. During this time, Diane didn't say much. Dave was mostly silent too, except to interject a New York–style quip to offset a classmate's joke, "Only a hick from the sticks would laugh at that!"

After the meal, the tables and chairs were pushed back to the walls in preparation for the dancing. Soon the orchestra started to play. The room filled with music, and the young couples immediately took to the floor and began to dance.

"Your date is pretty," whispered one of the upperclassmen to Dave as they went out onto the floor.

Dave gave him a passing look of superiority and uttered, "Naturally!"

While they were dancing, Diane looked up at Dave and asked, "How is Georgie Mitchell, your friend from Northfield?"

"He's fine. He came to New York City one weekend in August, and I showed him around. You should have seen him stretching his neck to look up at the tall buildings," Dave said and laughed. Then he told her that his father always had a suite at some hotel and that she could come and stay there.

Suddenly, a sixth-form boy cut in, and Diane danced with him. Looking over her shoulder, she saw Dave quickly retreat out a door and onto the outside patio.

From then on, Diane was cut in on over and over again. Some of the boys were good dancers, and that was fun; and others were not. However, she kept wondering what Dave was doing on the patio. Then a tall classmate of Dave's asked her to dance.

"Do you know that your date, Dave, is the most well-liked guy here at the school? He is really popular, and it is not just because his father is a bigwig. He is one of the best football players we have here. No one fights harder to win than Dave. He plays right guard, and those big shoulders of his make him a great tackler, and he is fast. Besides the football, he is funny—really funny—when he gets started."

"I know that," Diane said as the music stopped. "But where is Dave right now?" she asked.

"Don't worry about him. There's a long line of guys waiting to dance with you. Dave is just letting them have their chance."

"I saw him go outside!"

"Well, somebody might have a bottle stashed away in the shrubbery."

"I hope not. That's crazy! He might get kicked out of school."

"Forget I said that. He is just talking to some of the guys."

Finally, the strains of "Goodnight, Ladies" rang out, and Dave reappeared with a big grin on his face. Diane's partner stepped aside, and Dave grabbed her and began doing a high-stepping kind of dance. She followed as best she could. Then they started laughing, and she felt happy for the first time since she had arrived.

After the dance ended, the couples walked back to the guest dormitory. Dave held her hand tightly as they walked along. Some of them began singing.

But the singing stopped when they saw Professor Crawley, their English teacher, standing under the light by the entrance like a sentinel guarding a castle. The boys realized there would be no kissing the girls goodnight with him there; so they shook hands with their dates, and the girls went inside.

Diane felt happy as she climbed into bed. The girl who had been mean to her about her hat was in the other twin bed in the room, and she said, "Your date, Dave Hall, is very handsome. Everybody likes him. You are lucky."

"I guess so," Diane said, yawning, and instantly fell sound asleep.

Chapter 66

New York City
1943

BY APRIL OF 1943, the United States had been at war against Japan and Germany for over a year and a half; and thousands had been called up to serve in the army, navy, and marines.

During spring vacation from his senior year at the Hill School, Dave went to New York City to visit his father at his suite on the eleventh floor of the Ritz Hotel. His father had government business to do in the city but was glad to have his son stay with him.

Early one afternoon, they stood together by a window in the living room of the suite and admired the view of Central Park and the tall buildings on both sides.

"This is quite a city! And I want you to enjoy your vacation here."

"I'm sure I will. I am going to meet my girlfriend, Diane Thompson, this afternoon. She came in by train from Philadelphia this morning. She will be spending a night at the apartment of a friend of her mother's on Fifty-Second Street."

"So you told me," Martin said distractedly and immediately changed the subject. "You know, I have told people I work with about what some of your teachers are telling you."

"I didn't know that you remembered what I had said!"

"You're damn right I did."

"Was it because of what I said on the phone about one of the professors warning our class not to enlist in the regular army after graduation, but try to become officers?"

"That professor had a hell of a nerve to tell eighteen-year-olds not to go into the army when we are at war!"

"He said privates in the army are the first to get killed."

"This country needs every able-bodied man it can get to help us stop Hitler! I told my associates that the professor was dead wrong to tell the senior class not to enlist. You and all your friends will be needed to fight as soon as you graduate."

Dave faced his father and said, "Most of my friends are talking about going to Officers Candidate School after graduation."

"The war will be over by the time they get through OCS," Martin said as he turned away from the window. "I've got some telephone calls to make. Here is twenty dollars for you to use today," he said, reaching into his pocket and handing him the money. "Bring that girl up here later on. I'd like to get a look at her."

"I will, and thanks for the money," Dave said and then he went out.

After leaving the hotel, Dave turned onto Fifth Avenue and started walking toward Fifty-Third Street. The sun was shining and the wind was blowing, and there was still a chill in the air.

Diane rushed to the door of the apartment when she heard a knock. Earlier, when Dave had telephoned her to tell her when he would be there, she was excited to hear his voice. She hoped that nothing had changed and that their time together would be filled with the same fun and affection they had shared in Northfield in the summers.

She opened the door and saw him, but "hello" was all she could think to say.

"Are you ready to see New York?" Dave asked. "We are going to a movie first."

"Fine, I'm ready."

So they left the building and started walking toward Times Square.

"There is some kind of war movie at a theater a couple of blocks from here that should be good."

"Yes, I'll do that."

They didn't say much as they walked along the busy streets to the theater. Dave didn't hold her hand like he used to in Northfield.

Soon, they were seated in a crowded movie theater. The picture was called *Flight Command*. It began with naval officers giving orders from the bridge of an aircraft carrier. There were scenes of young pilots taking off from the deck of the ship.

After only fifteen minutes, Dave turned toward Diane in the dark and he nodded his head, and they both left their seats and walked out of the theater. Instinctively and without knowing the reason, they both had had the same urge to leave. The scenes of men firing machine guns at enemy planes and the general glorification of war on the screen was something neither wanted to look at for reasons they couldn't have put into words.

As they came out of the theater, Diane said, "The sun feels good. So where are we going now?"

"Didn't I tell you? We're going to the top of the Empire State Building!" Dave said, surprising her.

"That's wonderful!"

"And we are going to meet Bob Bradford and Barbara Ludlow there. You remember them from the house party."

"Oh yes, I remember Barbara. We shared a room there," Diane said, trying to sound pleased but remembering the girl's snobbishness toward her and how she had made fun of her hat in front of the others.

Dave walked faster, looking forward to seeing his friends, and she kept up with him. As they went through the revolving door at the main entrance of the Empire State Building, Dave shouted, "There they are, already!"

Bob rushed over to them, with Barbara following. "Hey, Harpo, we've been waiting for you—you are late!" Bob called out loudly.

"I thought you said three-thirty," Dave argued back.

"No, we agreed on three!" Bob said. And he added, "So you still can't tell time after all these years . . . That figures . . . but beside that, have you been behaving yourself?"

Dave didn't answer but crouched down in a boxing position and threw a few fake punches at his friend, and they both laughed.

Barbara seemed glad to see Diane. She even smiled at her, but as they rode up the elevator to the top floor of the Empire State Building, Diane could see Barbara looking at her closely. The red sweater, plaid skirt, and saddle shoes that she wore were no match for Barbara's finely tailored light blue coat and stylish shoes.

When they got off the elevator, they went outside and stood behind a railing to see the view.

"It's too bad that it's partly overcast," Bob said. "On a clear day, the view is spectacular."

"It's still spectacular," Diane said.

Then Dave and Bob started talking about their old school friends and what they were doing.

Suddenly, a strong gust of wind came down from the top of the tower, and Diane's long blond hair was blown into her face. It tangled badly. She tried to smooth her hair back into place, but the wind blew harder.

"Look at my hair!" she said, but nobody seemed to hear. She dug into her pocketbook for a comb, and then she hurried inside to the enclosed part of the observation tower and combed her hair.

From inside, she could see the others through the window. Barbara had moved closer to Dave, and they were talking to each other in an animated way, oblivious to the wind. All three were laughing at something Bob had said.

"I should go out there and join them," she said to herself. But she stayed where she was—still worrying about her hair and strangely feeling a little in the way.

Chapter 67

LATER ON, THEY stopped at the clubroom of a well-known hotel, where a popular orchestra was playing. As the four of them entered, they saw that the dance floor was very crowded. Then Bob found a table for them toward the back of the room, and they sat down. After they ordered drinks, Bob started to talk to Dave in earnest about the war.

"Do you know that many of our class, including me, have already received orders to report to Officer Candidate School right after graduation? I'm being sent to Princeton. Bill Hasslett has been ordered to Franklin and Marshall College. They tried to send the guys for this OCS program to a place near where they live. We report on July 1. Have you gotten any orders yet, Dave?"

"No, I was thinking of just enlisting in the marines."

"You can do better than that! You have to ask your dad to get you into Officer Candidate School as soon as possible."

"Dad has to be careful what he does," Dave explained. "If he pulls any special strings for me, the newspaper reporters will play it up. They are always looking for some dirt to spread around about important men. I don't think he would want to chance showing favoritism."

"That's crazy! I saw a picture in the paper of your father with the secretary of defense. One word and you can get into OCS with me. Don't be fooled. Those big shots in Washington are all seeing that their sons get safer assignments."

"Dad is not a real big shot. And it is important that he stays in good with the men he works for. Maybe having a son as a private in the marines will make dad look good."

"That doesn't seem right to me," Bob said.

"Anyway, it was my idea to join the marines."

"All right, if that's the way you feel about it. Anyway, it was nice of your father to say that we could have dinner at the hotel tonight on him. The girls will like that."

It was beginning to get dark when they arrived at the hotel.

Inside, Dave explained to Bob that his father wanted to meet Diane—so they had to go up to his suite, but they would be right back.

"We'll get a table in the dining room," Bob said. "Take your time!"

Dave and Diane took the elevator up to the eleventh floor. When they entered the suite, Diane drew a deep breath. "This is so luxurious!" she said.

Suddenly, a door off the main room opened, and Martin Hall came in.

"Dad, this is—"

Martin took one glance at Diane, and he shook his head in an obvious act of instant disapproval and dismissal. Quickly, he turned around and left the room without saying anything.

Diane was shocked at the sudden and unexpected rejection that Dave's father had shown toward her.

Dave said nothing but indicated that they should leave.

Dave's father's wanton affront to her was something Diane was not about to pardon or forget.

At dinner, Dave and Bob did most of the talking. Bob's date, Barbara, did remind Dave of the debutante party that was to be held the next night, to which he had been invited.

Later, without saying anything, Dave put Diane in a cab to go to the apartment where she was staying downtown. The next day, she took the train back to Philadelphia. On the long ride home, she wondered if she would ever hear from Dave again, or if she would ever see him again.

Chapter 68

Northfield
October 1943

WITHIN A MONTH after graduating, Dave enlisted in the Marine Corps; and by the end of October 1943, he had completed his combat training at Camp Lejeune, North Carolina. He was now a private first class in the US Marine Corps and had a two-week leave.

On the train from Camp Lejeune to New York City, a fellow marine who was sitting next to him asked him, "How do you plan to spend the two weeks here before we have to report to Camp Pendleton in California and then ship out to the war in the South Pacific?"

"I want to see the small town I grew up in."

"Not the big city? I thought you told us you knew some debutantes in New York City?"

"My dad's friends introduced me to some good-looking rich girls when I was there, but I got orders to basic training before I could get anything going with them."

"Call them up when we get there!"

"No, I'll stay one night with my mother, who lives in Greenwich Village, and then borrow her car and drive to Northfield."

"Do you have a girlfriend up there?"

"I did like a girl from Philadelphia who came to Northfield in the summers . . . but we lost touch."

"Well, it's the big city for me!"

Dave spent a day with his mother. Then he left the next morning in her car, heading north. After a four-hour drive, he turned off the highway onto Route 10, and he was soon on Main Street, Northfield. The leaves had started to fall, but there still were a few yellow and orange ones left on the trees that lined Main Street.

He drove slowly, looking first to the right and then to the left at the old colonial-style houses. Some of the houses were owned by people he had known well. He wondered if the Whiteside family still lived in the house with the pillars, or if Mrs. Abbott was having any luck selling antiques out of her house. Then he passed the town hall, where the Grange men used to organize square dances, and then passed Brown's Café where some of the local townsmen gathered for coffee each morning.

Dave stopped the car as he saw Fritz Kirschheimer hurrying across the street. Dave was tempted to blow the horn and yell to him, but he lost his chance as Fritz started running up the drive of the American Youth Hostel house. He remembered when he was growing up in Northfield, his friends didn't pay much attention to the youth-hostel people or the young men who came into town on bicycles and spent the night at the hostel and then went on.

Farther along, he passed the public grade school, and on the other side of the street was the old stone library. Then in front of him, to the right, he saw the Trinitarian Congregational Church. He was glad to see that the white puritan-style church was still there; and he smiled, remembering how some of the bad boys in town used to threaten to burn it down.

Soon, he turned into the Mitchells' driveway. He knew they were waiting for him because his mother had called them. Mrs. Mitchell had been a good friend of hers all the years she had lived in Northfield. As he got out of the car, the side door of the house opened quickly, and Georgie ran out with a big smile and shouted, "Hey, nice uniform!" Mrs. Mitchell came out next and gave Dave a hug and told him how glad she was to see him.

They went into the kitchen and sat down at a round table, and Dave remembered he had been welcomed there a hundred times when he was growing up. On one side of the kitchen was an old iron stove, with large pots and pans hanging on the wall beside it. On the other side was a tall cabinet that reached to the ceiling. On its shelves were sets of glasses, china, and serving dishes.

Looking down the wide hall from the kitchen to the front door, Dave realized that he never noticed before how large the Mitchells' house was. He liked the feeling of spaciousness. After two months of sleeping in barracks with hundreds of marine recruits, he felt a sense of relief at being in this large, familiar, quiet place.

"So you're a private first class in the marines now," Mrs. Mitchell said. "And you have ribbons already. What is this one for?"

"That is for sharpshooting."

"No good conduct medal?" Georgie asked.

"No, you get that later."

"If you get one," Georgie said, and they both laughed.

"Can you tell us what your training was like?" Mrs. Mitchell asked.

"It was mostly marching: left, left, right, left—left, right, left. An old drill sergeant instructor used to shout out screwy things while we marched. Like 'left right, left right . . . I left my wife with twenty-nine kids . . . I left, I left.' He was tough. Then we had to run the obstacle course. You had to do it right the first time or you would have to repeat it over and over. Then there were hours of rifle practice. We fired live ammunition. I did pretty well at that. They also showed us how to lower ourselves down the sides of a troopship and get into a landing craft."*

Then Georgie suddenly said excitedly, "I saw a picture of you in some magazine, aiming your rifle at something while you were lying on your stomach, just like you were fighting already. Remember I showed it to you, Mom."

"Yes, I remember. A lot of people here in Northfield saw it and were talking about it."

"Yeah, some photographer was following me around all one day, taking my picture," Dave said. "It was just because my father works for the government and knows a lot of top brass. Boy . . . the guys in my company kidded me something terrible about that guy taking my picture. They'd say things like 'here comes Mr. Important' or 'hey, can you get me a date with a movie star' or 'let's cut him down to size.' Actually, one day, two of them jumped on me and started wrestling me down, and I had to break out of both their holds. When they saw I could take it, they treated me OK, and I started to make some friends."

"Your mother must be very proud of you, Dave," Mrs. Mitchell said. And she added, "Georgie's enlistment has been delayed because of his allergies, but it's just a matter of time until he is called up."

Dave turned to Georgie and asked, "How's your girlfriend, Joan Brownell?"

"She's not my girlfriend, but she actually talks to me once in a while now. But soon, she will be leaving for Berkeley, California, where her brother is. He's a leader of some way-out peace movement there. Their grandfather always taught them to be citizens of the world."

"Hey, where's the draft board?" Dave asked.

"Don't ask me," Georgie said.

"Let's go outside," Dave said.

Chapter 69

"I WANT TO show you something," Georgie said. "It is out in the barn."

"What is it?"

"You will see!"

So they left the house and went across the yard to the barn. Through the open barn door, Dave could see a motorcycle. "Where did you get the bike?"

"Bill Patterson said I could use it while he was away with the marines. Do you want to take a spin with me?"

"Sure, but I want to drive," Dave said.

"Have you ever driven one of these before?"

"Marines can do anything—haven't you heard?"

"Where do you want to go?" Georgie asked.

"Let's go up on the Ridge and look at the summer cottages."

"Those roads aren't in good condition this time of year!"

"Don't worry! We won't tip over."

"There's nobody up there," Georgie reminded him. And then he said suspiciously, "Oh, I get it! You want to drive to the Thompsons' summer cottage so you can think about the times you walked Diane home after dark."

"Yeah, I liked her a lot. But I also remember those long, lonely three-mile walks home from her cottage."

"Do you ever hear from her?"

"Diane and I had a date in New York City last spring. But she left suddenly and went back to Philadelphia without saying good-bye."

"Didn't you call her up?"

"No, it's strange that I didn't call her—but by then, my dad and my school buddies were introducing me to a lot of rich debutantes. There was one that wasn't bad, but she kept throwing her chauffeurs at me and taking me around in her limousine, so I decided she was too fancy for me."

"Don't be a dope. You're a good-looking turkey. The Northfield girls would practically faint when you walked by."

"Oh, sure! But I have to tell you about this one woman I met in New York. She was a writer's wife, and her husband was away a lot. One night at a restaurant with her and some of my father's other friends, she started flirting with me and inviting me to come to her apartment."

"Did you go?"

"No, because I finally realized that all she wanted was for me to introduce her husband to my father. Writers need to know important people," Dave explained. And then he said, "Let's go. You get on the motorcycle behind me."

So they sped out of the driveway and up to North Lane that led to the seven ridges where the closed-up summer cottages were located. As they drove along the ridge, the loud noise of the motorcycle caused birds to take off from the pine trees and caused the squirrels to hurry away in all directions. The cottages were shut up tight and the curtains drawn closed. The porch rocking chairs were safely inside. In the front window of each cottage was a sign that read "No Trespassing—By the authority of the Rustic Ridge Association."

Dave went fast on the flat road and slowed down on the hills. He watched out for ruts, gullies, and downed branches.

They stopped when they came to the Thompson cottage. Georgie jumped off the back, and Dave leaned the motorcycle against a tree.

Looking up at the cottage porch, Georgie remembered something that had happened a few years back. "When I was fifteen, I worked at the hotel. Part of the job was delivering Western Union telegrams up here. I brought a lot to Mr. Thompson at this cottage. He was the president of some textile mill in Philadelphia.

"Well, one morning early, I arrived here on my bike. I had a telegram for him in my hand. I went up the steps to the screened-in porch of the cottage, and just inside, I saw two cots. Diane was sleeping in one, and her cousin Jenny was in the other. When I knocked loudly on the screen doors, the girls saw me and started screaming and pulling the covers over their heads. Finally, Mrs. Thompson came out and signed for the telegram, and I had to leave. I laughed all the way back to the hotel, remembering their loud screams."

"Remember the big Château dance?" Dave said.

"I remember it, but I didn't go."

"It was held for the hotel and conference employees at the end of the summer. My brother's gang went, and he fixed me up with Diane. I was just fourteen then and she was younger, and I didn't know how to dance, so we just sat outside on a balcony in the dark and talked . . . You say you didn't go to the dance, Georgie, but I remember seeing you spooking around outside the Château with some town boys when the dance was ending. I still say you should have asked Joan Brownell to the dance."

"Are you kidding? She would have kicked me off the back porch if I did. But I remember you pulling Diane by the hand up the steep hill outside the Château after the dance."

"I really liked her—but I didn't write to her, and she didn't write. So that was that."

"We better get back. Mom likes to have dinner early," Georgie said.

"Don't we have time for one ride down Main Street?"

"Sure."

So they left the Ridge and sped down the main street of Northfield from one end to the other, waving and shouting to anyone they happened to see. Finally, they drove back to the house.

They had hardly come in when Mrs. Mitchell rushed up to Dave to tell him that his mother had telephoned him. "You see, your father didn't know where you were and called your mother to ask her to find you and tell you that Admiral Wingate's daughter needed an escort to the Autumn

Debutante Ball at the Mayflower Hotel in Washington, DC, tomorrow night, and he wants you to get down there right away."

"Oh damn!" Dave swore.

"Do you know this girl? Is she cute?" Georgie asked.

"No, I don't know her. She would be a blind date. I wanted to stay here in Northfield for a week before being sent to the marine base in California."

"You know blind dates," Georgie said, laughing. "She's either too tall or too fat! Don't go!"

"Well, it's a disappointment," Mrs. Mitchell said, "but your mother was definite that you should go. We'll have a nice dinner together now, and then Georgie can ask some of your old Northfield friends to come over tonight to talk and catch up."

"I'd like that."

"Do you ever hear from Diane Thompson?" Mrs. Mitchell asked.

"Not lately, but did I tell you how popular she was at the house-party weekends at school? One of the professors said that she was the prettiest girl that ever came to dance weekend."

"Pretty Diane was always a favorite of mine among the summer girls," she said. And then she added, "I'll have dinner ready in a few minutes."

The next day, when Dave drove out of the driveway, there were two local women coming down the hill from the post office that was near the house.

"Isn't that the Hall boy driving out?" one asked.

"Yes, he's been visiting the Mitchells. In the old days, you never saw Dave without Georgie. They are great friends. Georgie's mother told me this afternoon when I saw her at the store that Dave had to leave sooner than they thought. And then she said to me, rather sadly, that she didn't think he actually knew where he belonged."

Chapter 70

Washington, DC
1943

THE COCKTAIL LOUNGE at the Mayflower Hotel in Washington, DC, was crowded on the evening of November 30, 1943. Dave sat on a stool at the end of the bar near the door so he could watch the main entrance. He was expecting his former roommate from school, Bob Bradford, to meet him there.

As the bartender put down Dave's second drink, he noticed his marine uniform, and he took a minute to say something to him. "I have a son who is a marine like you. All I know is that he is somewhere in the South Pacific in the thick of things."

"I'll be following him out there in a couple of days," Dave said, his eyes still on the door.

"Are you here for the big dance in the ballroom tonight?"

"Sort of . . ."

"Are you waiting for someone?"

"Yes, an old school friend of mine who said that he would meet me here."

From the far end of the bar, there came a sudden shout, "Refill, bartender!"

"I've gotta go," the bartender said to Dave. He added, "Good luck, kid."

Soon, Bob Bradford walked in. The new gold ensign stripe shone brightly on the sleeve of his dark navy blue uniform. He saw Dave and hurried over to him.

"Harpo, it's great to see you."

"Hey, Bob, old pal, old pal . . . what's it been . . . six months?"

"At least . . . of course, you couldn't write a fella a letter . . . oh no!"

"Me, write a letter? Sure! Sure! Come on and order a drink."

"I see I have some catching up to do," Bob said, looking at Dave's glass.

"I'm only on my second."

Bob took a seat on the barstool next to Dave and said, "No drink for me yet."

"How did you get to be an ensign in the navy so fast?"

"How did you get to be a private first class in the marines so fast?"

"Should I salute?" Dave asked, getting ready to stand up.

"Forget that!" Bob said quickly and then changed the subject. "I thought you had a date with some admiral's daughter tonight?"

"Don't remind me!"

"Do you or don't you have a date?" Bob asked.

"I didn't pick her up. My father thinks I have. When I got to my dad's place here in DC this afternoon, I saw he had left her phone number for me so I could call her. I did, and she answered and asked me to pick her up at her house out in Arlington. I suggested that she might come in with a friend, and I'd meet her for the dance here at the hotel. She said she did know a couple that was coming in, but she didn't want to bother them. I gave her my phone number and told her to do what she could to get a ride and call me back."

"I bet she loved that!" Bob said.

"I had just driven all the way down from Northfield, and I was bushed."

"So did she call back?"

"No, she didn't, but her mother did!"

"The admiral's wife called you—"

"Yes, and she wasn't at all happy about me not coming out to Arlington to pick up her daughter. I told her that I would never be able to find the house because I didn't know the streets in Arlington. I said 'If your daughter got to the hotel, I would meet her here and take her into the ball.' Then the mother went on and on about what a good friend the admiral was with my father. She said that I wasn't acting like my father's son. Then she asked to speak with my father, and I said that he wasn't home. The mother got very angry at me on the phone, and I was determined now not to pick up the girl, and I told the mother I wasn't driving way out there just to get lost, and hung up."

"You devil!" Bob said. "Think of the poor girl . . ."

"Well, I felt a little guilty about it, especially when I heard the girl screaming in the background and telling her mother that now she wouldn't go to the ball no matter what!"

"Those are the manners they taught us at school?" Bob asked sarcastically.

"I don't remember. Do you?" Dave said, and they both laughed.

"Don't worry about it. You can sit with Barbara and me at the dance tonight."

"Haven't you heard that officers are not allowed to fraternize with enlisted men?"

"Come on, Dave, don't say that. We had to get into uniform like everyone else. Listen, I'm proud of you, so cheer up. You are going to sit at our table tonight."

Chapter 71

TWO MEN WERE seated near them at the bar. Suddenly, one of them started talking to Bob and Dave. He was a well-dressed gray-haired man.

"I heard what you said about being forced into uniform. Do you want to know why? I'll tell you why!"

"Leave them alone, Frank," the other man said.

"Listen, Burt, they deserve to know the truth about what led this country into this war!"

Burt shook his head and then remarked to Bob and Dave, "This is Frank Rogers. He is in investments. He likes to talk and debate. I'm just warning you!"

"It began when the country repealed the Neutrality Act of 1935," Frank began. "Then in 1940, Congress passed the Selective Service Act that allowed for compulsory military training. At the same time, parents were assured that their sons were not going to be sent into any foreign war. Then the administration dreamed up the Lend-Lease Program that would help Great Britain. Most Americans at that time preferred to stay out of the trouble in Europe . . . but no!"

"Who is this guy?" Dave asked Bob. "He sounds crazy! And he is making me mad!"

"He makes some sense, but I don't agree with him," Bob said but was immediately interrupted by the man.

"Then someone got the bright idea to put embargoes on the Japanese for shipping oil. Then surprise, surprise . . . the Japs bomb Pearl Harbor."

"Well, we had to fight then!" Burt said.

"Then there is this man, Martin Hall," Frank Rogers said, "who has gotten himself all mixed up in this Lend-Lease business. Whoever elected him to anything!"

When Dave heard his father's name mentioned, he got to his feet. When Rogers saw the young marine coming toward him, he got up too.

"I don't like what you're saying," said Dave, and he made a fist and socked the man hard in the jaw. Then he quickly punched him in the stomach, and then he hit him again in the face, and the older man fell to the floor.

Bob grabbed Dave and told him to calm down. Dave shoved Bob away and shouted down at the man on the floor, "Get up and fight, you rich, ugly windbag!"

"Steady, Dave!" Bob said, trying to pull him back.

Then Dave looked down and kicked the man in the ribs, then turned and went back to the bar.

A customer in the bar shouted out, "Get the police!"

Another called out, "No, get the shore patrol!"

The bartender went to a phone behind the bar and dialed for the hotel security. "We need help here! There's a marine beating up a civilian!" he said.

The older man's friend asked Bob, "Why did that marine attack him like that?"

"He attacked him because he didn't like what he said about his father."

"His father—Frank didn't know he was Hall's son!"

"Well, he is."

Bob looked down at the man on the floor. "We had better help him up." So they grabbed him under his arms and brought him to his feet. Bob reached for a chair, and they sat Rogers down on it.

Dave looked back at him from the bar and said, "If you say one more rotten thing, I'll knock your head off."

"Stay away from me!" he shouted back.

Chapter 72

IN A FEW minutes, the hotel manager and two shore patrol officers walked in.

"Arrest that marine!" Rogers called out. "He viciously attacked me for no reason." Then he pressed a handkerchief to his nose to stop the bleeding.

"What exactly happened here?" one of the shore patrol officers asked.

Bob pointed at Rogers and said, "That man made derogatory remarks about the marine's father, so he hit him."

"Do you want me to get an ambulance?" the hotel manager asked Rogers.

"No, but I want to make an official complaint against this marine."

"All right, but why don't we go into my office where we can straighten this out in private."

The shore patrol men assisted Rogers across the lobby and into the manager's office. The others followed. When the door was closed, Bob said that he would be willing to telephone Dave's father—since he knew him slightly—and tell him about this and ask him if he would offer to make some kind of financial compensation to Mr. Rogers.

"I'm not sure I want you to tell my dad about this," Dave said.

"Go ahead and make the call," the shore patrol officer said firmly.

Bob picked up the phone on the desk and gave the operator Martin Hall's home phone number. Finally, Bob heard Martin's voice on the phone. Bob told him what had happened and mentioned Frank Rogers's name.

Then Hall shouted loudly through the phone, "This cannot get into the papers—do you hear me? There is to be no publicity about this, whatsoever!"

Bob listened carefully to what Hall intended to do and hung up.

"Mr. Hall says he will direct his lawyer to contact Mr. Rogers in the morning and offer him a generous settlement to compensate him for his injuries. He also said that a marine general, who is a friend of his, will see that Dave is flown out to California to his unit on the next available plane."

"That sounds fair," the hotel manager said.

"It is fair," Bob said, turning to Rogers. "This marine is only eighteen years old. He graduated from high school only five months ago. He has just finished a rigorous training at Camp Lejeune, where he was taught to fight first and ask questions later. He takes pride in his father's important government job. And now he is going off to fight in the front lines against a fierce enemy. So it would be greatly appreciated if you would make some fair agreement with Mr. Hall's lawyer tomorrow and leave it there."

"All right," Frank said gruffly. "I'll see what the lawyer has to say . . . but I will need these shore patrol fellows to help me out of here and get me a cab."

Dave and Bob left the office and watched Rogers being escorted out and onto the street, where cabs were waiting.

Suddenly, they heard a familiar voice. "Bob, Dave, where have you been?" Barbara Ludlow asked. "Everybody has gone into the dance. I couldn't find you!"

"Sorry we kept you waiting," Bob said. "Yes, let's go in."

The ballroom was filled with young people dancing, and soon, Bob and Barbara went onto the floor and joined them as the band played a popular number.

"You look beautiful tonight," Bob said, admiring Barbara's silver-and-white ball gown.

"I'm glad you like the dress."

"I like everything about you."

Bob held Barbara tightly as they danced.

Then Barbara said, "Dave looks kind of sad sitting over there at the table all by himself."

"You must remember that Harpo doesn't like to talk much. So don't ask him a lot of questions about what happened earlier . . . Okay?"

"Okay."

Dave was able to order a double scotch from a passing waiter, and he finally began to relax as he watched Barbara and Bob and the others dancing and laughing and having a good time.

Chapter 73

San Diego, California
1943

THE NEXT DAY, Dave arrived at Camp Pendleton, California, after obtaining space on a military transport plane from Washington, DC. He was assigned to a barrack at the camp and was informed that his division would be leaving for the South Pacific in two weeks.

Inside the barracks, he threw his Valpak on a bunk. Then he began seeing some of the marines he had known in basic training.

"Hey, here comes Mr. Popular!" one called out, seeing Dave.

"What have you been up to?" another asked.

Dave smiled and quipped, "It's just my luck to get thrown in with you guys again."

"You'll be glad to know that we have already started rifle practice—every day, all day."

"Well, somebody has to know how to shoot straight in this outfit," Dave bantered back.

Then one of the marines announced, "The good news is that we are all going to get passes to go up to Los Angeles this Saturday. They have a dance hall there called the Palladium. There are cute hostesses to talk to us, and famous movie stars show up." Then he continued, "Or does that sound too boring to you, Mr. Society?"

"No, it sounds great! We should have fun!" Dave replied.

So the next Saturday, the marines were given passes, and then they waited in line to board the buses that would take them to LA and to the Palladium.

While waiting in line, Dave felt a tug on his shoulder. When he looked around, he saw Bill Patterson from Northfield grinning at him. "Bill, is that really you?"

"Dave, I could hardly believe it when I saw you."

"What a coincidence to find each other in this mob scene."

"How long have you been here, Dave?" Bill asked.

"Not long, actually. I was in Northfield two weeks ago, but Georgie Mitchell didn't tell me where you were out here."

"I've been in the marines for over two years now. I'm older than you, remember! I've been doing guard duty around here mostly, but now I hear they are going to ship us out to the South Pacific soon."

"This is great running into you. Why don't we sit together on the bus and catch up."

"Is it OK to break into the line here? I was way in the back," Bill asked.

"Don't worry about it," Dave said. He shouted to the others, "Let this guy in!"

Then a marine standing nearby started yelling, "End of the line! End of the line!"

"He's from my hometown—Northfield, Massachusetts—so let him in," Dave called out.

"Northfield... where... never heard of it," one answered, but they let Bill get into the line.

On the bus, Bill and Dave talked about their years of growing up in Northfield and the mischief they had gotten into. They told each other stories about the neighbors—the nice ones and the grouchy ones—and they talked about the girls they knew.

"Of course, you knew Joan Brownell," Dave said.

"Oh sure, she was hot, but how about that summer girl that you liked?"

"You mean Diane Thompson? Well, we lost touch."

After an hour, the bus arrived at the Palladium. The place was crowded to the doors with servicemen. Bill and Dave pushed in and shouldered their way to a refreshment counter. Then Dave noticed two girls sitting at a small table. He grabbed Bill's arm, and together, they went up to them.

"Want some company?" Dave asked.

"Yes, that's why we're here," the girls answered in unison and laughed.

Chapter 74

Los Angeles, California
1943

DAVE AND BILL sat down and asked the girls their names.

"I'm Mary," one said. She had long brown hair and a pretty face.

"I'm Sally," said the blonde. She had a nice smile and a good figure.

"Where are you marines from?" Mary asked.

"We are both from Northfield, Massachusetts," Bill stated.

"Where's that?"

"Way back east in New England," Dave said.

"It's an important place," Bill said. "There were some German spies hiding out there recently."

"We have Japanese spies here," Sally mentioned.

"The spies back east were called German saboteurs."

"Saba-what?" Sally asked.

"Saboteurs are foreigners that sneak into the country and try to blow up defense plants and things like that."

Then Dave interrupted and said to Bill, "I don't remember hearing about German spies in Northfield."

"People didn't talk much about it. They weren't that sure that they were in Northfield . . . Anyway, you and Georgie were too young to care. It seems to me that, about then, you two were spending most of your time catching frogs in Perry Pond and trying to sell them as food to the summer people."

"No, honestly, how did foreign enemies get into Northfield without me hearing about it?" Dave asked.

"The rumor was that the spies had come ashore near Boston, off a German submarine. They had been rowed in on dinghies. And they had dynamite on board. When they were on the beach, they buried the dynamite to be used later.

"The story goes that a coast guardsman in a tower near the beach saw six men as they landed. He telephoned his superiors. Soon, three of the Germans were captured, but the other three were able to get away. Eventually, those three found railroad tracks—which they followed till they came to a station. They waited there until a train going west came along, and they got on board. They knew to get off at Northfield because they had been told that a man named Kirschheimer would be willing to help them if they could get that far," Bill said.

"You mean Otto Kirschheimer?" Dave asked. "You can't tell me he was in with the spies. I knew him from the golf house at the hotel. He was a good guy."

"This is all according to what my dad told me," Bill said. "He learned about it at the Kiwanis meetings. A member said he saw the three Germans hiding out at the Kirschheimer farm. Later, they found out that these men had set up radio connections there. German sympathizers in New York City would find out what US ships were leaving from New York. Then the contacts in New York would radio the men in Northfield, who would relay information to Detroit, Michigan, where it would be sent to a message center in Hamburg, Germany. The U-boat skippers in the Atlantic Ocean would then know the position of the US ships and could sink them at will."

"Did the three spies get caught?" Mary asked.

"No, they got away."

"What about Kirschheimer?" Dave asked.

"They couldn't get any proof that the men that were staying with him were spies. So he is all right, and he is still there!"

"Hey, listen—we are here to have a good time," Dave said. "I'll get some beer for us!"

"After that, can we dance?" Sally said, looking at Bill.

"Good idea!"

Dave started toward the bar, but he looked back and said to Mary at the table, "Hold on. I'll be back, and then we'll give those two a dancing lesson!"

"Don't believe it!" Bill said to Mary. "He has two left feet."

For the rest of the evening, the floor of the Palladium vibrated as hundreds of young servicemen, with the young girl volunteers, bounced up and down to the beat of the latest arrangement of swing-time and jazz music. They danced, not worrying about tomorrow or the next day or any time beyond that.

Chapter 75

South Pacific
December 1943

BY DECEMBER 15, 1943, a troopship with hundreds of marines from the Third Battalion, Fourth Division—plus the ship's company—left San Diego Harbor. As the men watched the California coastline disappear behind them, they were positive they would be returning when the war was over.

It took two weeks to get to Hawaii. When the ship dropped anchor in Hilo Bay, Hawaii, the marines disembarked and were taken to a training camp on the former Parker Ranch. The training period would take about a month. The rifle-range drills started up again, and the marines again practiced climbing down the side of the ships on ropes and getting into landing crafts below. Then they were shown how to wade ashore with their rifles held over their heads, and then to run to whatever safe position on the beach they could find to avoid enemy fire.

Dave, Bill, and a few of the other marines were surprised when they heard that their training in Hawaii would be cut short. They had been assigned to a special company. This company had been selected to be the first to land on the island of Kwajalein. They boarded another ship and headed out to make the initial attack. Kwajalein was sixty-six miles long and eighteen miles wide. They heard that the top admirals were taking no chance on a long engagement after what had happened at Tarawa and had ordered ships and planes to drop fifteen thousand tons of explosives there before the first marines would get ordered to go ashore.*

On the ship the night before they were scheduled to hit the beach, Dave, Bill, and a navy corpsman named Al—from Keene, New Hampshire—sat together on the deck with their backs supported against a gun mount.

Looking up, Bill said, "The stars are really bright up there. You can't see as many of them at night in Northfield because there are so many tall trees."

"I remember staring up at the stars when I was walking my girlfriend home," Dave said.

"I remember that girl . . . Diane Thompson, right? She was really young. What was she—about thirteen?" Bill said, laughing.

"No! She was fourteen . . . well, just fourteen."

Al then spoke up, "I got a girl at home in New Hampshire. Her parents are very strict, and they were always watching us, but she did let me kiss her good-bye at the station."

"My folks and half the town of Northfield came to see me and the other recruits off on the train the day we left," Bill said. "Even though I don't have a special girlfriend, I have been writing to some of the girls that were in my high school class there."

"How about that short blond girl who lives on the back road off Main Street . . . didn't she like you?" Dave asked.

"Oh, you mean Molly. I think she had a crush on Georgie Mitchell, not me."

"Georgie Mitchell!" Dave shouted in surprise. "You have to be kidding. He was too shy to ask a girl to do anything. To tell the truth, Georgie liked Joan Brownell, but she was always trying to avoid him."

"That reminds me," Bill said. "I got a letter from my mother, and she mentioned in it that Georgie has enlisted in the air force and is training at some base not far from Northfield."

Dave was quiet for a minute, thinking of his friend. "I hope he makes out OK," he thought to himself.

Chapter 76

Kwajalein Island
February 1944

ON FEBRUARY 1, 1944, the ship dropped anchor off the enemy-held island of Kwajalein. The marines climbed down the ropes on the side of the ship and boarded the waiting landing crafts.

Dave and Bill were in the same landing craft with thirty-six other marines. They crouched down in the boat so that they couldn't be seen from the shore. The boat bounced up and down in the rough surf. The men wore helmets and had packs on their backs and rifles in their hands.

As the landing craft drew near to the beach, Bill asked Dave, "What are you thinking about?"

"I don't know! My mother . . . a girl!"

"The Northfield summer girl you lost track of?"

"Yes, I guess so. I should have written to her. Oh well—I didn't," Dave said. Then he asked Bill, "What are you thinking about?"

"Northfield! My dad! And I wonder if he got that promotion at the factory where he works in Greenfield. He has worked so hard there and for so long."

Dave, who had looked over the side, interrupted Bill. "We're getting close! We better concentrate on what we're supposed to do."

"That's easy! We get in the water and slosh our way to the shore," Bill said. And then he asked, "Are you scared, Dave?"

"Who, me? Scared!" Dave shouted loudly. A few marines near him shook their heads knowingly.

Then one, who knew Dave had a well-known father, called out, "Show us how to do it, Mr. Somebody!"

"Just follow me!"

Suddenly, the heavy hinged ramp at the front of the landing craft crashed down, and the leathernecks moved forward and jumped into the water and waded as quickly as possible to the beach.**

When the first wave of marines was ashore, they were surprised that all was quiet on the beach. Immediately, they started setting up a beachhead, digging foxholes, and building machine-gun nests.

It was hard to know the strength of the Japanese forces, but they figured that they were hiding about two miles inland or possibly closer in small groups.

At midnight, the first enemy firestorm started with shells and bombs bursting on the beach. The marines fired back.

As the Japanese fired artillery, mortar, and machine guns, the marines began to take casualties. Dead and wounded marines now lay on the beach, and the medics hurried from one to the other.

Despite the casualties, the order came down that every man should move out and keep going. A young officer shouted, "We have to wipe out those Jap pillboxes!"

Dave and Bill were among the first to get up and run ahead into the line of fire. They threw hand grenades and shot at anything that moved. They were able to stay alive by running and dodging throughout the night, and they survived the next day's intensive attacks by the enemy. Finally, there was a lull, and they were able to rest.

Chapter 77

THE NEXT DAY, the sound of Japanese mortar shells bursting nearby was heard.

A marine captain came over to where Dave and Bill and some other marines were holding a position. The captain said, "We need a volunteer to run ammunition to our machine-gun unit on the high ground just beyond the wide part of the beach. Whoever goes will have to keep moving. They say there may be snipers in those trees over there." Then he asked, "Did any of you guys play football?"

"I did!" Dave answered quickly.

"OK, marine, you got the job," he said and handed Dave a bag full of machine-gun cartridges.

Dave slung the bag over his shoulder and picked up his rifle. Then he began running fast across the wide open beach. His only thought was to keep going forward and get the ammunition to the guys at the machine-gun placement.

A marine, watching him dash ahead, said, "He's sniper bait out there in the open!"

An enemy hand grenade dropped thirty feet behind Dave, and in a second, it exploded. Dave felt a sharp piece of shrapnel cut into his leg. He paused briefly and then began to run again, with the ammunition bag banging on his back as he went. He glanced up at the top of a tree bordering the beach and saw a Japanese soldier hiding there and aiming a rifle at him.

Dave kept going, but the bullets began to land closer and closer to him. He stopped and began to dig a foxhole with the butt of his rifle, but the volcanic ash mixed with the sand kept falling back into the hole. His helmet fell off as he kept digging. It was then that he was hit in the head by a sniper's bullet.

Bill saw Dave fall and called out loudly to Al, the corpsman. Then Bill raised his rifle, and seeing the Jap in the tree, he took aim and pulled the trigger. Then he watched the sniper plummet to the ground.

Al grabbed his medical bag and rushed out to Dave, with Bill following him.

They found Dave lying facedown in the sand. Al turned him over. "He's still breathing, but he is unconscious. It looks bad!" he said.

Bill crouched down beside Dave and whispered, "Don't die. Don't die!"

Then Bill and Al carried Dave down the beach to the landing area. There were other medics there tending to the wounded. Dave was lifted onto a straw litter and then put into the tender boat that was to transport the casualties to the hospital ship offshore.

"I'll stay with him," Al said to Bill, getting into the tender. "You have to get back."

"OK," Bill said reluctantly and turned and walked slowly back to his unit, oblivious to the constant enemy rifle fire that was coming in around him.

Chapter 78

WHEN THE TENDER reached the hospital ship, the litters were raised by pulleys to the main deck. Al got on board by climbing up a rope ladder. Al got a sailor to help him carry Dave to the end of the line of wounded men who were lying on the deck, waiting for treatment.

The sailor said to Al, "I hate to hear these guys moaning in pain."

"The ship's medics are injecting them with morphine as fast as they can," Al said.

"How's this guy doing?" the sailor asked, looking down at Dave.

"He's still unconscious. He has a head wound, and he was hit in other places."

"Well, I hope he makes it. Now I have to get back to work," the sailor said and left.

Al sat down on the deck next to Dave, watching him closely. Then he saw the chaplain nearby, whom he recognized from the troopship. He was kneeling by one of the badly injured men. Al got up and went over and spoke to him. "Hey, Padre, will you look at my friend over here?"

The chaplain got up slowly and said that he would. He followed Al over to where Dave was lying.

Then Al said, "This man has to get to a doctor immediately before the others. He's critical."

"No, that wouldn't be right!" the chaplain answered back. "The wounded are treated in the order in which they come on board. There are others here as bad off as your friend."

"You don't understand, Padre. This marine's father is way up in the government in Washington, DC. Believe me, he would be concerned if he knew how badly his son was hurt. He would want him to get the fastest and best treatment. If you tell the doctors who this marine's father is, I'm sure they will take him right away. This guy you're looking at is special! He helps out whenever he can, and he's funny."

Al went on, explaining, "All the marines in his company like him. He makes them laugh all the time. Sometimes he pretends to be talking to his dog and the dog talks back. Sometimes he pretends he is following a girl down a street, and he walks funny. The guys love him. He is always trying to cheer everyone up. We've got to help him!"

The chaplain looked down at Dave and asked, "How old is he?"

"He's just eighteen."

"I'm not sure it's the correct thing to do, but I'll go in and speak with the doctors. You stay here."

Soon two medics came out.

"All right, we'll take him," said one to Al. And he added, "Shouldn't you be back on the island, buddy?"

They carried Dave inside and lifted him onto one of the operating-room tables. In a few minutes, one of the senior surgeons came over and said loudly, "He's not breathing."

Another doctor took hold of the wrist. "There's no pulse. He took a bullet to his head, there's no bringing him back."

The senior doctor turned to the chaplain, who was standing inside the door. "Is this the son of the government man you mentioned?"

"Yes."

"I'm sorry, we couldn't save him, but he was gone before they brought him in."

Then the chaplain said, "I'll be conducting a 'burial at sea' service later in the day. His body will go into the ocean with the others."

Chapter 79

Fort Lauderdale, Florida
February 1944

MEANWHILE, IN FORT Lauderdale, Florida, Dave's father rested in a lounge chair on the patio of the oceanfront home of his friend Daniel Hunt, a financial analyst. Daniel sat at a table near him, looking over some papers.

"This sunshine and sea air is doing me a world of good," Martin said, lighting a cigarette. "My health has been a worry to me lately."

"I'm glad you're here. Florida is nice in February," Daniel said. "It's not hot yet, and the hectic social activities usually don't start until March."

"Lying here in the sun and watching the seagulls dive into the ocean to grab fish is all the activity I need."

"There's Barbara," Daniel said as his wife appeared around the side of the house and came toward them. She was a small blond woman who had on a yellow blouse and white shorts and brightly colored sandals. She hurried over to them.

"Forgive me for not getting up," Martin said as she joined them.

"Oh, don't be silly. You are here for a rest," Barbara commented. Then she said, "I have something to tell you two. A friend of mine called me a few minutes ago and told me some news. Guess who's getting a divorce? It's that rich airplane manufacturer that married the twenty-year-old girl last year. Of course, there is sure to be a nasty divorce, but she said that his grown daughters by the first wife are delighted about it."

Suddenly, the Hunts' butler came out, carrying a tray with a telegram on it. "Madam," he said, "this is a special official communication that has just been delivered at the door, marked urgent. It is addressed to Mr. Hall."

"I guess the administrators in DC have thought of something more for me to do," Martin said as he waited for the butler to bring him the telegram.

He opened the envelope and began to read—and then he shouted "NO!"

Daniel immediately got up and took the telegram from him and read it out loud:

"Your son, Dave, has been killed in action at Kwajalein. More details later. Deepest sympathies.

Chief of Staff, US Marine Corps."**

Martin struggled to his feet and stood, dazed in shock, for a few minutes; and then he began pacing up and down the patio. After some time, the Hunts were able to help him into a chair. They sat down near him, and Martin began to talk.

"I want to tell you about my son, Dave."

"Of course, go ahead," Daniel said.

"Dave wanted to get into the war. He even wanted to leave school so he could join up earlier, but I persuaded him to stay in school until graduation. It was immediately afterward that he joined the marines. He was barely eighteen. There was no holding him back," Martin said, choking up as he said it.

It was then that Daniel gave the butler a signal that meant for him to bring out some liquor.

"What can we do for you?" Barbara asked quietly.

"I want you to listen to me while I tell you about him."

"Yes, of course, we want to hear."

"Dave was about five years old when his mother and I got divorced, so I didn't see much of him for some years. His mother took him and his brother to live in a town in New England. But by the time he was fifteen years old, I was making enough money to be able to afford to send him to a good prep school. Also, he started spending his vacations with me in DC and in New York. We got to know each other well at last. There is so much that I want you to know about him."

"Yes, we want to hear about it," Daniel said.

For an hour, he talked about his son. He recalled his many antics, his successes and his failures, his good looks, his joy of life, and his best friends and how he loved to play football.

"He was right guard. For two years, his school team was undefeated. There was this one game he told me about that the score was tied, and he intercepted a pass and ran the whole length of the field for the winning touchdown. Ever since he was a boy, he had a fearless streak in him. He would try anything. He would do anything.

"I remember when he was only six. His mother had brought him and his brother to say good-bye to me at the pier in New York City, when I was leaving for a trip to England. Just as the ship was about to leave, Dave broke away from his mother and dashed up the gangway because he wanted to go with me—he wanted to be with me. Of course, he had to be stopped . . ."

Then Martin went on with more stories.

"He'll go on forever," Barbara whispered to her husband.

"Let him!" Daniel said. "We will just listen. It's the least we can do for him."

Chapter 80

Northfield
February 1944

TWO DAYS LATER, in Northfield, Fritz Kirschheimer was coming out of the IGA store with a newspaper in his hand. Suddenly, he saw Anne Mitchell coming up the steps toward him. Fritz stopped her. "Have you seen this?" he said, as he held up the front page of the *Boston Globe*.

"No, I haven't seen the paper, but I heard the news on the radio. The radio interrupted their regular programming to say that Dave Hall, son of Martin Hall, had been killed in action in the South Pacific. I feel so sorry about it! He just visited us in November. Georgie is devastated. I called him at the army airfield to tell him. He wanted to come home, but he couldn't. He is in the infirmary because of some minor training accident. Dave was his best friend," Anne said, letting out a deep sigh of grief as she looked down at Dave's picture in the newspaper.

"Dave's mother must be completely shattered," Fritz stated.

"Yes, I'm sure she is. Last week, before this happened, I talked to Mabel on the phone. She lives in Greenwich Village now, you know. She was hoping to come for a visit to Northfield soon. It seems the president's wife is starting an organization called the American Youth Congress. Mabel thought that the youth hostel and the Youth Congress could collaborate."**

"I've heard about that too, but I'm not sure it is a good fit," Fritz said.

"Of course, as soon as I heard the news about Dave this morning, I tried to telephone Mabel—but I was told by Boris Melikof, her old friend from the settlement house, that she couldn't talk to anyone. He was at her apartment, and he told me that she was in her bedroom, and he could hear her saying over and over: 'It couldn't have happened! It's too soon! He couldn't have gotten there so fast. It's too soon!' Boris told me that a marine officer had come to tell Mabel that Dave had been killed. Strangely enough, Bill Patterson from Northfield was in the same marine company as Dave, but he is all right. Did you know Bill?" Anne asked.

"Yes, I remember Bill," Fritz said, and then he shook his head as he looked down at the picture of Dave once more in the paper, and then he left.

Two Northfield women came up the steps to the porch of the store and began to talk to Anne Mitchell.

"Is it true, that Mabel Hall's son was killed?" asked one.

"Yes, he was killed in action. He was Georgie's best friend."

"I heard that he got kind of wild after he left Northfield."

"I never heard that," Anne said, hastily, and frowned at the woman.

"I wonder if he would have come back here to live," the other woman asked.

"I don't think he would," replied the other. And she added, "The young people in town who knew Dave will feel sorry when they hear about this. They all liked him. He had a handsome face and curly brown hair. He had a kind of loose way of walking, and people always said good things about him."

"He'll be remembered," said the first woman.

"There is one thing though," said the other. "His family . . . I mean his mother . . . she was actually a newcomer here. She came in the midthirties, didn't she? I mean, she wasn't a real Northfield person."

"That's true," said Anne. "You are right, not a real Northfield person from way back! But she was well liked and respected."

At the same time, in Philadelphia, Diane Thompson was coming home from school. She hurried up the walkway to the front door of the house. She was shivering because a cold February wind was blowing.

She was surprised to see her mother waiting for her at the door, holding a newspaper in her hand.

Suddenly, Diane heard the words: "Dave was killed." When her mother tried to show her the article in the newspaper, Diane turned and ran up the two flights of stairs to her third-floor bedroom and slammed the door. Then she sat down on the side of her bed and stared at the blank wall in front of her, not moving . . . just staring.

Chapter 81

ON SEPTEMBER 2, 1945, the Second World War ended. The Japanese surrendered aboard the USS *Missouri* in Tokyo Bay. Soon the soldiers, sailors, and marines started returning home.

In Northfield, the townspeople welcomed back the servicemen who had enlisted from there. Bill Patterson was given a job at the Northfield Bank. Others found work at the post office, the Ford dealership on Main Street, and maintenance jobs at the schools. The ones who took jobs at the Northfield School for Girls and the Mount Herman School for Boys hoped for an increase in the enrollment, which would mean better pay. Some went back to farming and did carpentry work.

In the years after WWII, the United States became a world power—partly as a result of the Truman Doctrine, the Marshall Plan, the Berlin Airlift, and the North Atlantic Treaty Organization. Also, nationally, an enlargement of the government's social and economic departments was taking place.**

After WWII, life went on as usual. The Main Street Diner filled up each morning with the town men who came in for coffee.

Georgie Mitchell regularly joined the others.

The topic of conversation was usually about the results of the Boston Red Sox baseball game the day before. One morning, after the game had been completely discussed, an "old regular" brought up a new subject.

"Bill Patterson at the bank wants us to build a World War II monument next to the town hall. It would have the names on it of all the Northfield boys who fought in the war. And at the top part of the monument would be the names of the ones who were killed."

"That's a good idea," one man said.

"Yes, that's a decent thing to do," said another. "But it will take a long time to get the townspeople to warm up to the idea—especially if it means their taxes will be raised to pay for it!"

"I think the people will agree to it eventually," said the first man, "if you give them enough time to talk it over and think about it."

Then a man sitting on a stool at the end of the counter said, sarcastically, "Enough time? How about ten years? Northfield people don't rush into things."

And they all laughed.

The same man called over to Georgie and said, "How do you like that job you got raising money for the girls' school here?"

"It's OK. I help write letters to all the old graduates, asking them for donations. Some give . . . some don't. Actually, I just assist the main fund-raiser, but a job is a job."

Then they went back to talking about the baseball game.

Chapter 82

Northfield
1934–1952

THE FIRST AMERICAN Youth Hostel had been located on Main Street in Northfield since 1935. Over the years, it became a very popular stopping-off place for young bicycle riders. Groups of them would start their bike trips in Northfield and circle up north through New England and then return to the Northfield hostel on their way back.

The youth-hostel movement gained momentum as the founders would send out messages about hosteling to the high schools, to the college students, and the Boy Scout troops across the country. The message told of the physical and spiritual benefit that came from bicycling, hiking, and canoeing under one's own steam. As a result, the youth hostel on Main Street began to fill up during the summer months with young bikers who needed a place to sleep.

In the evenings, there would be gabfests around the fire in the large common room of the hostel. The importance of international friendship was emphasized by those in charge, and the needs of the entire globe were discussed.

Fritz Kirschheimer, nephew to Otto Kirschheimer, arrived in Northfield in 1936 from Germany and was offered a job as assistant to the leaders of the hostel, which he gladly accepted. Fritz, who lived at the hostel, greeted the new bikers enthusiastically. He took pride in maintaining the building and kept everything running efficiently—sometimes alone since the leaders were often away.

In the spring of 1939, Fritz began to plan a three-month summer bike trip to Germany. Dick and Carl Newberg, Hank Snyder, and four others, all former bikers, signed up for the trip. Fritz would be their leader. The experiences the group had on the European trip in the summer of 1939 have been related in detail in previous chapters.

When the United States declared war on Japan in 1941, thousands of young men were drafted into the armed forces. Because of this, there were fewer young people taking biking vacations. But Fritz kept the hostel going, and the doors were always open; and some still came, and some stayed on.

At this time, word got around in Northfield that the youth hostel was harboring both conscientious objectors and expatriate Germans. Some of the more conservative townspeople didn't hide their suspicions that international liberalism was being fostered there. Others saw the hostel as a place that brought strangers and drifters into town with no visible means of support, while their sons were being drafted into the army.

But the talk calmed down after WWII ended. Also, a new highway had been built across the river, several miles away from Northfield—so fewer bikers went there, and it became known around town that the youth hostel was for sale.

A large family from another town bought the house and moved in. Since the youth hostel was still listed in newspapers and on college campuses, many small groups of bikers and hikers still arrived at the door. When this happened, they were welcomed in because the new owners liked young people with independent leanings and new ideas. Of course, many who found their way there had little money and often stayed on for some time.

Chapter 83

Northfield
1960

IN 1960, THERE was a summer camp located on Forest Lake, New Hampshire, not far from Northfield. Most of the campers were African American children from Harlem in New York City. In the summer of 1960, the camp was filled to capacity.

Many college students who wanted to help disadvantaged children, and to earn money and get an outdoor job, signed up to be counselors. The camp activities were well organized. The campers swam in Forest Lake, took hikes in the woods, did craftwork, played softball, and sang around the campfire in the evenings. Their dining room and camp kitchen were located in a renovated barn, and they slept in tents on canvas cots. Bedtime was at ten o'clock, and it was then that a bugler played Taps. The solemn notes rang out across the lake and the mountains beyond. Then an eerie silence came over the camp, for the most part—except for an occasional whisper, giggle, or shriek, which came from the campers inside the tents.

Kathy Ford, the younger sister of Jenny and also the cousin of Diane Thompson, had heard about the camp and immediately applied to be a counselor there for the summer. She had just graduated from a Midwestern college.

From the first day of camp, Kathy was followed around by another counselor: Aaron Clavir, who was in charge of some of the boys. He would show up suddenly when she was leading the young girl campers from one activity to the next. The children would laugh when they saw him coming and whispered about how he liked Kathy.

However, there was another young man at the camp. He was from Boston and would be going to medical school in the fall. His name was Mark Stewart. He was in charge of the grounds, building, and equipment at the camp. He also drove both the camp truck and bus. Mark was tall and handsome, with broad shoulders and brown hair and eyes. It didn't take long for Kathy to notice him—or for him to notice her, since she was prettiest of the girl counselors. As Kathy and Mark got to know each other, Aaron was all but completely ignored.

Often at night, when the campers had gone to sleep, Kathy and Mark would sit in the dark and talk about their lives so far. Later, exhausted from the day's work, they would say goodnight. Mark would go to his room behind the kitchen, and Kathy would go to one of the campers' tents. Her cot was just inside the entrance flap. The sound of children breathing heavily in unison was the last sound she would hear before falling sound asleep.

One morning, Mark passed Kathy with a group of little girls on their way to breakfast. He stopped her and said, "Did you know we have a half a day off each week? So next Wednesday, after lunch, we could take some free time off together. I can get the camp truck."

Kathy agreed quickly and then told him she would like to go and see her relatives in Northfield, if they could. And she added, she knew he would like them.

So the next Wednesday afternoon, they climbed into the camp truck and started toward Northfield, happy like escaped prisoners.

On the way, Kathy asked, "Have you ever been in Northfield?"

"No, but I've heard about it. There used to be a youth hostel there, wasn't there?"

"Yes, it was well known. Lots of bikers stopped there, but I'm not sure it is a real youth hostel anymore," Kathy said.

"I think my mother took a bike trip from there years ago."

Chapter 84

THEY HAD TO drive down a steep, curving mountain road on their way. Mark pumped the brake pedal hard so he wouldn't lose control of the truck.

"We turn left on a dirt road at the bottom of the hill," Kathy said.

Then Mark suggested that after they've visited her aunt and cousin at their cottage, he would like to drive past the old youth hostel on Main Street.

"My mother took a youth-hostel bike trip north from Northfield one summer, as I remember it," Mark said. "She told me that there were two girl friends with her. They had quite a time! Halfway through the trip, one of the girls' bikes lost a wheel, so they were forced to hitchhike. A truck driver stopped for them, and they all piled into the back. He dropped them off in Hanover, New Hampshire. They had no idea if there was a youth hostel in town, where they could sleep that night. They went into a drugstore and told the girl behind the soda fountain their troubles. She said they could sleep on the floor of her one-room apartment, which they did. The next day, they hitched another truck ride. This time going south, and they got back to Northfield safely. Mother loved telling that story."

"Oh, that reminds me," Kathy said. "Diane's husband, Dick Newberg, who was an enthusiastic biker, went on a youth-hostel trip to Europe in the summer of 1939. He was only fifteen years old. His brother, Carl, and some others were with him. Eventually, they saw hundreds of men and boys in uniform in Germany while they were there."

"That was just before Germany invaded Poland," Mark said.

"Yes, but he got home two weeks before that happened, I've been told."

"It was a close call!"

"Then two years later," Kathy continued, "when he was seventeen and a senior in high school, he came to Northfield for a youth-hostel Christmas reunion with his friend, Hank Snyder. The Thompsons were guests at the Northfield Hotel at the same time, and Diane and my sister, Jenny, were with them. They met on the hotel skating pond. Dick was able to get Diane's address in Philadelphia."

Kathy continued, "In June 1941, Dick had been appointed to the Naval Academy in Annapolis, Maryland. It was then that he began sending letters to Diane in Philadelphia, and she began visiting him for weekend dance parties, and soon they became engaged. After graduation, Dick was assigned to the battleship *South Dakota* and spent eighteen months on active duty in the pacific. When World War II ended, Diane and Dick were married, and now they have three little girls. Dick has a job in Groton, Connecticut, where the submarines are built. Diane and the children spend the summers at the family cottage in Northfield, and Dick drives up every weekend to be with them."

After two miles on the dirt road, they turned up onto Rustic Ridge and were soon at the Thompsons' cottage.

Helen Thompson and her daughter, Diane, were sitting in rocking chairs on the screened-in porch. Suddenly, they heard a truck rumble to a stop on the road below them.

"It's Kathy!" Diane shouted, getting up.

"Yes, it is," Helen said. "But who is that with her? It's not that Aaron that came with her before!"

"I don't think so!"

Kathy jumped out of the truck and waved up at them, and Mark followed her. They walked up toward the cottage on a path covered with pine needles, with thick banks of ferns on each side. They climbed up the wooden steps to the porch, and Helen and Diane hurried over to welcome them.

"You should have told us you were coming, Kathy," her aunt said.

"We didn't have time, Aunt Helen. I wanted you to meet Mark Stewart. He works at the camp with me, and he was kind enough to drive me over."

They shook hands.

"This is my cousin, Diane," Kathy said.

Diane smiled and said, "Let's all sit down. I want to hear about camp."

"Camp is so interesting and fun, but it's hard work too," Kathy said. "When I take the young Harlem girls on a hike in the woods, they scream and huddle around me because they say they see ghosts behind the trees. But I can usually calm them down. They are fun!"

Then Mark said with a smile, "Yesterday, I was showing the boys a big black snake I had caught, and one of them was so scared of it that he ran way out of the camp without stopping or looking back. Finally, he came back."

"How is that other counselor you brought by a few weeks ago—the one with the beard?" Diane asked.

"Oh, you mean Aaron Clavir... he's OK," Kathy answered.

"That's my competition!" Mark said. And he added, "He is a real radical and is part of a peace movement whose members are trying to keep the country out of the Vietnam War. I guess that's all right, but Aaron is too serious for me!"

"Uncle Bob had a long friendly conversation with Aaron when he was here," Diane mentioned.

"Uncle Bob likes to talk to everyone and anyone, and he always makes them feel good," Kathy said. Then she asked, "Where is Uncle Bob?"

"He is at the Northfield dump," Helen informed them. "He takes tree-slash down there. He trims branches and trees for me out in front so we can get a better mountain view. And, of course, when he goes to the dump, he spends an hour or so talking to the old man who is in charge there. If you two will stay for supper, you will see him. He'll be home by then."

"Thank you, but we have to be back at camp at six o'clock," Kathy said. "And we want to drive by the old youth-hostel house. Mark's mother took a bike trip from there years back and often talks about it."

"It's not a real hostel anymore," Helen informed them. "There are still young people coming and going from there, like in the old days."

Soon it was time to go, so Kathy and Mark said good-bye and went down the path to the truck. They waved back to them as they drove away.

Diane then turned to her mother and exclaimed, "That guy is definitely the one for Kathy! I'm sure of it, and I'm so glad." Then she did a little dance around the porch, adding, "He's perfect for her!"

"You do have a kind heart," Helen said to her daughter.

Chapter 85

THE SUMMER SUN shone brightly on the houses on Main Street as Kathy and Mark drove along.

Suddenly, Kathy called out, "There's the old youth-hostel house!"

Mark swerved the truck into the driveway and stopped by the side door. "This is a big place," he said.

"Yes, I heard that the back part of the house has enough sleeping spaces for forty, but not many come anymore."

After they got out of the truck, Mark pointed to a car that was parked nearby. "I'll be darned," he said in surprise. "That's Aaron Clavir's old Plymouth. Did you know he was coming over here?"

"No, but he did mention once that two of his antiwar friends would be here soon, and he planned to see them."

Mark looked toward the back lawn that sloped down toward the river. "There's Aaron now! He is sitting at a wooden table with two other guys."

"Let's go down and surprise him," Kathy suggested, laughing.

As they hurried toward them, Mark shouted loudly, "Hi, Aaron, I thought you were on kid duty at the camp this afternoon?"

"Kathy, Mark—what are you doing here?" Aaron called back, getting up from the table.

"What are *you* doing here?" Mark mimicked back.

"I got permission to come over to see my friends. Why aren't you two taking care of the kids?"

"Afternoon off," Mark said.

"Listen, I want you to meet these guys," Aaron said. "The one with the beard is Paul, and the one with the long hair is Mo."

They looked up and nodded. Mark and Kathy smiled at them.

"These two have been out in San Francisco and just got here yesterday. I met them at an SDS—Students for Democratic Society—meeting last year. The group was working on a peace plan," Aaron said. "They were hoping to get the government to stop making nuclear weapons. Also, they were against the Vietnam War."

Then Paul spoke up, "Aaron and I were in New York City in 1955 when we were asked to take shelter during a civil defense exercise in order to be ready in case of a nuclear attack on the city. It was known as Operation Alert. It was like a practice. Everyone was supposed to participate. But it was stupid! Well, our group of pacifists refused to do it. We stood our ground at City Hall Park and protested loudly. A few of the group were arrested, including us. The arraigning magistrate gave us a tongue-lashing, and some hard-liners were put in jail."

"Was there one special leader of the protest?" Mark asked.

"No, not that day," Aaron answered. "But there were a few antiwar groups there. There were some from the Fellowship of Reconciliation, the American Friends Service, Catholic Workers Movement, and others."

Then Paul spoke up, "There is a Student Peace Union at the University of Chicago that has been formed by a young Quaker activist. He sponsors informal meetings for Chicago-area pacifists and left-wing students within the campus. He hopes to inspire them to work for the cause of disarmament."

Mark looked straight at Paul and said, "I heard that some of the Communists are trying to infiltrate into these student groups."

"No, that's not right!" Paul answered. "The National Committee for Sane Nuclear Policy in New York City now prohibits card-carrying Communists from joining the national organization."

"Paul and Mo are leaving for Boston tomorrow, but I hope they will come back," Aaron said.

Then Kathy stood up and said in a slightly confused way, "I learned a lot by listening to you, although I don't understand it all very well. But it is getting late. We have to get back to the camp."

So Mark and Kathy walked quickly up to the driveway and got into the truck and left. Just as they were driving away, Anne Mitchell and Minnie Johnson were walking along the sidewalk past the house.

"Did you see those young people that just drove away? Do you know them?" Anne asked.

"I think I have seen the girl before . . ." Minnie answered. "Her relatives have a summer cottage on the Ridge. She and that boy with her are counselors at the Forest Lake camp."

Then Minnie suddenly stopped talking and pointed to the backyard of the house. "And who are those long-haired idlers sitting at the picnic table?"

"I don't know them, but they are probably some of those strangers that always seem to show up here. There is something about our town that attracts them, and some of them stay for quite a while," Anne said. She continued, "You know, it's not just outsiders that gather at this house . . . our own Northfield young people like to congregate at this house and talk about world problems with whoever shows up."

"Yes, I know the strangers come to town, but they always seem to leave in the end."

"Let's hurry and get to the store," Anne said, as she remembered that they had to buy some of the food for the church supper that night.

A warm July breeze came up and rustled the leaves on the tall trees along Main Street as the two Northfield women climbed the steps of the IGA store and went inside.

Chapter 86

IT IS HARD to say whether the ideas of a few idealists in Northfield resulted in the gradual influx of a large number of young antiwar protesters to the area over the next ten years. But as the Kennedy administration increased the country's involvement in the struggle between North and South Vietnam, opposition began to grow, mainly among the college-age students.

In 1961, President John F. Kennedy began to assist the South Vietnamese government in their struggle against the North Vietnamese Communists. US helicopters were sent there to transfer the South Vietnamese soldiers to the front.

On November 22, President Kennedy was killed while riding in a motorcade in Dallas, Texas. The new president, Lyndon Johnson, continued the US involvement in Vietnam. Then Congress initiated a draft by lottery, which caused considerable anger among the young men who would be forced into the army. It was then that further opposition to the war began. Protesters marched in many of the large cities, and there were rallies where they blasphemed the government's military action.

In Northfield in the mid-1960s, a group of high school students and some disgruntled young people from nearby towns began to meet at the old youth-hostel house. This was the house that was always open to young people who objected to the old ideas of the establishment. It was a place where the group could express their fears and concerns. Soon, the group was joined by more idealistic college students and antiwar activists, all of whom heard of the movement in Northfield.

The idea of a commune, where like-thinking young people could live together, took form. The first one was located in an old vacant house in Warwick, Massachusetts, not far from Northfield. And as word spread of its existence, large numbers of young people arrived, and the commune grew quickly in size.

Some of the most radical members who came believed that society as it was would soon be in chaos, and they would be there to save it. Joan Brownell was one of them. She was older than most of the others and had finished at a college in Maine. Now she willingly left her grandfather's house on Pine Street and joined the antiwar and anticultural activists at the Warwick commune.

Chapter 87

WHEN *LOOK* MAGAZINE published a cover story about the commune in Warwick, Massachusetts, many young people who read the article decided to leave home and join the commune. Some of those that swarmed toward Warwick would stop by the old youth-hostel house in Northfield to get directions since they had heard of its open-door policy.

In Warwick, the commune leaders were taken by surprise by the sheer number of eager new groups that showed up and moved in. They came in trucks, cars, and on foot. The young liberals and radicals that arrived at the Warwick house were mostly from the Mid-Atlantic and New England states. Some were college educated. Others were poor and had come from families whose members worked for low wages in the textile factories. Some were revolutionary zealots, who came from the slums of New York. There were moderate socialists who were simply against capitalism.

As they moved in, they were cooperative with each other and followed the rules of the commune—often explained to them by Joan Brownell. It became a community of young reformers, talkers, and dreamers; and indiscriminate sexual activity was the accepted norm.

The old members did what they could to accommodate them and started building a new dormitory. Because of the crowding, the commune leaders would often make the short trip back to the old youth-hostel house in Northfield. They would make themselves at home there and eat whatever was offered to them.

For this and other reasons, the family decided to move away, and the house was put on the market. It was advertised for sale in many city newspapers, but after six months, there wasn't one offer. This news surprised the family; and after some thought, they decided to give the house, free and clear, to the commune people.

The title of the house was handed over in a casual way, with a handshake and a smile—but unfortunately, there was no time given for the family to move out in a proper way. The same day that the word-of-mouth settlement was made, the commune young people (or hippies, as they were now being called) rushed into the house and began taking over everything.

The commune crowd now took off the doors to all the rooms to show togetherness. As their number began to increase, every closet in the house had to be used as a sleeping space. They painted the walls in dark colors.

To some of the citizens of the town of Northfield, they were the invaders.

Chapter 88

ON THE NIGHT of May 20, 1969, light shone through the windows of the Northfield town hall. A meeting was being held. All the seats in the main room were taken. Some of the men had to stand in the back. Those gathered there were mostly Northfield farmers, but there were also shopkeepers and businessmen who worked in Greenfield, and lumbermen. There were teachers from the school and retired people as well. The first selectman of the town—with the fire chief and tax collector—sat at a table in the front.

After the meeting had gone on for a while, the first selectman asked, "Now that we have settled which roads will be repaired and blacktopped, are there any other concerns?"

Bill Patterson, from the bank, stood up and began to speak. "As you know, I am a marine veteran. My concern is about the gang of radicals and hippies that are living here in a large house on Main Street, which they call a commune. I believe they have the potential to corrupt the morals of decent youngsters in town. There are at least forty of them living in that one house. They sit around in there and verbally tear down every known tradition that we have always lived by. They are against marriage. They are against working for a living. They are against the fairly elected town and state officials. They burn their selective service cards. They say proudly that they are suspicious of anyone that is over thirty years of age. I think we should start enforcing some town restrictions on them."

Then an old retired teacher named Andrew Brownell, grandfather of Joan Brownell, struggled to his feet. "Those young people have a right to be there. They were given the house free and clear."

At that comment, Anne Mitchell stood up and said firmly, "Those commune kids are ruining that house. They are ripping out all the doors inside, and they plan to paint the outside purple. That was known as one of the oldest and was one of the finest houses on Main Street. A famous founder of Northfield lived there."

"Mrs. Mitchell, you are missing the point," Andrew said from his seat. "Those young people have joined together to live a new kind of life. They are searching for a new philosophy, and they thrive on being with people of their same age."

Georgie Mitchell, who was standing in the back, called out, "Isn't there a law against forty people living in one house?"

Andrew was quick to respond. "An attached sleeping area that was built during the youth-hostel days is being used. And why do you call them 'commune kids'? There are some intelligent older college graduates living there. You would recognize some of the names of their wealthy fathers, who are doctors and lawyers."

Bill Patterson answered back, "I still say it's unfortunate that this group moved in on us. Why did they pick our town to settle in? Aren't most of them from other places?"

"No, that is not right," Brownell continued. "There are some town youngsters who have moved into the commune. My granddaughter, Joan, is one of them." Then pointing to Georgie Mitchell, he added, "I thought you were a friend of hers."

"Sure, Joan is all right. It's the other ones that I don't like."

Then a deep voice from the back of the hall was heard. "I am the water commissioner here, as you know, and I can tell you that those people are breaking the sewage code. Forty people using two toilets *is* breaking the law!"

At that, there was some laughter and some muttering; but suddenly, a thin, balding man stood up. He was dressed in a black suit and wore glasses. "Most of you know already that I am the new minister of the Unitarian Church here. I have visited the commune several times. I accept their new thinking. Many are peace activists, and they are against the Vietnam War. They were also adamant against the stockpiling of atomic weapons. It is true that most of them are immature. Some seem quite confused, actually. The older ones seem more focused. But even they are unsure of where they are heading. They are searching and seeking. That is good. We should reach out in friendship to them."

Then the owner of the local general store raised her hand and said, "Excuse me . . . but when they come into the store to buy food, they are more likely to be demanding than friendly. Also, most of them look unclean and malnourished. They are not interested in assimilating themselves into the town or in making friends . . . they prefer to keep to themselves."

"How did all this get started?" asked one farmer's wife.

"It began some years ago when rebellious students organized demonstrations at hundreds of high schools," Patterson said. "They were protesting against the Vietnam War and society in general. At the protest events, many began to hear about the commune in Warwick and, afterwards, the one here in Northfield."

Then a widow who was sitting in the front row got up. "There are perfectly nice Northfield youngsters living there at the commune, like your granddaughter Joan," she said, pointing at Brownell. "I don't see what all the fuss is about."

"Frankly, I don't see how those few can get along with the wild radicals that come in from different places."

Then the widow in the front row spoke up again, "Some of them have begun taking odd jobs around town. What's wrong with that?"

"That's all right," Patterson admitted. "But since they are members of the commune, they have to hand over whatever money they have earned to the leaders, who had taught them about the negative side of having money."

Then a man's voice came loudly from the back. "I've heard that a lot of them have figured out how to go on to public welfare. They get regular federal handouts."

There were moans from the crowd.

Another person shouted out, "I have heard they are starting a rock band. The guitars and drums can be heard banging away at all hours of the night. And someone told me that they plan to hire out for school dances and for gigs at local restaurants."

"What is next!" said Anne Mitchell dejectedly.

Then the first selectman stood up and said loudly, "That's enough for tonight. There will be another town meeting in four weeks. We will continue to discuss this problem then. Can I hear a motion to adjourn the meeting?"

"So moved," Patterson uttered quietly.

"All in favor say 'aye.'"

A few said "aye," and the others began to get up and leave.

Outside, the night's silence was broken by the sound of cars starting up as the people started to make their way home.

The Wilson brothers, Pat and Dan, left with the others and walked north on Main Street. They were in their early twenties and had lived in Northfield all their lives. All evening, they had ducked in and out of the meeting in order to smoke.

"You know that commune over there," Dan said, looking across the street.

"Yeah!"

"I heard that the guys that live there now are hitting on a different girl every night. And besides that, I hear they know where to buy cheap drugs."

"Does that mean you want to join them, stupid?" Pat said, hitting his brother on the side of his head.

"Hell no, they are weird. Anyway, I like the girls at the dance hall in Greenfield better. But it's hard to get Mother to let us have the car to go there every Saturday night," Dan said.

"Don't worry, I can talk her into anything."

"Let's cut through the church property."

Soon they were gone, and silence returned again to Main Street.

Chapter 89

ON A JANUARY afternoon in 1975, Bill Patterson sat at his desk in his office at the Northfield Bank. Five years earlier, he had become the manager of the bank. He was fifty-two years old now, and he was stouter; but he still had a head of thick brown hair. He wore a dark suit with a blue shirt and tie.

There were loan applications and other bank papers on his desk that he was putting in order. The door to the main part of the bank was half-open. Occasionally, he would look up and see who was coming in and walking over to the tellers' windows. When he finished with his work, he put his feet up on the desk and shook out the local newspaper and began to read.

Suddenly, Andrew Brownell was standing at the door. "Can I speak to you?" he asked.

"Certainly, come right in and have a seat," Patterson said, putting down the newspaper and getting up and pointing to the chair across from the desk.

Andrew propped his cane against the wall and sat down. His face was deeply lined, and his white hair was uncombed. He wore a stained plaid jacket and old corduroy pants. The wool scarf around his neck was frayed. His cracked leather boots were unlaced.

"I guess you know that my granddaughter, Joan, is living at the commune, in the old youth-hostel house with the others," Brownell began as Bill took his seat behind the desk.

"Yes, I know that, and I have seen Joan around town recently."

"She was in California for a while but came back and moved into the commune. She has been with those people for several months now," Brownell explained.

"Since you have mentioned her, I would like to say something to you. I have noticed that Joan is not only with the commune group, but she has taken up with Pat and Dan Wilson. I don't think that's wise. Those boys are up to no good."

"I know those two. I don't think they are really bad," Brownell said. "Anyway, Joan is involved with one of the big shots at the commune. She is always following him around."

"I wonder if you know that our local policeman has his eye on the Wilson boys. He suspects that they have been stealing things from the IGA store, and he told me that those boys go into Greenfield on Saturday night and get drunk and buy drugs. I tell you this because your granddaughter has been seen walking with them on Main Street late at night."

Brownell shifted in his chair and said angrily, "Who told you that? Some town busybody, I suppose. Some of them are always spying on the boys and trying to find out what they are doing, and hoping it is something bad."

"People in town have to know what's going on," Patterson said and then changed the subject. "Tell me, Andrew, have you heard from your grandson? I liked him, and we were friends—but then he left Northfield suddenly, and I haven't heard from him. As I remember it, he went out to Berkeley, California. Correct me if I am wrong, but I heard from someone that he became a leader of an antiwar organization called Act for Peace at Berkeley. And Joan went out there herself for a while."

"Yes, that's right. My grandchildren have always been pacifists like me, and I'm proud of them!"

"I read recently that the 'Act for Peace' organization has turned into an 'acts of violence' group now. I read they don't mind breaking windows and turning over cars."

"I don't know where you read that, but it's not true," Brownell said loudly, leaning forward in the chair and shaking his fist.

"Look, the Vietnam War is all but over now—so the sooner the antiwar protesters stop attacking the establishment, the better."

"The establishment should be attacked if it continues to promote senseless wars," Brownell said belligerently.

Patterson shook his head in frustration and then asked, "Why did you come to see me today?"

"I need a loan of one thousand dollars."

"What is the money for?"

"My granddaughter says they need money for food and heat at the commune."

"Is that so? I thought they had a rock band and were making money."

"No, the band is not known well enough yet."

"What would you use as collateral for the loan?" Patterson asked.

"I will put up my house on Pine Street."

"Look, I know your situation. Your Social Security check is all you have to live on. I am not going to let you put yourself in debt for that thoughtless gang, even if Joan wants it. Sorry, but I can't do it. That's final!"

Brownell reached for his cane and slowly pulled himself out of his chair. Suddenly, he began to sway and lose his balance. Patterson hurried around his desk and reached out to steady him.

"I'm all right!" Brownell said, pulling back.

"Do you think you can make it home?"

The old man didn't answer and left the office.

He limped slowly across the main room of the bank toward the door. The two young women tellers watched him go and shook their heads with concern. Georgie Mitchell was entering the bank just as the old man was leaving. Brownell ignored him and kept going.

Georgie saw Patterson standing by the door of his office and went over to him. "I came to tell you that they have postponed the Kiwanis meeting because there is a big snowstorm coming tonight."

"Thanks for telling me, Georgie, but I can't talk to you right now. I'm busy." Patterson went back into the office and closed the door.

One of the young tellers smiled at Georgie, so he immediately walked over to her. Then he said, laughing and pretending to have a gun in his pocket, "Give me all your money!"

"We don't joke about things like that in here," she said, trying to suppress a smile.

"How about you and me going ice-skating tonight?"

"No, it's too cold!"

"We could go to a movie in Greenfield."

"No," she said again. "Anyway, you just said it's going to snow tonight. By the way, why aren't you at the alumni office at the school, doing your job? Do you want to get fired?"

"Me . . . get fired? No, they like me over there," Georgie said and shrugged his shoulders as he headed for the door.

Outside, a few small snowflakes were already coming down, and the wind had picked up. Georgie pulled up the collar of his jacket and put on his gloves. Before he got into the car, he looked up and saw old man Brownell, some distance away, walking unsteadily along Holton Street. Georgie watched as he turned onto Highland Avenue, and he said to himself, "I wonder if he'll make it to his house on Pine Street in this stiff wind."

Then he got into the car and drove to Highland Avenue and caught up to him. He got out and insisted he let him drive him home.

Brownell gave in and said softly, "I remember when you used to come over to see my granddaughter, Joan."

"That was a long time ago."

Chapter 90

A YEAR LATER, on a cold night in February, Pat Wilson drove a black pickup truck into the driveway of the Northfield commune. His brother, Dan, sat next to him, finishing off a can of beer.

"I hope that's not the last can?" Pat asked as he pulled on the brake.

"No, I brought some extras. We are celebrating, remember, because we were able to buy this truck."

"That was lucky that we got paid the day before we were fired from the construction job in Springfield. It was just enough money for the down payment on the truck."

"We would still be working there for those builders if you hadn't brought that drug dealer around, you lamebrain!" Pat said.

"I didn't know anyone was watching—"

"Well, forget it . . . I had better honk the horn so that Joan and her friends know that we are here."

"Not too loud! We'll wake up everyone on Main Street."

Pat ignored that remark and blew the horn. Then they both got out the truck.

"Joan's room is on the third floor," Pat said, looking up. "She must have heard us. She's waving from the window. I'll signal her to come down."

"How many friends is she bringing with her?" Dan asked.

"She said about eight—three guys, and the rest are girls. Some of the older ones, Joan's age, who live here, turned her down when she invited them because they knew what kind of a party it was going to be."

"Does Joan and her other friends know where we are going?"

"Yes, I told her. She knows that we will be breaking into one of the summer cottages on the Ridge to have the party."

"Does she know that some of the commune rock-band guys are coming?"

"Sure, she does. She sees them all the time. Joan knows how to have fun. She told me that when she was in California, she would go from one party to another every night."

"I'm sure you didn't tell her that we owe the band leader three hundred bucks for the stuff he bought for us," Dan asked Pat.

"She doesn't need to know everything."

The third-floor window was dark now, and soon, a light came on by a side door of the house. Joan was the first one to come out. She had on a winter parka and a turtleneck sweater and blue jeans. She was followed out by the others.

"There aren't too many of us, are there?" Joan asked as she hurried over to Pat.

"No," Pat answered and signaled to the crowd to get into the open back of the truck.

Then he asked Joan, "Where did you get that parka? You look nice in it."

"I bought it at a Goodwill Store in Turners Falls. I know there's no heat in those closed-up summer cottages, and it's cold tonight, so I dressed warmly."

"Don't worry, we'll get a fire going."

Then looking toward the group that had begun climbing into the back of the truck, Pat suddenly shouted, "That girl over there is carrying a baby."

"The baby won't be any trouble, and I promised her that she could come and bring her baby."

"Some party . . . with a baby!" Pat said and then walked to the back of the truck to help the last ones climb in.

"Is everybody in now?"

"Yes!" was the loud cheerful yell.

Pat went around and got in the truck behind the wheel. Joan sat between him and Dan. Pat backed out of the drive onto Main Street and headed north. Soon they were on Moody Street and then North Lane that led up to Rustic Ridge.

There were squeals of laughter coming from the back as the truck bounced over the ruts and potholes on the ridge roads.

"It's dark and spooky up here this time of year," Joan remarked.

Chapter 91

"LOOK, THERE'S THE cottage!" Dan shouted, rolling down the window. "The front door is open. I guess the band guys are here already."

"I hope they have started a fire," Joan said, shivering as the cold air blew in through the window.

Pat parked close to the front door. The commune gang jumped down from the back of the truck and rushed into the cottage. Inside, they were greeted by the band members, whom they thanked for starting the fire in the stone fireplace. Then they all sat in a semi-circle on the floor in front of it.

Some of the rock-band members sat at a table nearby. A few of them had long hair and beards. They had lit a kerosene lamp to see by. They were busy melting heroin into liquid using two cigarette lighters. As the liquid formed, they poured it into syringes.

Soon, they were passing the syringes around to the waiting group.

The two main leaders of the commune sat in two large Morris chairs in the corner. One of the crowd called out and asked, "Why don't you come over and sit with us?"

"No, we're waiting for Pat Wilson," was the answer.

Then Dan said to the gang sitting around him, "My brother is checking something out on the truck. He will be here in a minute." And then he turned to Joan and whispered, "Why does everyone bow and scrape in front of those guys? What's so great about them?"

"They and some of the others started the commune," Joan answered. "Those two actually dropped out of high school at the same time, and they got a few kids to hang out with them. Soon, the kids were convinced to leave their homes. The group started off living in a tree house in a town near Northfield. Gradually, their dislike for law and middle-class conventions won them over. Then they became a real breakaway group. More and more youths wanted to join—and not just high school kids, but radical college students too. As a result, the first commune was started up in a vacant house in Warwick, Massachusetts, and dozens would show up and move in. Then another commune was started here on the Main Street in Northfield. Other young people kept coming to both places, and they liked living together and sleeping together with no rules. Later, some came with guitars, and there was a lot of singing and dancing. That led to the forming of the rock band."

Suddenly, the door opened, and Pat Wilson came in.

"Hey, Wilson," one of the leaders called out, "I hope you brought the money you owe me for the stuff I bought for you, that we're using tonight. I had to pay the whole tab to that smart-aleck drug dealer you put me on to. Now I'd like to get back the three hundred dollars you owe me."

"Sure! Sure!" Pat said nervously.

"So . . . when?"

"Why don't you and I go out on the porch and talk about it and let everyone enjoy themselves in here."

So they went outside.

"Boy, it's cold out here," Pat commented.

"Never mind that—where's my three hundred bucks?"

"I don't have it right now. But if you were to give me a couple of weeks, you'll be paid."

"I don't want to wait a couple of weeks. If you don't have the money now, then steal something and sell it." Then he softened his tone and said, "Actually, if you are fair with me about this, I may have a job for you and your brother."

"That would be swell!" Pat said in surprise.

"We need two guys to make posters to advertise the band concerts. You would have to print them up and then tack them on telephone poles and put them in store windows in the towns where we are going to give our next concert. The posters will help us to get a good crowd."

"Yeah, Dan and I can do that."

"But remember—I get the money first, then you get the job. I mean it! Now let's get out of this cold wind."

So Pat pushed open the door for him, and they went inside, where the fire in the fireplace was blazing up brightly.

One of the commune guys—whose name was Joe, and who had been standing by the door—came over to Pat. "I could hear what he said to you. I know how you can get the money. It's easy. Just break into the church. I've done it plenty of times in Brooklyn. Me and my pal Mike will help you and your brother. Mike is sitting over there."

"Hey thanks, that might work! I hear they leave the collection plates with the money in them in the church office, and there are gold candlesticks and stuff like that around in there."

"OK, as long as Mike and I get our cut," Joe said.

"Sure, you will!"

"Let's meet tomorrow night at midnight at the back of the church!" Pat said.

"We'll be there," Joe agreed.

Then they sat down with the others in front of the fire.

Chapter 92

LATE THE NEXT night, Joe and Mike were crouching down by the back door of the Congregational Church. Joe was holding a crowbar and a burlap bag in his hand. "Where are those guys, anyway?" Joe asked.

"Hey, look, they are coming now," Mike said, seeing Pat and Dan running across the church parking lot in the dark. Soon they joined them.

"We thought you changed your mind," Joe said.

"No, we had to wait until our old lady went to sleep."

"So how are you going to bust in this door?" Dan asked.

"We're not going to bust it in. We're going to pry it open with this crowbar."

"Will that work?"

"I've pried open plenty of doors," Joe said.

"Well, go ahead and do it!" Dan said impatiently.

"Yes, but we had better wait until a big truck goes by. They make a lot of noise, and then no one will hear us break in."

"There aren't many trucks going past at this time of night," Dan said.

"No, there are some trucks. I seen them. The drivers of the big rigs get off the highway across the river and use the main street of Northfield as a shortcut to Vermont. Let's just wait."

"Are you sure there is money in the church office?" Mike asked.

"Yes, there is money there from the Sunday collection. I heard they only put it in the bank once a week—and don't forget about the gold candlesticks," Pat answered.

"Listen, there's a truck coming now," Joe said.

As the truck rumbled by, Joe wedged the crowbar into the side crack of the door and pulled back hard on it. The wood split lengthwise, and the lock broke. Then the four of them went inside.

"Boy, it's dark in here," Mike said.

"You brought a flashlight, didn't you?" Joe asked.

"No, but I brought some candles," Mike said, reaching into his pocket. "And I brought cardboard squares to hold the candles. You stick the end of the candles through the hole so the hot wax won't burn your hand."

Then Pat took one of the candles and handed the rest to the others. They lit the candles, and he said, "The church office is inside on the right, and the money should be in there. You and Joe look around in the office, and Dan and I will go to the main part of the church."

Pat and Dan went along the hallway that led to the sanctuary. Inside, they could barely make out the rows of pews, but they could see dimly the large gold candlesticks high up on the church altar.

"Let's get them!" Pat said. So they climbed over the altar rail, and reaching up high, they each took one.

"Boy, they're heavy," Dan said.

"We should get a good price for these," Pat said. He added, "Let's go back to the church office and see if those guys have found the money."

They walked fast along the dark hallway that led to the office, shielding their lighted candles.

As they entered the office, they saw papers all over the floor as Joe and Mike busily rifled through the drawers of the desk. Pat and Dan put their candles on the windowsill, and Pat suggested that they try opening the drawers in the wall cabinet.

"They're locked," Joe said.

"Well, use your crowbar."

Joe went over and pried open the top drawer. Pat, looking in, suddenly shouted, "There are the collection plates, and the money is still in them."

"Let's put the money into this bag," Joe said.

"No, let's count it out and divide it up first," Pat suggested.

Suddenly, there was a swooshing sound behind them. Looking back, Dan cried out, "The window curtain is on fire!"

"You stupid dopes," Mike shouted in disgust, "you left the candles on the sill!"

"Look what you've done!" Joe said.

Dan picked up a small rug off the floor and tried to smother the flames. As he swung at the fire with the rug, there was another sound behind them.

"Oh no, the other curtain has burst into flames," Pat shouted.

The fire began spreading up the walls and down to the papers on the floor.

Joe grabbed the money out of the drawer and stuffed it in the bag and yelled, "Let's get out of here!"

The four of them dashed out the back door as the fire spread. They ran across the field behind the church and into the woods.

Chapter 93

THE MITCHELLS' HOUSE was two blocks away from the church on Main Street. Late that night, Anne Mitchell was awakened by a strange light shining through the window. She got up and was surprise to see that the night sky outside had turned bright red.

"It must be a big fire," Anne said to herself and then rushed to her son's bedroom.

"Get up, Georgie! There's a fire on Main Street!"

"Fire," he said sleepily.

"Come look out the window."

He got up and looked for himself. "It might be the church!" he said.

"How can you tell?"

"It's the tallest building on the street."

"I hope not! You know that Cousin Minnie lives right across from the church."

"Look, Mom, you'll have to call the fire chief and tell him to phone the volunteers if they are not there already. I have to get there fast myself," he said as he put on his clothes and rushed down the stairs.

"Don't go into the burning building," Anne shouted after him.

"Mom, I'm a volunteer fireman! I have to go in! That's what firemen do!"

"Don't go in!"

She heard the back door slam closed and the car starting up. Then she hurried to the phone and dialed the fire emergency number. She soon learned that other townspeople had seen the flames and had called in and that the firemen were on their way.

Then Anne called her cousin Minnie, who answered the phone immediately. "Anne, it's awful! The church is on fire."

"I know. Some noise woke me, and then I saw the red in the sky. It's not threatening your house, is it?" Anne asked.

"No, it hasn't crossed Main Street yet, but the church is ablaze."

"I wonder how it ever got started," Anne asked.

"I'm not sure, but I saw four boys running into the woods behind the church right after the fire began."

"You'll have to tell the police about those boys."

"I will when I get a chance," Minnie said, her voice cracking.

"Are you crying?" Anne asked.

"Yes. It's so sad to see the church burning."

"Be calm, dear. Don't watch it."

And they hung up.

The Town and the Troublesome Strangers, 1880-1980

Georgie Mitchell and Bill Patterson were among the first to get there. But soon, the other volunteer firemen began arriving. Not long afterward, the Northfield fire engine pulled up with the siren blaring. The fire chief jumped out of the truck and began giving orders.

Georgie and Bill got axes out of the back of the truck and raced up to the front door. They broke it down, and the other men followed them into the church.

"This is one fire we have to put out," Bill said.

"The smoke in here is so thick, it is hard to see anything," Georgie said.

One of the men with them said, "All the pew cushions are burning—and the hymnbooks too."

"Look over there. The fire is spreading up the wall to the balcony and will soon reach up to the steeple."

"We have to get the hoses in here," Bill said anxiously.

The chief, who was at the door, called to the others, "There's not enough water pressure in the hydrant. We hooked up the hoses, but there is only a trickle of water coming out. Without water, this is hopeless. You guys have to get out of the church. It is too dangerous for you to be in here now. There is nothing we can do."

"Isn't there anything we can save?" Bill asked, trying to peer through the dense smoke around the altar.

Georgie moved back toward the door with the other men. They were all coughing and rubbing their eyes.

"Come on, Bill, we can't save anything. You will get hurt," Georgie said.

But Bill waited a few minutes after the others had left to take a last look. Then the heat of the fire became unbearable, and he reluctantly left.

The townspeople had begun to gather out front to watch the fire. Some had thrown their coats over their pajamas. Some had shoved their bare feet into boots before they rushed to the scene. They stood in groups, looking up at the burning church. As the fire became intense, glass started bursting out of the windows. Soon, the church became a mass of flames, blazing and crackling, with sparks shooting into the sky.

Georgie walked up to the chief and asked, "How do you think the fire got started?"

"We don't know yet."

Then Georgie felt someone pulling on his shoulder. He turned around and said in surprise, "Cousin Minnie, you shouldn't be out here."

"I came to tell the fire chief that I saw four boys running away. They ran across the field into the woods. That was the same time the fire started."

"Four boys—what boys!" asked the chief, who had overheard her.

"I couldn't see who they were," Minnie said, pulling her old coat around her tightly.

"I have a good idea who they were. But I won't say anything until I have proof," Bill said.

"Why would anyone want to burn down a church?" Minnie asked.

"There are some kids in this town that might do it, and that crowd of youngsters that are living in the old hostel house are kind of wild," Bill said angrily.

The Town and the Troublesome Strangers, 1880-1980

The chief answered, "There are always some bad kids in any town, but there are a lot of good kids with decent parents in Northfield."

Then they all stood there and watched the church burn to the ground.

The next morning, Bill and Georgie and some of the firemen joined the chief of police at the town hall and laid out a plan to catch whoever had started the fire.

Soon, Pat and Dan Wilson were arrested as they were seen trying to get out of town that afternoon. They were taken to the Franklin County Jail in Orange and put behind bars. On the way, they told the police that Joe and Mike, from the commune, were in on it. When the police went to the commune to arrest them, they were told they had left. They had wanted to go back to Brooklyn, where they came from.

In less than a week, Bill Patterson was able to tell the town that money was already being donated to build a new church.

Chapter 94

FOR DAYS, PEOPLE talked about the fire that had destroyed the ninety-year-old church. And when they heard that the Wilson brothers were partly responsible, some of the old-timers shook their heads knowingly. Others whispered that they had heard there was also a connection between the fire and the commune.

A few nights later, in the living room of the commune, Joan Brownell was very distraught and complained loudly to everyone who would listen that a mistake had been made. She told them that Pat, Dan, Mike, and Joey were all innocent. "They didn't do it! They didn't start the fire," she insisted.

"The police think they did," one of the girls said to her.

"Oh, I hate the police. They just listen to the old people in this town—the ones that have never liked us from the beginning," Joan replied.

"I was told that somebody saw all four boys running away from the church after the fire started," another girl mentioned.

"I heard that too," the first girl said.

"I know who made that up! It was that old half-blind, snoopy neighbor—Minnie Johnson—that lives across from the church. She said it," Joan said accusingly.

"The police believed her."

"It was pitch-dark. How could she see anything? If the police trust her, they are as stupid as she is!" Joan continued angrily.

"I give up!" one of the girls said and changed the subject. "When is the Indian chief getting here to give his speech?"

"Very soon, now," Joan replied, having lightened her tone. "My granddad, Andrew Brownell, is bringing him over. They have been friends for years."

"What is he going to talk about?"

"The chief always talks about peace making."

In a little while, Andrew arrived with the chief.

"Do any of the people in the Mohawk National remember me?" Andrew asked as they entered the main room.

"Yes, they talk about you often. You were learning our language and helping them in the fields."

"I had a good summer there," Andrew said. Then pointing ahead, he remarked, "Look, the youngsters are filling up the room. And there are some older townspeople here too."

Most of the people sat on the floor. The chief and Andrew went and stood by the fireplace.

Andrew introduced the chief, who was tall with black hair and broad shoulders. He wore a gray shirt with a wide ribbon across his chest that was covered with colorful Indian symbols. He had on black trousers, and he wore moccasins.

"This is my friend from Akwesasne," Andrew said. "He is a Mohawk chief and is the spiritual leader for the Mohawk Nation. He is an advocate for world peace and for environmental conscientiousness. So I know you will welcome him and be interested in what he has to say."

The people clapped, and some whistled.

Then the chief started to speak. "I have been told that a Tree of Peace was planted here—"

Suddenly, there was a loud noise and a commotion in the back of the room, near the door. Two of the rock-band members had just come in. They sat down on the floor with the others, who shouted greetings to them and began talking to them, completely ignoring the chief. One of the commune young men asked them, "How do you like living in the new commune in Gill?"

"Fine, it was about time we got another commune going. It's working out great!" he said.

Andrew, now sitting in a chair in the front, called out loudly, "Quiet back there! Let our Indian friend speak."

Chapter 95

THE INDIAN BEGAN to talk again, and the crowd turned and paid attention to him.

"I have been told that a 'Tree of Peace' was planted here behind this building years ago. I know about 'Trees of Peace.' Over a thousand years ago, a Peace Tree was planted in the Iroquois Nation. It was the action of a Great Peacemaker who appeared among the native people of the Iroquois Tribe. Some of those people still live in Upstate New York. The Peacemaker I speak of appeared during a dark age in the history of the Iroquois. Some people of the tribe had become violent and destructive. From the Great Lakes region, the Peacemaker appeared and urged the people to stop abusing one another. He told them that human beings are capable of reason, and through the power of reason, everyone desires peace. He inspired the warriors to bury their weapons, and on top of the weapons, they planted a sacred Tree of Peace."*

One of the newer members of the commune called out, "Who planted the Peace Tree we have here?"

The chief didn't answer, but Andrew got to his feet. "I had better answer that question. I don't believe that the chief knows much about the early days, in the 1930s and 1940s when the First American Youth Hostel was here. The founders from New York City were looking for a good spot for the first hostel, and they picked Northfield. They realized that the town was a gateway to White Mountains and was away from the more densely populated parts of southern New England. Northfield was well suited to be the headquarters of the AYH, which promoted recreational pursuits for bikers, hikers, and mountain climbers. Gradually, a chain of hostels was established . . . each providing a place to sleep for the young travelers. Farmers' barns were often used."

"Yeah, we know all that!" shouted one of the boys in the front, but Andrew kept talking.

"In 1936, a German named Richard Schireman came to the United States and was invited to be present at the initial dedication of the Northfield youth hostel. Some wanted it to be named after Richard, the founder and originator of the youth hostels in Germany. It would be called the Richard Schireman International Youth Hostel. However, he preferred that it be called the International Youth Hostel. Later, however, the financial supporters in New York City determined that it would be named the American Youth Hostel.

"When Richard was here, he asked if he could plant a tree in honor of the dedication. A hole was dug, and a tree was brought in by truck and planted by two sturdy nursery men. I remember that Richard spoke entirely in German to the large group of hostelers and friends of hosteling who were here. Photographers and newspaper reporters came also. When his message was translated, it was a simple and sincere one. Its meaning was that 'as the tree grows, youthful friendships will grow—that can make the world one kinship."**

The chief ended his talk by saying that the Mohawk tribes invite people to their campgrounds to share in their Peace Tree–planting ceremonies and to listen to the stories about the Great Peacemaker. It is a story that tells of burying old bad feelings, thoughts, and ways. The chief's last words were "Remember, the Indian is as strong as water and as flexible as the wind."**

As the chief finished, many crowded around him and asked questions. Andrew called out to his granddaughter, Joan, and beckoned for her to come over to him. But she shouted back, "No, I have to see someone! It's important!"

Chapter 96

JOAN WENT OVER to where two of the band members were standing and talking to some friends. She interrupted them and took hold of the arm of one of them and said anxiously, "Come outside with me. I want to talk to you."

"What's this all about?" he asked, stepping back in an annoyed way.

"Please come out with me," she pleaded.

He reluctantly followed her out the door to the driveway.

"Let's get in the truck," Joan suggested.

"No, say what you want to say to me right here and get it over with."

"Why did you start that new commune in Gill and leave me here in Northfield?"

"I didn't leave you! You stayed here!"

"You left me. You made me look like a fool after all the time we have spent together!"

"As I remember it, the times we spent together recently were always your idea! Anyway, I heard you were running around with one of the Wilson boys."

"He was just a friend."

"That's not what I heard!"

"Anyway, he's in jail now. It's awful! Some people are saying Pat and Dan Wilson and also Joe and Mike from the commune were the ones that burned down the church. I still don't believe it was them."

"Well, when the police came looking for Joe and Mike here, those two were long gone. So that was the end of that."

"Pat and Dan were forced to steal money from the church because you were hustling them to pay a debt they owed you."

"You don't know what you're talking about!" he said and started walking toward his truck.

"Don't turn away from me!" Joan shouted. "I still say you shouldn't have left me here when you moved to the new commune. You took some other people from here with you."

"Calm down, will you? All I care about now is making money with the band. We got the down payment for the house in Gill with band money, and now we need more to keep going."

"Just a minute!" Joan said. "Speaking of money . . . how about all the money I gave you ten years ago, when I first joined the commune? I begged that money off my parents and my grandfather."

He looked straight at her and said angrily, "You knew from the start that if anyone wanted to join up, they had to put in as much money as they could get their hands on, and the leaders would use it as it was needed."

"But I gave you much more money than the others did! Don't you remember?"

He groaned impatiently and mumbled, "Whatever you say."

"Also, before you left Northfield, you were mean to me. You treated me as if you disliked me, resented me, and despised me!"

"Whatever you say."

"The others told me that you called me a drug addict and a drinker behind my back. You made me look bad. That was terrible of you! Don't forget, I have seen you high on drugs and booze plenty of times! So why point a finger at me?"

"Whatever you say."

"Don't repeat that over and over," Joan said. "I remember when you decided it was over between us, you would turn away from me when I would try to give you a pat on the shoulder. You would pull back and say, 'That hurts.' It seemed like you couldn't stand me."

"Are you through?" he snapped back at her. "For years, you have tried to boss me around and in front of the others. 'Do this, do that'—it became unbearable, and you were always screaming about the money you put in. Then you started fooling around with those town boys."

"I didn't fool around."

"And another thing, do you know how ugly you look when you get mad like this? Now leave me alone!"

He went over to his truck and got in. Then he honked the horn three times to let his band friend know he wanted to leave. He soon came out and quickly climbed into the truck, saying cheerfully, "I got a picture taken of that Indian chief and me. That will be good publicity for the band."

"Sure," the other muttered as he started the motor and began to back up the truck.

Joan ran up to bang on the door with her fist, but she was too late. He quickly turned onto Main Street and headed toward the highway that crossed the bridge that spanned the Connecticut River and continued on toward the new commune in Gill.

Chapter 97

JOAN BURST INTO tears as she watched them drive away. Then she turned and went into the house by the kitchen door.

A girl stopped her. "Why don't you go back into the main room with the others? They are having a good time in there."

"No, not now! I'll just go upstairs," she said as she started to climb up the narrow, curving back stairway to the third floor.

Her tiny bedroom was at the far end of the hall, under the eaves. When she got there, she realized that the room was very cold, so she plugged in the small electric heater that was by the wall.

Then Joan remembered she had a bottle of wine under the bed. She got it out and took a long swig from it. After that, she lay down on the bed and tried to sleep; but she couldn't, and she began to cry again.

The noise coming from downstairs went on until late that night. Finally, the loud noise stopped, and she heard a scrambling sound as the people climbed the stairs to the bedrooms.

Then Joan noticed a small pile of laundry on the floor in the corner of the room. She picked it up and went out into the hall and walked to the small bathroom at the far end. There she washed the things out in the sink, using cold water and a piece of white soap that somebody had left there. Returning with the wet laundry to her room, she decided that the best way to dry the laundry was to put it on top of the electric heater, which she did. Then she lay down and fell asleep.

It took a while for the laundry to dry enough to catch fire, but when it did, the flames spread quickly.

Joan woke up with a feeling of heat on her face. Seeing half the room ablaze, she jumped out of bed and raced out into the hall, screaming, "Fire! Fire!"

Chapter 98

MOST OF THE people in the house were awakened by Joan's screams. Seeing the flames on the third floor, they fled downstairs and escaped to the outside. There they stood in the darkness—dumbfounded, looking up at the house in disbelief. They could see fire inside the upper-floor windows.

By the time the first fire engine arrived, the attic was ablaze, and the fire was burning through parts of the roof. A call for help went out to neighboring towns. Within two hours, there were eighty firemen from eleven communities fighting the stubborn blaze, which kept rekindling itself through the night. Their efforts were hampered by the lack of water pressure from the hydrants, so the fire chief ordered water brought in by tankers.**

At daybreak, many of the townspeople had come to see what was left of the house. Bill Patterson stood talking to the Northfield fire chief, who was still directing his men to put out hot spots. "You wouldn't think that we would have another big fire this soon after the church burned."

"No, that's never happened here before," the chief answered, shaking his head.

"Of course, everybody in the house got out, didn't they?" Bill asked.

"Yes, we figured there were forty people living in there. They were driven out fast by the smoke and flames. I went inside myself to make sure. I found a couple upstairs still asleep, oblivious to what was going on, and we evacuated them quickly."

"Do you know how it started?"

"One of the young women said they thought it started when somebody left clothes on an electric heater, but she wasn't sure."

Georgie Mitchell, who had been fighting the fire with the other volunteers most of the night, came up to Bill and the chief. "The second and third floors are burned out," he announced.

"Did Andrew Brownell's granddaughter get out all right?" Bill asked Georgie.

"Yes, I saw her. She and some others were piling into the back of a truck, and I was told that they were heading for the new commune in Gill. But just as they started up, someone pushed Joan out of the truck, and they drove off without her. I tried to go over to help her, but she was crying and screaming 'No! No! No!' And she was saying 'I've given years of my life to them. How can they just dump me? How can they ride off and leave me here alone? I was one of the ones that kept it all going.'"

"She said all that?" Bill asked.

"She's still over there by a tree now. I'm keeping an eye on her."

There was an article about the fire in the *Greenfield Record* of March 2, 1978:

> Northfield—a fire, reportedly caused by an electrical heater, heavily damaged the Commune House, 88 Main Street, Northfield, Wednesday night. More than 40 people were driven from the historic three-story wooden structure, which gained distinction as "America's First Youth Hostel." Also, it was Northfield's first Post Office and home of the eighteenth-century Yankee musician Timothy Swan, considered one of America's finest early composers. The fire chief reported that the firefighters attacked the blaze but were forced back many times. They used large hoses and ladders and pumped water from the large tanker into the attic area. There were double ceilings, dead air spaces, and nooks and crannies that had to be gotten into. The firemen continued to pump water into the structure through the night and into the next day.

Later that morning, Anne Mitchell and her cousin, Minnie Johnson, hurried down Main Street to see what was left of the two-century-old house.

Anne told Minnie, "That was Solomon Vose's house, built in 1795. He was the son of General Vose of Revolutionary War fame and a classmate of John Adams at Harvard. Solomon Vose was the first postmaster of Northfield."

"Look, there's Georgie. He is helping with the cleanup."

"My boy is always there when there is something that is needed to be done."

Chapter 99

AS THEY LOOKED up at what was left of the burned-out house, Anne said, "I can't believe it. This was one of Northfield's finest old homesteads."

"Well, you can blame those commune people that lived there and their careless ways for what happened. Ever since they moved in, I knew something would go wrong and they would leave."

"They stayed ten years!" Anne said. "Now, many of them are over in Gill."

"Mark my words, they'll be thinning out over there too. That kind of loose, undisciplined living never lasts."

"Well, I guess I have to agree with you. But you know, Minnie, it takes all kinds to make up the world," Anne said and changed the subject. "Bill Patterson told me some news when I saw him. He said they have some money donated already to rebuild the church, and more money is promised."

"That's good to hear," Minnie said.

"As I think back, we have had our share of strangers that come and go."

"That's what I've been telling you."

Anne continued, "First, there were the summer-conference people who came around 1890 and returned year after year until the late 1930s. They were the ones that built the summer cottages on Rustic Ridge. Then the youth-hostel people came, who were bikers and hikers, and who had international ideas and leanings. Then the commune people arrived with their objections to the staid ideas of the older generation and their aversion to the Vietnam War."

Suddenly, they saw Joan Brownell sitting alone under a tree, and they could hear her repeating over and over again, "No! No! No!"

Chapter 100

JOAN SAW GEORGIE'S mother and Minnie Johnson staring at her, so she wiped the tears off her face and stood up. Then, being sure to avoid them, she hurried out to the sidewalk and began running in the direction of Pine Street. Georgie saw her and started chasing after her.

She finally slowed down, and he caught up to her.

"What do you want?" Joan asked him abruptly.

"Nothing . . . are you going back to your grandfather's?"

"I suppose so . . . now go away!"

"Yeah, I know, but—"

"All my so-called friends from the commune have deserted me. They think I started the fire—"

"You did, didn't you?"

"Leave me alone, will you?" she screamed at him and walked faster.

He stayed close behind her, and neither of them said anything for a while.

Approaching the house on Pine Street, they saw the Indian chief standing by the front doorsteps.

"Where's Grandfather?" Joan asked.

"He's in the good hunting ground."

Georgie pushed past her and shouted, "What did you say?"

"He died in his sleep last night. The undertaker took him away. I will leave now." And he went off.

Georgie looked at Joan and saw the stricken stare on her face, and he moved toward her. "You come home with me now. My mother likes you and will help you."

Joan slowly went up the steps and opened the front door. "No," she said. "I feel so bad, but I'll stay here by myself. It's my house now."

"Do you want me to come in with you?"

"No," she said loudly. And then she added, "No, not now. But I've gotten so used to you following me around town all these years, I guess you can come over in a few days."

There was a burial service for Andrew Brownell at the old cemetery, at the foot of Parker Street by the river. Georgie stood at the back during the service.

Two months later, Georgie was able to arrange with the Northfield School for Joan to become one of the history professors.

After that, as was his usual way, Georgie continued to tag around after her.

The End

Acknowledgments

I WOULD LIKE to express my gratitude to the staff at Xlibris Corporation, for their assistance in getting this work published.

I want to thank my daughters—to whom I have dedicated this book—for their encouragement during the twelve years I have worked on this historical saga spanning one hundred years.

Also, my sincere gratitude goes to Michael Nagel, who tirelessly typed the book and often made constructive suggestions to improve it.

Mary Helen Neuendorffer

Sources and Notes

Chapter 1   Moody, Paul. My Father. Little, Brown and Company. 1938.
Philbrick, Nathaniel. *Mayflower*. Penguin Group, USA. 2006.
Kidder, Tracy. *House*. Mariner Books. 1999.
Chapter 2   Mabie, Janet. Heaven on Earth. Harper and Brother. 1951.
Pollen, Dorothy. *Rivertown Review*. Published by The Tricentarian Committee. 1973.
Chapter 3   Fèrre, Maria; Ross, Susan and Stora, Joan. Northfield. Arcadia Publishing. 2014.
Moore, Helen Peck. *A Shepherd's Heart*. Livingston Publishing Co, Narberth PA. 1957.
Chapter 4   Ibid.

Chapter 5   Moore, Helen Peck. A Shepherd's Heart. Livingston Publishing Co, Narberth PA. 1957.
Mabie, Janet. *Heaven on Earth.* Harper and Brother. 1951.
Chapter 6   Friends of Dickenson Memorial Library, Northfield MA. Our Town. Published by the town. 2002.
Chapter 7   Ibid.
Chapter 8   Moore, Helen Peck. A Shepherd's Heart. Livingston Publishing Co, Narberth PA. 1957.
Chapter 9   Mabie, Janet. Heaven on Earth. Harper and Brother. 1951.
Chapter 10 Ibid.
Chapter 11 Ibid.
Chapter 12 Ibid.
Chapter 13 Morrow, William. Ala-rah, Ala-rah. Northfield Mount Herman School, 1988.
Chapter 14 Moore, Helen Peck. A Shepherd's Heart. Livingston Publishing Company. Narberth PA. 1957.
Chapter 15 Moore, Helen Peck. A Shepherd's Heart. Livingston Publishing Company. Narberth PA. 1957.
Chapter 16 Ibid.
Chapter 17 Ibid.
Chapter 18 Ibid.
Chapter 19 Ibid.

Chapter 20 Stansell, Christine. American Moderns. Henry Holt and Company. 2000.
Chapter 21 Ibid.
Chapter 22 Ibid.
Chapter 23 Morris, Edmund. Colonel Roosevelt. Random House. 1918.
Chapter 24 Ibid.
Chapter 25 Morris, Edmund. Colonel Roosevelt. Random House. 1918.
Chapter 26 Ibid.
Chapter 27 Pollen, Dorothy. Rivertown Review. Published by The Tricentarian Committee. 1973.
Chapter 28 Hansen, Arlen. American Ambulance Drivers. Arcade Publishing. 2011
Chapter 29 Gurd, Fraser N. The Gurds. The General Store Publishing House. 1996
Morris, Edmund. *Colonel Roosevelt*. Random House. 1918.
Chapter 30 Gurd, Fraser N. The Gurds. The General Store Publishing House. 1996
Chapter 31 Ibid.
Chapter 32 Lash, Joseph. Eleanor and Franklin. W. W. Norton. 1971
Chapter 33 Ibid.
Chapter 34 Perkins, Frances. The Roosevelt I knew. Viking Press. 1946
Stansell, Christine. *American Moderns*. Henry Holt & Co. 2000

Chapter 35   Moore, Helen Peck. A Shepherd's Heart. Livingston Publishing. Narberth, PA. 1957
Chapter 36   Ibid.
Chapter 37   Ibid.
Chapter 38   Ibid.
Chapter 39   Perkins, Frances. The Roosevelt I knew. Viking Press. 1946
Chapter 40   Ibid.
Chapter 41   Hapgood, Beth. 88 Main Street. One World Fellowship. Greenfield, MA. 1989
Chapter 42   Perkins, Frances. The Roosevelt I knew. Viking Press. 1946
Chapter 43   Alsop, Joseph. FDR 1882–1945. Viking Press. 1982
Chapter 44   Ibid.
Chapter 45   Ferré, Ross, Stoia. Northfield. Arcadia Publishing. 2014
Chapter 46   Ibid.
Chapter 47   Hamilton, Sally. Lift Thine Eyes. Northfield Mount Herman Publishers. 1996
Chapter 48   Ibid.
Chapter 49   Shirer, William. The Rise and Fall of the Third Reich. Simon and Schuster. 1960.
Chapter 50   From Youth Hosteler's Diary of Bicycle Trip through Germany. 06-1939/08-1939
Chapter 51   Ardagh, Evans, etc. Fodor's Exploring Germany. Random House. 2002

Chapter 52 Hunt, Ivory, etc. Fodor's Exploring Germany. Random House 2002
Chapter 53 Kallanbach, Locke, Locke, etc. Fodor's Exploring Germany. Random House 2002
Chapter 54 Colin, Speakman. Fodor's Exploring Germany. Random House. 2002
Chapter 55 Pagel, Horne, Tilley. Fodor's Exploring Germany. Random House. 2002.
Chapter 56 Ferré, Ross, Stoia. Northfield. Arcadia Publishing. 2014
Chapter 57 Alsop, Joseph. FDR 1882-1945. Viking Press. 1982
Chapter 58 Moore, Helen Peck. A Shepherd's Heart. Livingston Publishing. Narberth, PA. 1957
Chapter 59 Alsop, Joseph. FDR 1882-1945. Viking Press. 1982
Chapter 60 Ferré, Ross, Stoia. Northfield. Arcadia Publishing. 2014
Chapter 61 Friends of Dickinson Memorial Library. Our Town. Published by the town. Northfield, MA. 2002
Chapter 62 Ibid.
Chapter 63 Ibid.
Chapter 64 Alsop, Joseph. FDR 1882-1945. Viking Press. 1982
Chapter 65 Ibid.

Chapter 66 Alsop, Joseph. FDR 1882-1945. Viking Press. 1982
Chapter 67 Ibid.
Chapter 68 Hapgood, Beth. 88 Main Street. One World Fellowship. Greenfield, MA. 1989
Chapter 69 Ibid.
Chapter 70 Ibid.
Chapter 71 Moley, Raymond. The First New Deal. Harcourt, Brace, & World. 1933
Chapter 72 Ibid.
Chapter 73 Bradley, James with Powers, Ron. Flags of Our Fathers. Bantam Books, 2000
Chapter 74 Shirer, William L. The Rise and Fall of the Third Reich. Simon & Schuster. 1960
Chapter 75 Bradley, James with Powers, Ron. Flags of Our Fathers. Bantam Books, 2000
Chapter 76 Ibid.
Chapter 77 Ibid.
Chapter 78 Ibid.
Chapter 79 Ibid.
Chapter 80 Ibid.
Chapter 81 Ibid.
Chapter 82 Hapgood, Beth. 88 Main Street. One World Fellowship. Greenfield, MA. 1989
Chapter 83 Ibid.
Chapter 84 DeBenedetti, Charles/Chalfield, Charles. An American Ordeal. Syracuse University Press. 1990

Chapter 85　DeBenedetti, Charles/Chalfield, Charles. An American Ordeal. Syracuse University Press. 1990

Chapter 86　Manchester, William. The Death of a President. Harper Row. 1967
　　　　　　Bohlen, Charles E. *Witness to History.* W. W. Norton and Co. 1973

Chapter 87　Hapgood, Beth. 88 Main Street. One World Fellowship. Greenfield, MA. 1989

Chapter 88　Town Meeting

Chapter 89　DeBenedetti, Charles/Chalfield, Charles. An American Ordeal. Syracuse University Press. 1990

Chapter 90　Ibid.

Chapter 91　Shavelson, Lonny. Hooked. The New Press NY, 2001 PP20-21
　　　　　　Ketcham, Katherine/Pace, Nicholas. *Teens Under the Influence.* Random House. 2003

Chapter 92　Ibid.

Chapter 93　Ferré, Ross, Stoia. Northfield. Arcadia Publishing. 2014

Chapter 94　Hapgood, Beth. 88 Main Street. One World Fellowship. Greenfield, MA. 1989

Chapter 95　Ibid.

Chapter 96　Ibid.

Chapter 97　Ibid.

Chapter 98　Greenfield MA Recorder Newspaper, Commune House Fire. March 2, 1978

Hapgood, Beth. *88 Main Street.* One World Fellowship. Greenfield, MA. 1989

Chapter 99　Ibid.

Chapter 100　Northfield School. A New History Professor. 1980.

Index

Bowman, Albert; president of the Northfield Grange, respected town father

Bradford, Bob; Dave Hall's good friend from prep school. Bob becomes an ensign in the navy. Dave enlists in the marines as a private. They meet on leave in New York City

Brownell, Andrew; Elderly, lifelong resident of Northfield—a liberal thinker, never had much money. His granddaughter, Joan Brownell, moves in to the first commune.

Brownell, Joan; A Northfield girl from birth; in her teens she begins to like the free ideas of her contemporaries in the '60s and '70s. Her grandfather makes no objection to this. She helps to establish the second commune in the old youth-hostel house in Northfield. She ignores Georgie Mitchell, a Northfield boy who has always followed her around.

Conference Attendance

Conference Begins;

Congregational Church, Corona, Long Island, NY

Corona, Long Island, NY, Detective's Surveillance

Clavir, Aaron; counselor at camp, antiwar activist

Crawford, James; fourth-generation farmer on the Crawford land in Northfield

Crawford, Marie; wife to James Crawford

Donkey Baseball Game

Drivers; 7

First Commune Established

Ford, Jenny; Cousin of Diane Thompson, lives with the Thompsons

Ford, Kathy; Sister of Jenny Ford, she is a summer camp counselor. Her boyfriend at the camp is Mark Stewart; they visit the old youth-hostel house in Northfield

Ford, William; Bachelor minister of the Congregational Church in Corona, Long Island, NY; he later marries Grace White. They are summer residents of Northfield, MA, where he could rest from the church's financial problems and parishioners' sad troubles, he marries his daughter, Helen, to Bob Thompson

Forest Lake Camp

Fort Lauderdale, FL

Fuller, Nat; Bob Thompson's army friend, served in World War I together

Gibbs, Ruth; Sarah Nelson's sister

Hall, Mabel; New immigrant worker at the East Side settlement house

Hall, Martin; Young social worker at the settlement house; marries Mabel, new immigrant. Martin later becomes hospital manager in New York City, then he is promoted to a government position in Washington, DC. Divorces Mabel, who moves to Northfield with their two sons, Tom and Dave

Hall, Dave; son of Martin and Mabel Hall, grows up in Northfield, attends prep school in Pennsylvania, joins US Marine Corps in 1943, Battle of Kwajalein

Hall, Tom; son of Martin and Mabel Hall, grows up in Northfield, plans 'get-togethers' for the teenagers

Heron, Chief (Indian Chief); friend of Andrew Brownell, chief of tribe in Akwesasne, comes to talk to commune members in Northfield

Higgins, Chuck; discouraged teenager from poor family in Northfield

Higgins, Mrs.; Poverty-stricken mother of Chuck Higgins

Hospital, Bellevue

Hunt, Barbara; Wife of Daniel Hunt, hostess

Hunt, Daniel; Wealthy businessman, friend of Martin Hall

International Dinner at Settlement House, NYC

Johnson, Minnie; Older woman, cousin of Anne Mitchell, objects to changes in Northfield

Jones, Al; Medical corpsman with marines at Kwajalein, makes friends with Bill Patterson and Dave Hall before the battle,

Kirschheimer, Fritz; New immigrant from Germany, gets assistant job at American youth hostel in Northfield, leads summer 1939 bike trip through Germany

Kirschheimer, Otto; Foreman of construction job in Northfield, Pro Shop manager, later farmer and weaver

Kwajalein Island, Battle, WWII

Levering, Charles; Important member of the Corona, Long Island, NY, church, president of a bank in New York City, marries Clara Lovett

Lewis, Mrs.; Friend of Mrs. Winters who has come to her to get away from abusive husband

Lieberman, Nat; Friend of Dave Hall's father, entertains Dave in NYC during preschool vacation

Lieberman, Sylvia; Wife of Nat Lieberman

Lovett, Clara; Rents a room in her house in Corona to Rev. Wm. Ford. She is a church member, and she also attends Northfield summer conferences with her daughter, Liza. Later married Charles Levering

Lovett, Liza; Daughter of Clara Lovett, is a nurse in France during WWI. Later works at Bellevue Hospital, NYC, then marries Boris Melikof

Ludlow, Barbara; Bob Bradford's girlfriend. She and Bob meet Dave and Diane in NYC.

Marines Third Battalion, Fourth Division, leaves San Diego, CA, for war in Pacific

Mayflower Hotel, Washington, DC, 1943

Melikof, Boris; Manager of the East Side settlement house in NYC, earlier lived in Corona, friend of Wm. Ford, later moves permanently to settlement house in NYC, eventually married Liza Lovett

Men's Camp, Northfield Conference

Mitchell, Anne; Well-respected matron in Northfield, mother of Georgie Mitchell, who is friends with Dave Hall and Joan Brownell

Mitchell, Georgie; Son of Anne Mitchell, best friend of Dave Hall, likes Joan Brownell

Moody, Dwight; Famous evangelist, founder of Northfield Mount Herman School and summer conferences

Thompson, Bob; Son of E. B. Thompson, enlists in Army Medical Corps in 1917, sent to France, on return works at Bellevue Hospital Mental Ward. Married Helen Ford, whom he met in summers in Northfield. Works for his father in a textile mill in Philadelphia and later has daughter, Diane Thompson

Thompson, Diane; Daughter of Bob and Helen Thompson, falls in love with Dave Hall, Mabel Hall's son, during summer vacations in Northfield. Attends his prep-school dance weekend in PA

Thompson, E. B.; Wealthy manufacturer, owns textile factory in Philadelphia. Father of Bob Thompson, takes family to Northfield each summer

Thompson, Georgina; Wife of E. B. Thompson, mother of Bob Thompson

Thompson, Helen Ford; Daughter of Wm Jay Ford and Grace White Ford; meets Bob Thompson in Northfield,

MA. They marry after WWI; they have daughter named Diane

Murphy, Patrolman; Corona, Long Island, NY, police officer who joins Detectives Reily and O'Toole to try to catch a "Black Hand" criminal. Murphy later becomes Mr. Levering's chauffeur

Nelson, Ernest; Northfield farmer, James Crawford's cousin**Nelson, Sarah**; Ernest Nelson's wife

Newberg, Carl; Brother of Dick Newberg, takes an AYH trip to Germany in the summer of 1939 with his brother and friend, Hank Snyder and others, Fritz Kirschheimer is leader of the group

Newberg, Dick; Brother of Carl Newberg, from Tarrytown, NY. He took many bike trips through New England at a young age, starting in Northfield. Took trip to Germany with brother and others led by Fritz K. in 1939. Entered United States Naval Academy in 1941—Lt. USN battleship in WW2. Returns and marries Diane Thompson, whom he met in Northfield

Northfield, Château Dance, 1938

Northfield, Commune House burns

Northfield, MA, Historic farming town

Northfield, Robbery and fire at church

Northfield School, New Director of Admissions

Northfield, Summer cottages

Northfield, Town Hall meeting

Northfield, Winter sports

O'Toole, Detective; employed by Peterson Agency

Palladium Dance Hall, Los Angeles, CA

Patterson, Bill; Bill and Dave Hall, old friends from Northfield, meet unexpectedly at Camp Pendleton in California; both are marines. They enjoy one evening at the Palladium Dance Hall. They are both sent to the Pacific, and they fight side by side on Kwajalein Island. WW2 ends, later Bill works at the bank on Main Street in Northfield and keeps an eye on the anti-Vietnam War hippies that start showing up

Peterson, John; Owner of Peterson Detective Agency in NYC, also has summer home in Northfield, told that Wm. Ford receives threatening letter from "Black Hand" mob. Wm meets Peterson and Levering at bank in New York City

Potter, Ben; Son of Zeke Potter

Potter, Rob; Son of Zeke Potter

Potter, Zeke; Town employee, leader of three-man band that plays at the Grange Hall square dances

Reily, Detective; Employee of Peterson Detective Agency

Rogers, Frank; Man at Washington, DC, hotel bar, seated near Dave Hall and Bob Bradford. The man talks against the war, Dave takes objection to what the man is saying and attacks him. Dave's friend talks the authorities into letting Dave go

Saunders (Chauffeur); John Peterson's chauffeur

Smith, Fatty; Lives near settlement house in NYC, knows Boris Melikof

Snyder, Hank; Friend of Dick and Carl Newberg from Tarrytown, NY, who takes trip to Germany with them in the summer of 1939

SS *Bremen*, Transportation between US and Germany, 1939

Stewart, Mark; Counselor at camp near Northfield, likes girl counselor Kathy Ford. They visit her family on the Ridge and go to the old youth-hostel house

Union Club, NYC, 1919

United States enters WWI in Europe

Wagoner, Charlotte; Unmarried woman who lives with parents in a house next to Clara Lovett's boardinghouse, hopes to marry Wm Ford

Wagoner, Mr. and Mrs.; Parents of Charlotte

Waldorf Hotel charity ball, NYC

White, Grace; nineteen-year-old niece of Otis White from Boonton, NJ. Meets Wm. Jay Ford on train to Northfield conference. Later marries him and moves into the parsonage in Corona, Long Island, New York

White, Otis; Uncle of Grace White Ford, friend of Wm. Jay Ford, also a minister from Long Island, attends Northfield summer conferences

Wilson, Dan; Brother of Pat, local Northfield youth, needs money for drug debt, robs church

Wilson, Pat; Brother of Dan, local Northfield youth, helps rob church

Winters, Fred; A drunkard and wife beater who attacks Wm. Ford

Winters, Mrs.; Wife of Fred, afraid of her husband, Wm. Ford tries to intervene

Wood, Mike; Brother of Joe, commune member, helps Pat and Dan rob church

Wood, Joe; Brother of Mike, commune member, helps Pat and Dan rob church

WWI Ends, November 1918

Youth Hostel, American

Youth Hostel Bicycle trip to Germany 1939

Edwards Brothers Malloy
Thorofare, NJ USA
December 17, 2015